THE PRAIRIE BARONESS

ROBERT J. STEELMAN

SAGEBRUSH
Large Print Westerns

First published in the United States by
Doubleday & Company, Inc.

First Isis Edition
published 2017
by arrangement with
Golden West Literary Agency

A catalogue record for this book is available
from the British Library.

ISBN 978–1–78541–226–4 (pb)

Published by
F. A. Thorpe (Publishing)
Anstey, Leicestershire

Set by Words & Graphics Ltd.
Anstey, Leicestershire
Printed and bound in Great Britain by
T. J. International Ltd., Padstow, Cornwall

This book is printed on acid-free paper

Foreword

The Old West was peopled with picturesque and romantic characters, not the least of whom were the Europeans who came in the seventies and eighties in search of adventure and fortune.

There was Darrell Duppa, son of an English diplomat, who spoke several languages and would not say quit in any of them when Apaches attacked him in the Agua Fria country of the Arizona Territory. He stayed put, and helped build a great new state.

There was the Scotsman Murdo Mackenzie, doyen of the immense Matador Land and Cattle Company of Texas, Montana, and Dakota. Mackenzie lived affluently in mansions in Denver and Trinidad, sent his son to Princeton, and traveled widely.

There was Pierre Wibaux, the Frenchman. The first home in the wilderness for Pierre and his pretty wife Nellie was a log cabin with a sod roof. For Christmas they had turkey, plum pudding, and mince pie, Nellie Wibaux hovering over the cookstove in an evening gown, Pierre with a glass of champagne in his hand and dressed in stiff shirt and swallow-tailed coat. Eventually Pierre, successful in the cattle business, built a great castle of a house with carved woodwork, a billiards room, a wine cellar, and real wallpaper, a curiosity on the frontier.

There was the German Conrad Kohrs. In the eastern

part of Montana Kohrs controlled a million acres of rangeland. Every year he sent his wife East to enjoy the Metropolitan Opera; she last attended it in 1942 at the age of ninety-three.

There was Morton Frewen, the "sublime failure." Frewen was an Englishman who lost money consistently in various ventures in India, Australia, Canada, and the United States. The story is told that Frewen once bought the same herd of cattle twice when the seller simply drove the steers around a hill and brought them back as a second batch. Daily Frewen had fresh flowers cut and sent to his ranch houses. A titled foreigner invited to one of the Englishman's lavish parties rode thirty miles through a blizzard to get there, nearly frozen but immaculate in white tie and tails.

There was Sir Horace Plunkett, son of Lord Dunsany of the famous EK Ranch. Plunkett was a member of the exclusive Cheyenne Club, where wealthy cattlemen could enjoy rare wines from the vaults and the cuisine of great chefs. The Cheyenne Club had two grand staircases, a dining room, hardwood floors, and tennis courts. Legend has it that Sir Horace could play tennis and simultaneously call out winning moves to two opponents playing chess on the veranda.

Picturesque characters all, they helped paint the colorful picture of the Old West that has come down to us. Everything in this book happened at one time or another to men like these. They were brilliant successes and abominable failures. They were wise and courageous; they were foolish and timid. They were honorable men, and sometimes rascals. They built great empires and lost fortunes. They lived in luxurious mansions, and they lived in hovels. Some of their European-style dwellings were attacked, ransacked, and burned; some of the sod shanties still survive. Some died rich and greatly mourned, others perished penniless and alone. But in one respect they were all alike. They had style.

In *The Prairie Baroness*, the Baron de Fleury is a composite of all these men. Lutie Hamlin is, of course, sheer invention. No woman could ever have been like Lutie. Or could she?

Robert J. Steelman

CHAPTER
ONE

With shining eyes Lutie stared at the great iron animal, awesome in its steamy power. The locomotive's brasswork winked in the light from hurrying lanterns in the cavernous Chicago station. Metalwork was painted in bright colors; polished brass shone like gold. Above the great spread of the cowcatcher loomed an iron figure looking like the hitching-post boy that stood before the great houses on Broad Street in Columbus, where the rich people lived. It reminded Lutie of one of the old statues in Papa's mythology book, an iron maiden with proudly spread wings.

"A sight, ain't it, young miss?" a voice inquired at her elbow.

She heard the voice, but in her spell she did not take account of the words. Instead, she watched the man coming across the tracks, a man puffing under the weight of a huge box he carried, a box decorated with antlers and painted orange and green and red. Seeing her gaze, the conductor said, "That's Mr. Slocum, the engineer for the run to St. Paul. I seen you watching my train. She's a beauty, ain't she?"

"Yes!" Lutie turned, excited. The engine was a beauty, a powerful beauty. She thrilled at the

1

steam-smelling force of the engine. High above all towered the diamond stack, puffing gray-white smoke. The smell reminded her of coal burning in the kitchen range at home, the home she and Papa and Mama and Sid had now left forever. "Oh, yes!"

"That's the Pacific Express," the pleasant gray-haired man in brass buttons told her. "You traveling west on her?"

"Y — yes, sir," she stammered, brought unwillingly back to reality. "To St. Paul, then on to Bismarck and the Dakota Territory."

This Pacific Express was nothing like the rusty Baltimore and Ohio relic that had jolted them all the way from Columbus. Entranced, Lutie watched Mr. Slocum, in high starched collar and derby hat, mount the cowcatcher, puffing under the weight of the colorful box. "What's he doing, then?" she asked.

The conductor was amused at her ignorance. "All the engineers got their own headlight. Slocum puts his on at Chicago. At St. Paul there's a change of crew, so Slocum takes his light down and goes home with it. The new engineer puts up his own, then, for the run west."

Nodding, he left her to watch Mr. Slocum wrestle the heavy box into place on a high iron shelf. There was indeed a big brass lamp in the box, and a polished-metal lens behind it. With the help of a mechanic, Mr. Slocum finally got the box bolted in place and lit the wick. A bright golden beam shone down the tracks, illuminating the polished twin ribbons of rail.

For a while Lutie remained beside the engine, even dared to feel its hot flanks. When a bell clanged, she drew nervously back. Then, from somewhere within the iron beast, a roaring plume of steam escaped and the whistle shrieked. In delighted terror she shrank back, clasping the new plumed and cherried hat tight to her ginger-tinted curls. Running down the platform, she lifted her skirts with one hand and held out the other in an effort to thread her way through the swarm of people. What if the engineer — the magnificent Mr. Slocum — were even now pulling back the throttle, or whatever it was called, to leave her alone on the platform while Papa and Mama and Sid rolled out of her life?

In headlong flight she unknowingly passed the shabby "Zulu car," where their seats were, and found herself at the "varnish," the luxurious sleeping cars and private coaches at the end of the Pacific Express, far from the smoke and ashes and noise of the engine. She did not know why her own coach was called a Zulu car, unless it was thought fit only for jungle savages in Africa. The Zulu cars were boxlike affairs with two tiers of wooden cubicles built along each side. There was a cooking stove so emigrants to the west could fix their own food, and wooden straight-backed seats in pairs facing each other so boards could be placed across them to form rude beds. There was no upholstery.

The cars were beginning to rumble and jerk as she ran by; the train was starting to pull out. "Damn!" she muttered between clenched teeth.

"'Boooooard!" the conductor shouted. Far down the tracks she saw him waving his lantern.

3

"Jesus!" she added, frantic. Mama did not allow profanity in her house, but when Lutie was alone and distraught she used a lot of bad words. Where was their Zulu car? She must have passed it. Gasping for breath, she ran back a ways and pulled herself aboard just as the iron wheels started to grind their way west, and was relieved to find herself in her own car. "More luck than sense" she muttered to herself.

Sidney, fourteen going on fifteen, looked at her with owlish eyes, dim behind spectacles. "Where you been?" he demanded, laying down Mr. Stevenson's *Sea Cook*, now running as a serial in Sid's precious *Young Folks* magazine. "Why you so out of breath, Lutie?"

She fanned herself with her new hat, careful of the cherries and feathers atop the straw crown. "None of your beeswax!" Inside the crowded emigrant car with its cooking odors and brass cuspidors the air seemed stifling. In sudden alarm she stared round. "Where's Papa and Mama?"

"Gone to look for you," Sidney leered. "You're going to catch it when they get back. Mama was real mad!"

She sighed in relief as she saw them open the door at the end of the car, and was willing to take the scolding she knew would follow.

"Lutecia!" Indignant, Mama sank down on the wooden bench, fanning herself. "Girl, where on earth have you been?"

Papa was severe also, not a common thing with him. Lutie loved Papa. "We looked all through the cars for you."

4

"I told you not to be long!" Mama insisted. "Wherever were you?"

Lutie looked into the precious hat. There was an unladylike dark rim around the inside where she had perspired. "I — I walked down to look at the engine. It's *such* a beauty! I guess I stayed too long. I'm sorry."

Mama was still indignant. "A dirty old engine is no place for a young girl! Besides, all kinds of people are running around this smoky old station, and who knows what —"

Papa placed a hand on Mama's arm. "Now, Mattie, the girl's sorry. Let's let it go at that, eh?"

Mama set her lips, and pulled away from Papa's placating touch. "I declare, I don't know how that girl is ever going to learn responsibility. You're no model, Lorenzo, I must say that!"

Lutie did not regret straying up the tracks to visit the great engine. The engine had thrilled her, touched something in her bosom she did not know was there. It was, she decided, as if some great experience, not concerned with Uncle Milo and his Dakota farm, were upon her. An opening of life had suddenly stirred — too beautiful, too marvelous, to know completely, with only her nineteen years of living to encompass it. Something had happened and she could not hold all of it in her eager hands. It was too much, draining away, sifting through her fingers. She wanted to cry out to God, saying, "Stop — it's too much — wait a minute, please!" Almost, she wept.

Papa leaned forward. "Lutie, you all right?"

She nodded, breathing deep. "Yes, Papa."

Lorenzo Hamlin had tried a little of everything, and failed. Bank clerk, part owner of a dry-goods store, violin teacher, printer — at last he had sold all their household goods and was now sure the Dakota Territory held a new and vibrant promise. His brother Milo, Lutie's uncle, had written enthusiastic letters from his quarter section on the banks of the Little Missouri River, and sent glowing prospectuses printed by the railroad.

"Listen to this, now — just listen!" Papa said, spreading wide the Northern Pacific's folder as the train gathered speed. "Mattie, listen — and you too, Lutie and Sid." Papa always wanted to go to Paris, France, and named his daughter after the old Roman name for that fabulous city. Now he smoothed thinning brown hair, adjusted his pince-nez: "'Dakota is a land fair enough to tempt angels in their flight to —'"

"You've read that folder a thousand times!" Mama protested.

Papa smiled. "Each time it sounds better, doesn't it?" Unperturbed, he went on:

"' . . . tempt angels in their flight to pause and wonder whether a new and better Eden has not been formed, and roofed with sapphire skies. People have come here to die of bronchitis and consumption, and have lived to become glowing embodiments of soundness and strength, with throats like firemen's trumpets and lungs like blacksmiths' bellows.'"

Papa himself had always had weak lungs, and at night wheezed a lot. Grumbling, Mama took out her knitting. "I know all that by heart. I declare, if I hear it once more I'll scream."

Lutie's mother was a Dysart, from Bedford County in Virginia. Her father had been Major Edmund Randall Dysart, CSA. The Dysarts were vexed when Mattie Dysart married beneath her. Their vexation had at last consumed their daughter. She had opposed the Dakota journey from the first, predicting no good would come from it, in spite of Milo Hamlin's enthusiasm.

"Those railroad pamphlets are just puffery. Lorenzo, you've been taken in so many times I wonder you don't finally smarten up!" She rapped Sidney on the head with her knuckles. "Boy, put on those spectacles again. I didn't pay three dollars for them to have you ruin your eyes reading that trash." To Lutie she said, "Don't sit there and stare out the window. There's nothing to see now but the dark, anyway. Pick up that sampler and finish it, please. I want you to have something nice to give Papa's brother when we get there — if we ever do."

With Mama intent on her knitting, Lutie instead picked up her precious volume of poems. Mama wouldn't notice, now that she had had her say. Beside her, Sidney stared down the aisle toward the cooking stove where emigrants were cooking cabbage and frying side meat. The bowl of the stove glowed a dull red but it was cold in the Zulu car and he shivered, leaning against Lutie for warmth.

"If it's this cold in April, right here," he observed, drawing the new coat tighter about his thin frame, "what must it be like out in Dakota in the winter, the *real* winter?"

Papa was reassuring. "Of course it gets cold, Sid. It got cold in Columbus, too, didn't it? But listen here!" Pleased at the opportunity, he unfolded a new page of the prospectus, adjusted his pincenez again. "'The howling blizzards, of which outside worldlings delight to prate, blow all miasma and contagion from Dakota's favored plains and valleys to breathe new life into dilapidated nostrils.'" He looked up, triumphantly. "And how's this?" He read again. "'The productive capacity of Dakota is as limitless as her extent is great. Any land will pay for itself at present prices in one or two crops.'"

Knitting faster, Mama pursed her lips. "If Milo is doing all that well, why didn't he send us some money when you wrote that letter telling we were coming out? He never even answered."

Papa folded the precious railroad literature, placing it, dogeared, in an inside pocket of his new coat. "Well, you know how the mails are, Mattie. Then this is almost spring. A man's bound to be busy plowing and harrowing and disking and all those things." Lorenzo Hamlin knew little of farming, but he was a voracious reader. "Maybe we left Columbus just before his letter got there. Right now it's probably in the dead-letter office. But don't worry — everything is as fine as frog hair."

Lutie took her banjo from its case under the seat. Mama had wanted to sell it to get money for the trip. "After all," she argued, "there'll be a lot of hard work

8

after we get there, and no time for fumadiddles like music. Anyway, the banjo is an instrument for darkies, and we need money." But Papa had bought Lutie the banjo, and taught her how to strum and chord. Really, she was quite good at it, and sang also to her own accompaniment: "Belle Mahone," "Jordan Am a Hard Road to Trabbel," "Bird of the Wilderness." Papa had come to her defense, and she still had the banjo. Softly she plucked a few chords, but Mama was still in a bad mood.

"It's late, girl. People are already trying to go to sleep. A sampler doesn't make any noise, you know. Work on that!"

Sighing, Lutie returned the precious instrument to its velvet-lined case. "Yes, ma'am."

The next evening they reached St. Paul, where a fresh train crew took over. Mr. Slocum removed his big box of a searchlight, and the new man erected his own. During the night the Pacific Express thundered over the Red River Bridge — Papa followed the train's progress on his map — and the wooded countryside of Minnesota gave way to dawn-lit prairie. Mama had not slept well; she dozed, swaying on the hard wooden seat. Papa and Sid slept also, Sid curled up like a small animal with his head in Papa's lap, his precious new copper-toed boots with their red tops clasped tight to his meager stomach. Lutie, wide awake, abandoned the sampler and pressed her face against the cold window glass.

Potholes and sloughs punctuated this strange new land. Flocks of wild ducks and geese, startled by the coming of the locomotive, rose in alarm. Rabbits bounded endlessly about. Gophers, she thought they were, looked out of their burrows and without fear watched the passing of the Pacific Express. Once or twice she saw a shanty made of earthen slabs and shuddered. How awful to live in such a den! She was glad Uncle Milo had built a house.

While there were no trees in this land, the soil was nevertheless black and fertile in appearance. Lutie waved to a lonely woman hanging clothes on a line in the stiff wind. A dog barked, and ran furiously after the speeding cars. Yawning, Lutie picked up her reticule and rose, careful not to wake the rest of the family. In the gray cold light she went to the water butt. Dipping a handkerchief into the water she freshened her face, pinching her cheeks to bring a little color back into them. All around her lay hopeful emigrants, stirring restlessly, contorted into positions that made her think of Mr. Doré's pictures in Grandpa Dysart's family Bible that Mama treasured so, with all the births and deaths and marriages of the Dysart clan back to ancient times, clear to seventeen hundred and something.

The Zulu car smelled bad: tobacco fumes, stale food, the sharp sweet odor of whiskey. A young man with slicked-down black hair, long and straggly, was watching her from the narrow bench where he lay, hands locked behind his head. He smiled at her, but she only tossed her head and opened the door to the next car.

10

That was no better. People sprawled on benches, in the aisles, behind the now cold and lifeless cooking stove. One man had had the foresight to bring along a sailor's hammock, which he stretched across the car. He snored rhythmically as the hammock swung to the motion of the train. Waking children whimpered. A woman with a nursing child looked up with sleep-heavy eyes as Lutie passed, then pressed the child tighter to a sagging breast.

When so many people died in the War, many of the survivors turned to spiritualism, encouraged by the preaching of Mrs. Fox-Jencken and her sister. Now, in the aisles, a fat woman in a taffeta dress was holding an early-morning service. Her listeners closed their eyes and swayed back and forth, holding hands in a ring, while the fat lady declared that even now her spirit guide was hovering over them.

"Don't you feel it? Can't you feel the brush of his wings?"

"Excuse me, ma'am," Lutie said politely, trying to get by.

They had to break the ring, then, and the fat lady glared at Lutie, who fled to the next car like a wraith herself, passing silently through a wilderness of sleep-drugged flesh. People, so many people, and all going out to the new land! Had they been so unhappy and unprospering back home, in Columbus or Pittsburgh or Utica or wherever they came from?

Almost before she knew it she had come to the sleeping cars and parlor cars and private coaches of the wealthy. The varnish was forbidden territory for Zulu car riders but no one barred her way. Curious, she tiptoed through the elegant accommodations, wondering who lay sleeping behind the green baize curtains — senators, railroad magnates, great financiers like Jay Gould, perhaps?

In the vestibule of the next car a conductor dozed atop a stool. On the glass-windowed door leading into the elegant car was painted CALIFORNIA in gold letters. Daringly, Lutie slipped past the man and opened the inner door.

No Zulu car, this! She caught her breath at the luxury. Fringed curtains hung at the windows. The floor was deep in the rich pile of a red and gold and green Turkey carpet. There were oriental-looking divans, elegant lamps shaded by multicolored glass veined with gold, wicks still burning wastefully from the night before. The air smelled clean and pure, laced with the scent of flowers in cut-glass vases. Awed, she stood just inside the door, reticule clutched in both hands, staring at the incredible palace on wheels. Even the hum and click of the wheels on the iron rails was muted, softened, and the chuffing of the distant engine was lost in the rich draperies. What manner of people lived in such magnificent surroundings? They must be magnificent also, to match the atmosphere!

Frightened, yet deliciously propelled by curiosity, she stole forward into the car, feet making no sound on the heavy pile. Midway of the car was a partition, hung with oil paintings of lightly clad maidens drinking at a forest spring. At one side of the partition a narrow corridor led farther into the depths of the California

12

car. Quaking, she entered the dark aisle. Was there no one here to enjoy all this opulence?

Suddenly a door opened off the corridor. Almost losing her balance as the car swayed around a curve, she stopped dead. The breath caught in her throat as she stared at the tableau within the small room that opened to her gaze. It was a bedroom, apparently, with a washstand and a gilt mirror. A man — a dark foreign-looking man — stood before the mirror, face lathered, shaving. Beside him on a leather seat lolled a beautiful lady, clad in the most gossamer of gowns.

Pausing in his shaving, long razor poised, the man smiled at the beautiful lady. Lifting a corner of the flimsy robe, he laid a fond hand on her knee, and she did not flinch; he talked to her in some foreign language, spoken seemingly through the nose. Lutie did not understand the words, but there was no mistaking their amorous quality.

The lady saw Lutie first. Her huge dark eyes widened; hastily she drew the diaphanous fabric about her limbs and murmured something.

"Eh?" The bearded man turned, stared at Lutie.

She fled. Running back through the narrow passageway, she stumbled in the deep carpeting, fumbled at the cold nickel-plated handle of the door. It slipped in her grasp, would not open.

The lather-faced man followed her. While she struggled with the knob she felt it suddenly turn in her grasp. The once-dozing conductor stood sternly in the doorway, brass buttons gleaming.

"Here, now!" he barked. "What's all this?" He turned to the foreign man. "Baron, has this little snip been bothering you?"

The baron looked at Lutie with dark eyes agleam with malice. She twisted in authority's grasp but the burly official held her fast.

"I didn't mean any harm!" she wailed. "I was just — just —"

"She's from one of those emigrant cars," the conductor said. "I recognize her now! She's with one of those Zulu families traveling out to the prairie."

"Ah!" The baron's heavy brows twitched. "That is it!" His words were weighted with accent; *that* sounded like *zat*. Behind him the woman appeared, now with a figured robe of Chinese silk over the flimsy nightgown.

"Charles!" she demanded. "Whatever is happening? How did she get in here? I think you should write a letter of complaint to the division manager!"

The baron frowned, a scowl that stitched the heavy brows together, furrowed his face in malignant wrinkles. Putting his countenance close to Lutie's, he shouted.

"Boo!"

Openmouthed, she stared at him, petrified with fright.

"Boo!" he cried again, and waved the terrible razor.

Panic-stricken, she wrested her arm free of the conductor's grasp, and fled.

Behind her she heard diminishing laughter; a deep voice, the man, and then shrill merriment from the woman. Never in her life had she run so fast, even when hurrying to catch the Pacific Express when it was abandoning her in Chicago. Breathless, she caromed through the other private cars, knocking down a servant in a white coat who carried a silver teapot on a tray. Headlong she ran through the emigrant cars, hopscotching over babies crawling in the aisles, dodging women cooking breakfast on the again-glowing stove. Rough-looking men chewing toothpicks strolled the aisle, and she pushed them aside, all the time fearing the bearded man was pursuing, or the angry conductor. Once again she broke the spiritualist's circle, and they made unreligious remarks. At last, at long last, she saw her own car. Casting a relieved glance behind her and finding no pursuer, she slowed to a walk, adjusting the cherried hat and tucking in her hair. Casually, although heart still pounded, she strolled to her seat.

"Where in heaven's name have you been?" Mama demanded crossly. "I don't know of any young girl can disappear into thin air the way you do, Lutie!"

Papa handed Lutie a tin plate with fried sausages on it along with a piece of bread. Sidney leered again and said, "I know where she's been. She's been lallygagging around looking for boys!"

"You shut your mouth!" Lutie snapped.

"That's no way to talk," Papa said gently. "We were worried about you, Lutie! There are some rough people on this train."

In spite of the attempt to calm herself, her breast still heaved with the effort of running. She took a deep breath.

"I was just strolling through the cars, that's all. I thought it would be a good idea to stretch my legs."

Mama looked at Papa. Papa looked at Mama. Sidney — damned brat — snickered. She'd fix *his* clock when she got a chance.

"Limbs!" Mama snapped.

"Ma'am?"

"Stretch your *limbs*, girl! It's indecent for a female to talk about her legs. At least, they don't in Bedford County, Virginia, though what the rule is out here in this benighted frontier I don't know and don't care to know!" For a moment Mama looked out the window, at landscape, seeming to see something beyond the passing dun landscape. Papa grasped her hand. For a moment she let it lie in his, then pulled it away. "What you'd better do, child," she added in a softer tone, "is get to work on that sampler again. It's not far now, Papa says, to where we get off, at Little Missouri."

Meekly Lutie took out sampler, thread, needles, and thimble from the cigar box. *That foreigner*, she thought indignantly. Baron or count or whatever he was, and the fallen woman! Even rich people ought to have a little respect for appearances! But in spite of herself she giggled at the memory of his lathery face when she caught him stroking that wicked hussy's thigh. Guiltily she wondered how her own thigh would feel if a man were to stroke it like that, such a very private part of her own body!

"Lutie!" Mama protested. "Whatever is the matter with you? You keep twisting and twitching. Can't you sit still like your brother Sidney?"

16

Sid snickered. Under cover of the spread sampler Lutie pinched him, hard.

"Yes, Mama," she agreed. "I'll try. I — I'm sorry."

But she was not sorry. Actually, she felt gay and wicked. She longed to play a lively tune on her banjo, but wisely decided this was not the time. Instead, she took out her book of Mr. Sidney Lanier's poems (Mama had named Sid after the Southern poet) and read her favorite, "The Marshes of Glynn," although she had long known it by heart.

Shortly after sundown the Pacific Express passed over the Little Missouri River. The big locomotive — Sid claimed it was called a 4-4-0, for some reason Lutie didn't understand — ground to a halt. Steam sighed from valves and the bell rang as they came to a shuddering halt at the station.

"This is it, family!" Papa said cheerily. "We're here!"

With the other emigrants they clambered wearily down, all carrying sacks, parcels, blanket rolls, firearms, valises. One man staggered under the weight of a steamer trunk.

"We're at the edge of what they call the Badlands," Papa explained, helping Mama down from the high iron step. "That doesn't mean there's really anything bad about them," he added hastily. "It's just that the early French explorers found them hard to travel through because of the buttes and gullies and water courses. *Mauvaises terres à traverser*, they said; bad lands to travel through. But we're not going to travel anymore, just out to Milo's place, that's all." The way

Papa said "Milo's place" was like someone would say "the Garden of Eden." Papa, dear Papa!

"Well," Mama said grimly, "it looks pretty bad to me, no matter what the French called it."

The station was a newly built structure of raw wood with a bay window giving a view of the tracks in both directions. Inside, it smelled of kerosene and new lumber. Wanted bills giving descriptions of Dakota Territory outlaws and mail robbers were tacked on the walls, along with multicolored Northern Pacific posters extolling the virtues of Dakota farmland.

When they had recovered their luggage from the baggage car, the town itself appeared no better. Little Missouri, they learned from overheard conversations, was better known as "Little Misery." It was a straggling town of badly carpentered buildings, tents, lean-tos, and a few Indian *tipis*. Sid was entranced.

"It's the Wild West!" he enthused. "Look, Lutie!" Excitedly he snatched her sleeve, indicating an evil-looking man lounging before a false-fronted livery stable. "See that rifle he's got? That's a Remington! The Scourge of the Sioux carried one just like it, and killed over a hundred Indians when they scalped his sweetheart!"

"You and that trash you read!" she said witheringly.

Together the little family trudged down the dirt street, carrying their few belongings.

"It's so late," Papa said, "there's no use trying to get out to Milo's place tonight." He looked around. "Appears there's only one hotel in town. The Antlers, over there."

18

The Pacific Express, ready to depart westward, whistled; a plume of steam hissed. They turned to watch the locomotive, wheels grinding and slipping and then grinding again, draw away from the station on the balance of its run. Mama began to cry.

"Now, Mattie." Papa dropped the valises and held her in his arms. "It's not an end, you see. It's a new beginning! In a few weeks we'll all be nicely settled in, and glad we came."

He gave the clerk at the Antlers Hotel a dollar for the family to sit all night in the rude "lobby," taking turns dozing on a rump-sprung sofa. They could not afford two rooms, or even one. For a late supper they ate leftover bread and sausage, drinking from a pot of tea Papa bought at a Chinese eating house across the tracks. Papa finally agreed that Little Misery seemed to be a rough place, but was sure that the country around Milo's place was much nicer. During the long night they slept restlessly, roused often by scuffles in the street, a piano in the Empire Saloon, and once, a scattered burst of gunfire that frightened everybody but Sid.

"If they come in here with their shooting," Mama said fiercely, clutching her umbrella, "I'll give them what for. I wasn't born a Dysart for nothing!"

Papa slept through most of the commotion, pale and weary after the long journey. Strands of thinning hair lay innocently across his brow, and his face was like that of a tired child. Toward dawn Mama found a blanket and put it over him.

In the morning he arranged with a drover to take them out to Milo's farm, eight miles south, along the banks of the Little Missouri River.

"Hamlin?" the whiskered driver asked, scratching his chin. "Milo Hamlin? Sure I know him. Kind of a crazy feller, ain't he, with a cast in one eye? Eddicated, sort of? Reads books?"

"He's my brother," Papa said proudly. "We all read, in my family. Yes, that's Milo, all right!"

The man demanded five dollars in advance. Mama was indignant but they had to pay him. "Ain't no stage line or anything runs out that way," the driver explained. "Seems to me you ain't got no other choice."

After the fare, Mama covertly counted what remained. Twenty-three dollars and some loose change; that and a few pieces of Dysart silverware in the battered trunk constituted their fortune. But Papa was cheerful.

"We'll be with Milo soon," he promised. "Everything will be all right then. Milo was always the smartest one of us boys. He'll have a fine crop coming along already, I vow!"

In the sunny dawn they embarked on the high-wheeled wagon. Papa and Mama sat beside the driver. Lutie and Sid made do among the freight in the wagon bed.

"Couldn't take you all the way out there for only five dollars," the whiskered bandit explained, "without I had a few barrels of flour and lard and some new harness for the Griffins up the river."

20

At this altitude — two thousand feet, Papa said — the spring air was dry and bracing, smelling of wild sage. Fringed with budding cottonwoods, a pale haze of green, the Little Missouri looped along its eccentric course. "We had an early spring," the driver remarked, indicating the cottonwoods. "Usually they don't sprout till late May, or mebbe June."

From the water's edge a plain sloped gently upward to snow-covered peaks varied in form and color. The high cliffs resembled scenes of the Grand Canyon of the Colorado River Lutie had gazed at in a stereopticon at the Columbus Public Library. Papa, reading from one of his numerous pamphlets, explained that the river and its tributaries had carved out the bizarre pinnacles and crags in ancient geological time.

"That's so," the driver agreed, impressed by Papa's skill in pronouncing the big words.

All along their route the Little Missouri had left rich dark soil. "Looks like the land will raise a fine graze," Papa said, though he knew little of animal husbandry.

A white-tailed deer bounded across the wagon ruts. Birds flitted ahead, regrouping with soft calls after they passed. From one of the high peaks a pair of mountain sheep stared curiously down.

"*Macha sicha*, the Indians call them colored buttes," the driver offered. "Think bad spirits live there." He guffawed. "None of old Yellow Hat's people wouldn't go into those buttes for a silver dollar and a jug of booze, dearly as a Sioux loves his tot!"

In midmorning they reached Milo Hamlin's place. Papa stared.

"This is it? I mean — Milo Hamlin's? Are you sure?"

Against a craggy butte was a ramshackle structure of chunks of withered sod laid up like bricks, roofed over with poles on which was plastered mud, topped off with more sod, bright with new grass. The primitive dwelling was dug halfway into the base of the cliff. From a brush corral a melancholy mule stared at them, and a bony cow wandered among sagging outbuildings. From the dwelling to the river stretched a patch of recently plowed land, but there was no sign of humanity, no Uncle Milo Hamlin.

Mama sounded worried. "Are you *sure* this is it? Milo wrote that he built a *house!*"

The driver again scratched his bristled chin. "Well, ma'am, it's a kind of house. Dug back in the hill that way, it'll stay warmer in winter than a lot of fine clapboard structures. And if the roof leaks" — he slapped his thigh, chuckling — "there's plenty more material around to patch it!"

"Milo!" Papa called. He got down from the wagon, approached the sod shanty diffidently. "Milo, you in there?"

The driver was impatient. "Got to be gettin' on," he grumbled. "Better get your stuff down, mister."

"Wait a minute," Mama pleaded. "There must be some mistake!"

"No mistake, ma'am. There surely ain't no other Milo Hamlin around here." The driver raised his own voice. "Milo? You got company out here!"

There was no response. "Probably out shooting a rabbit for our supper," Papa said nervously. He walked to the door of the shack, which sagged on leather hinges.

"Milo!" he announced. "We're here! Lorenzo and Mattie and the children! Are you in there?"

The sunny morning was suddenly quiet. Even the birds seemed to have stopped their quiet conversations. The only sound was the rushing of the Little Missouri, intent on its own business, unconcerned with human affairs.

Papa stepped inside the door.

"I dunno where Milo can be," the driver said, perplexed, a note of concern in his voice. "Usually tinkerin' around, or inside, reading them books of his."

Sidney began to whimper. Lutie cuffed him, feeling uneasy. Mama only wet her lips, staring at the black eye of the door.

"I'm going in there to see!" Lutie decided. Mama didn't say anything, so she jumped down. Hiking up her skirts, she ran to the ugly shanty, stopped just outside the door.

"Papa?"

There was no answer.

"Papa!" she called again. This time there was panic in her voice.

She was about to enter when her father came out. His face was pale and his lip quivered. In his hand he held a crumpled piece of wrapping paper.

"What's wrong?" Lutie asked.

Curious, she started to look inside when he caught her wrist and pulled her back. "Don't!" he said in a harsh voice she had never before heard. But she had already seen enough. Uncle Milo hung by his neck from the ridgepole, sightless eyes scanning the mud-chinked wall as he revolved.

"Milo's hanged himself," Papa murmured, staring at the crumpled paper.

From the wagon Mama must have heard his words. "Oh, God!" she said softly. Sidney started to cry.

"There's this note," Papa went on in the harsh voice. He read:

"Lorenzo, I'm sorry about this. I never could make a go of it in spite of all the nonsense I wrote to you and Mattie. I just wasn't cut out to be a farmer, I guess, or anything else worthwhile. Goodbye, all."

There was an inky stain where the pen had failed poor Milo, then a scribbled postscript, almost illegible:

"I'm truly sorry it had to end this way. As an older brother I guess I'm a poor example. But I just couldn't face you and Mattie and the children after all the big blathering I did."

The driver climbed down, peered in the door, and whistled between his few remaining snaggle teeth. "Gets a lot of 'em this way," he remarked. "There was a Dutchman, over toward Wibaux, that —" Taking a fresh plug of tobacco from his pocket, he snicked off a piece with his jackknife. "There's an undertaker in Little Misery. Lots of business for him what with all the shootings and such. Want I should send him out with the hearse?"

Papa folded the paper, put it in his waistcoat, the new flowered one Mama had made him buy for the trip west.

"No," he said heavily. "We'll bury him ourselves. Thank you, though."

CHAPTER
TWO

The baron's private car, California, rented from the Northern Pacific Railroad, was spotted on a siding at Little Missouri. The voluptuous Marie de Courcy who had accompanied the baron from Chicago was sent back to Chicago in a private drawing room. The baron spent most of the forenoon choosing a costume for the momentous day. At last, smoothing his leather coat, he spoke in French to Murdoch. "*Tiens*; how do I appear to you, eh?"

The valet knew he pleased his master when he tried the Gallic tongue. "*Très bien*," he said, Scots burr wrestling with the French uvular trill. "*Magnifique, monsieur!*"

Rolling the points of his mustache between thumb and forefinger, the baron strolled into the lavishly appointed drawing room. Emile Durand sat in a pool of sunlight reading the Chicago *Daily News*, a copy of which had been especially delivered to the California by the conductor of a passing freight.

"I am approved by Murdoch," Charles announced. "Emile, how do I look to you, old friend?"

Tall and well knit, of a military bearing, the baron's figure was well set off by the hunting coat of many pockets and a wide-brimmed felt hat with leather band. Around his waist was a canvas belt filled with cartridges. From it hung a holster with a long-barreled Colt's revolver; a hunting knife in a beaded sheath was on the other side. A leather water bottle hung also from the belt, and he carried a double-barreled French shotgun of expensive make in the crook of his arm.

Lawyer Durand took off steel-rimmed spectacles and ran a hand through his blond hair.

"You want my opinion?"

"Of course!"

Emile's blue eyes twinkled. "As friend, Charles, or as legal adviser?"

The baron was impatient with small talk. "Come, come! We have not got all day, you know! There are horses to rent, arrangements to make!"

"As a friend," Emile said, "I consider you a dashing and imposing figure. As your lawyer, dedicated to the pursuit of truth, I believe the citizens of this Little Misery place will be amused. You must expect some snickers."

Charles's heavy brows drew together. He tugged at his beard. " 'Sneekers'? I do not understand that word!"

Emile folded the paper, reached for his hat.

"Perhaps it is just as well. Are you ready? Then let us go."

After the previous night's bacchanal, Little Misery lay quiet in the morning sun. During the night a rattle of gunfire and thudding of hooves had been clearly audible on the Northern Pacific siding a quarter mile away. Now the cowhands slept off their spree, the prostitutes were in bed, and the last drunken army private had been dragged back to the cantonment by comrades. The baron stopped to pick up an object glinting in the sun, a brass shell. All about, in the warming dust, lay the shiny tubes. Nearby was a dusty black patch that might be congealed blood.

"Go away!" Emile cried, swinging the folded *Daily News* to drive away a sniffing cur.

"There must have been a battle," Charles observed. "The scene reminds me of Algiers and the Tenth Hussars."

Emile took his arm and pulled him toward the livery stable. "It reminds me," he said, "of nothing so much as absolute stupidity! These people are hardly civilized!"

The editor of the Little Missouri *Gazette* rose early. Seeing visitors, he hurried from the shop, untying an ink-stained apron and wiping his hands on the seat of his trousers.

"Name's Oates," he said. "Sam Oates. Editor of the paper." Quickly he produced a notebook and a stub of pencil. "You two gentlemen have business in the Territory? What's your names? Come in from Chicago?" He looked down the tracks. "That your car down there, the California?"

Charles was annoyed, but Emile spoke to him in a low voice. "Be calm, my friend! It is the custom of the country to be forthright." In accented but fluent English he spoke to the editor. "This is Charles Jean Jacques Ferrier de Marigny, Baron de Fleury. I am his lawyer, Emile Durand, of Chicago. The baron has bought several thousand acres of land from the

28

Northern Pacific Railroad and intends to raise cattle. We are about to secure horses and ride along the river to inspect the land. Now, sir, we must hurry about our business!"

"Yes," Charles grumbled in English. "Our business! We hurry quick. No time!"

Mr. Oates trotted beside them as they approached Sigafoos' Livery Stable — Feed, Grain, Horses Rented — with hitching post in front and a straggling corral in the rear. "Where is this land?" he demanded.

"Along the river," Emile said.

"How much land?"

In the shade of the sloping porch roof, Emile pushed open the sagging door and tipped his hat. "A great deal of land, sir," he said. "Now we leave you. Good day!"

Oates remained rooted in the dust, pencil poised above the notebook. He seemed concerned.

"Yep?" a voice inquired from a cavernous darkness within the sagging building.

"I search for the proprietor," Emile explained.

From a cot in one corner the owner of the voice arose, throwing aside a ragged quilt. He yawned, stretched, scratched an armpit. "That's me."

"Horses," Emile announced. "My friend and I want to rent riding horses for a trip of several days along the river, Mr. Sigafoos. Good horses, your best — and pack animals. You can accommodate us?"

"All I handle is good horses!" Jake Sigafoos grumbled. For a moment he stared unbelievingly at the baron, then shook his head. Hitching suspenders over his shoulders, he took a swig from a bottle beside the cot and motioned them to follow.

Charles stared at the animals in the corral. They were small, having mulish hocks and slanting quarters, their hides fantastically blotched with patches of brown and white and black. They rolled their eyes at Emile and tried to bite him when he examined their withers. A mare with ears laid back kicked out at the baron and Charles drew back, cursing. "These are strange animals. *Mon Dieu*, they belong in a zoo, along with aardvarks and zebras!"

Emile had been conferring with the livery-stable proprietor. "They are all we are likely to get. Mr. Sigafoos assures me they are sound, with good wind, and can carry heavy loads or a person such as yourself all day without fatigue."

Leading the rented animals, they went back to the California parlor car. Murdoch, familiar with horses, helped them pack their belongings in canvas sacks which he then roped to the backs of the strange mounts.

"We will be gone several days," Charles said. "Hold the fort, Murdoch — fight off the natives if they attack, and have a lamp burning in the window to guide us home! *Au revoir!*"

Emile buttoned his coat and set his hat firmly on his head. "So long!"

Murdoch was puzzled. "So — long, sir?"

"It is an American expression. You will get used to exotic phrases like that."

Little Misery was just coming to life as they rode out on the land. Wagon wheels ground in the dust, mules brayed, a teamster rolled beer barrels down a ramp and into the dark confines of the New West Bar and Music Hall — Show Nightly at 8p.m. From somewhere they could hear the wheeze of a concertina and a shrill soprano practicing scales. Charles shrugged, made a face.

"Let us," Emile said, smiling, "look forward to nature, rather than backward toward man."

In a short while they left the town and were riding along the banks of the Little Missouri. The baron became enthused, then excited.

"Look at it, Emile, just look! Did you ever see anything like it? So different from France, from Switzerland, from anything! In his book on cattle raising, Mr. Brisbin was right." Charles quoted from memory; Brisbin's book was a constant companion. "'Where the broad rivers flow and the boundless prairie stretches away for thousands of miles.'"

Rich buffalo grass grew knee-deep. The meandering course of the river was fringed with budding cottonwoods, towering trees with roots set deep in the fertile soil. There were gentle hills and valleys, canyons floored with new grass where water from beaver dams had backed up. Away from the river the land sloped to a wall of bluffs, serrated like the turrets of a castle and varied in color — white, gray, chocolate brown. Emile dismounted and dug with his penknife in a ledge, coming away with a chunk of black dirt.

"Lignite," he decided.

"Eh?"

"A primitive form of coal. It will burn, too."

At noon, still on Charles's land, they tied their animals in the shade of a grove of box elders and opened the picnic hamper Murdoch had prepared. There were tins of pâté de foie gras, sardines, cheese, crackers with sweet butter, and a liter of Haut Médoc.

"Look!" Charles cried, pointing with the neck of the tall bottle.

Only a hundred yards away a spotted fawn rose from the grass. It looked at them with liquid eyes, then ambled into the cover of alders choking the draw.

"Paradise!" Charles marveled, breathing deep of the sweet air. "Thank God for room to move about without stepping on others!"

That afternoon they ambled along the course of the river, not yet needing the map Emile had prepared. They saw fat elk, and antelope. Once, on a chiseled peak, a solitary mountain goat stared down. Below, in a thick stand of willows was a conical lodge. Naked children ran and hid.

"Sioux," Emile explained. "Poor people — ever since they destroyed General Custer, they have paid for it! Now they are reduced to beggary!"

"And living on my land!" Charles complained.

"You signed a contract for it. The Indians had no contract."

Charles slapped him on the back. "My friend, you have a tender heart, and think I do not! But look!" He pointed toward the river, where a crude shelter roofed with sod was dug into the bank. Smoke rose from a mud-and-twig chimney. "Over there is someone else living on my land. Am I put down by this? No!" he chuckled. "I will live here as a *grand seigneur*, surrounded by my vassals. If they acknowledge my authority as landlord, I will be very kind to them, you will see!"

That night they camped on the high bluffs overlooking the Little Missouri River. While Emile pitched the patent canvas tent and started a fire to boil coffee, Charles roamed the grassy plateau.

"This is it!" he exclaimed. "This is the very place!"

Emile pounded in the last stake and straightened a painful back. He was unaccustomed to long hours in the saddle. Charles was the cavalryman.

"What do you mean?"

"This level place on top! What a magnificent location for the chateau I shall build!" Charles swept out his arms. "Up here a man can look forever and see nothing but his own land! Imagine a great house where I sit on the veranda and watch thousands of cattle — my cattle, my fortune! After a century of losing causes, the de Fleury banner will wave high once more!"

Wearily Emile poured ground coffee in the bubbling pot. "If you are lucky."

Seeing his friend's fatigue, Charles was contrite. He smote his brow with the back of a hand.

"Emile, I am sorry!" he apologized. "Here you have been toiling like a slave while I make speeches! But you know me, *mon ami*. When I am on the verge of a great undertaking, I become thoughtless."

"I forgive you," Emile smiled. "And now let us dine."

For supper they ate cold chicken, pickled artichokes, and a peeled orange apiece. In the dry air the bread had mummified. They threw pieces of it to the birds watching them from the thickets. The night lay like black velvet, pricked by myriads of stars. A gentle wind blew; leaves rustled, a rind of moon sailed overhead. In the distance they heard the murmur of the river as it spread over sandbars, coiled into eddies and backwaters, foamed through basaltic rocks. Emile, hands locked behind his head, stared at the night sky. By the light of a candle Charles read from M. Brisbin's volume, *The Beef Bonanza*.

"Listen, Emile! 'No region in the United States or the world is attracting more widespread and favorable attention today than Dakota, and none is or could be more worthy of such regard. Dakota unites in herself all the capabilities of a glorious statehood, all that is requi —'" He hesitated, sounding out the unfamiliar English word.

"Requisite," Emile said drowsily.

"' — all that is requisite to render her, ere long, the imperial commonwealth of the New Northwest, and the cherished homeland of contented and happy millions!'" Reluctantly the baron closed the book. "I am more excited than the day I chose a military career and entered St. Cyr! Are you not — can you not share in my feelings? I want for you too to feel as I do."

Emile did not answer.

"Are you sleeping?"

Emile still did not answer. The baron sighed. "Lawyers! They have no vision." Pulling a blanket from

34

a pack, he laid it over Emile's sleeping form against the chill that gave an edge to the night. He drew another blanket over his shoulders and sat for a long time on a campstool while the fire burned low and then glimmered out. *Cattle. As far as he could see. His cattle.*

Next morning, waking early while Emile was still rolled in his blanket, the baron built a fire. He tried to fry bacon from the inexhaustible picnic basket but succeeded only in burning it, searing his thumb on the hot skillet, and splashing grease on his boots. The cursing woke Emile, who came yawning and stretching to the fire. The morning was chill. Emile squatted before the blaze, holding out his hands to the heat.

"*Ma foi*, Charles — whatever are you doing?"

Helplessly the baron rolled his eyes.

"Here! Give me that!" Emile took the skillet, wiped it clean with a handful of grass, and laid in fresh strips of bacon. "There! That is the way to do it! A hot fire, at first, to sear in the juices. *Then* lower heat!"

Charles sucked his burned thumb. "My friend, I admire you. Always you are so methodical, so unruffled!"

Emile turned the bacon with a fork. "That, my dear Charles, is domestic training. A married man with four children has to learn a lot of things."

"There are advantages to the domestic life," the baron conceded. "But the life of the bachelor has its advantages also, my Emile. Perhaps I cannot fry bacon to perfection, but there are other things I can do."

35

Emile laid strips of crisp brown bacon on the baron's plate, poured him coffee. "I know. You can see a pretty ankle a league away!"

"And what is more," Charles said joyfully, "have the stocking off and the ankle in bed within an hour!" He spun the spikes of his mustache. "As the poet has told us, the destination is nothing; the road is all!" He chewed with sensual pleasure on the bacon. "And speaking of roads — look there, my friend! The highroad to adventure awaits on us!"

Up the river morning sun broke from the clouds and shone on rippling waves of grass. Dappled in shade and sun, the land stirred. Green, green, green — as far as the eye could see; new green, broken only by the darker green of burgeoning box elder, willow, and cottonwood. The cliffs, now pastel in the morning sun, loomed high and proud, marking the path through the baron's new fiefdom.

"Then let us get on with it," Emile sighed.

He offered the baron the last of the bacon but Charles refused. "I am too excited to eat, Emile! With your domestic skills, perhaps you will clean up the household while I saddle our hammerheaded horse brutes."

Emile munched on the bacon. "If there were only brioche to go with it," he said, "or perhaps a croissant or two —" The baron was peering up the valley with his brass-bound spyglass. "What are you looking at?"

"Cattle," Charles said. "Oh, a lot of cattle! They are on the other side of the river, though — not on my side, fortunately."

Emile unrolled his map. Consulting his pocket compass, he looked again at the map. "That is what they call the Slash G land."

Looking puzzled, the baron telescoped the glass.

"Slash G is their 'brand,'" Emile explained. With a stub of pencil he drew a large G, transfixed with an arrowlike bar. "For Griffin, you see. A Mr. Henry Griffin owns the land on the east side of the river. It is a very large cattle operation, the Slash G."

Charles was fascinated. "You know, my friend, I too must have a — what is it called? — a brand?" He took the pencil and map from Emile and drew designs on the back. "Of course, there must be an F, for Fleury." He sketched varieties of the letter F, attaching bars, crescents, curlicues. "What do you think of this, Emile?" Before Emile could answer he shook his head and scratched out the design. "No, too complicated! There must be something both grand and simple about the de Fleury brand. Grand, for our lineage — and simple, for our faith in God."

Emile smiled, retrieved his map. "There is time for that later, Charles."

All morning they saw Slash G cattle as they rode up the valley of the Little Missouri River. "It is the spring roundup," Emile explained, pointing to distant riders. From across the river they could hear distant hallooing as a cowboy spurred his mount to head off a steer. "During the winter the cattle have wandered far away. Now it is necessary to round them up, as they call it — brand the new calves, make a count, cull the herd, do all the things you yourself will soon have to do."

Near noon they ambled down a grassy slope toward the river. The high bluffs at this point crowded the course of the Little Missouri, forming a narrow pass. Swollen by spring rains, the stream ran muddily through high-piled rocks. Beyond the pass lay another rude sod shanty, a sagging barn, and a pole corral.

"I am parched," Charles said, rubbing his throat. "Perhaps those people over there have a well. A cup of cold water would go nicely with the tinned stew Murdoch provided for our lunch."

Charles waved his hat and shouted to the little group standing before the sod dwelling. "*Bonjour, mes amis!*"

"Hello!" Emile called. "Good morning!"

As they rode closer they saw a man digging a hole. Beside the hole stood a severe-looking matron, arms folded over her bosom. A towheaded boy hung behind the woman's skirts. In the doorway of the hut a young girl stood, watching their arrival.

"Hello," Emile repeated, dismounting. "We are travelers, and we thought —"

It was then they saw the sheet-wrapped body, lying on a plank supported by sawhorses. The baron took off his big hat, and Emile muttered an apology. "Madame, we did not know —"

"It's all right," the gravedigger gasped, climbing from the hole and wiping his brow. He was a small man with a wreath of sweat-dank hair surrounding a bald spot, and was dressed in a faded black suit turned green with age. He might have been an accountant, or a clerk; certainly with hands so white and slender he was not used to hard labor. "It's all right," he repeated, looking at the woman as if for approval.

The baron took the shovel. The man protested, but gave it over. The hard-faced woman was less tractable.

"We don't need any help!" she snapped. "We always do for ourselves!"

While Charles continued to dig Emile explained. "This is Baron de Fleury. He owns considerable land around here. We were just riding by. I am Emile Durand, madame — the baron's lawyer. We — we were about to have lunch, and hoped to get a glass of cold water from you."

"I'm Lorenzo Hamlin." The man slumped on the board at the feet of the corpse. He was winded; breath rattled in his throat. "My wife Mattie, gentlemen! The boy is Sidney — we call him Sid." Shading his eyes, he looked toward the hut. "Yonder is my daughter Lutie."

The baron's shovel paused; he looked toward the doorway.

"You find us at a very unfortunate moment," Lorenzo Hamlin said, brushing dirt from his trousers. "We — my family and I came out from Columbus, Ohio, to join my brother Milo." He waved toward the shanty, the corral, the windmill, the chickens, a forlorn cow. "But when we got here —"

"When we got here," Mrs. Hamlin interrupted, "we found Milo had died unexpectedly. So we are burying him, as you see. I guess we'll have to make do on this place ourselves, though the Lord knows we haven't got much experience and it's a forbidding land."

"Sidney," Mr. Hamlin said, "go and bring a jug of water and a tin cup." He tried to take the shovel from the baron, but Charles shook his head. Mr. Hamlin sank gratefully back on the board. "You gentlemen French? Seems to me I recognize the accent."

Smeared with clay, Charles looked up from the hole. "Accsong?" he joked in English. "Me? I have an accsong? Monsieur Hamlin, I do speak the perfect English." He jerked his head toward Emile. "That man there — he have an accent *incroyable!* Talk through his nose!"

Sidney brought a glass jug. The water on top sparkled in the sun; in the bottom lay a thick brown ooze. "River water is all we have," Hamlin apologized. "Got to let it settle. What do they say? 'Too thick to drink and too thin to plow.' Back in Columbus we had a municipal filtration plant."

Sweating, Charles finally had dug the hole deep enough to suit Mrs. Hamlin. The girl, Lutie, was bashful before strangers, but in response to her mother's command walked slowly from the sod shanty and joined them. She was tall and angular, like her mother, with a wealth of shining hair, tinged with bronze in the sunlight. She stood near her father, blue eyes downcast, wearing a soiled traveling dress of gray serge. They all gathered bareheaded while Lorenzo Hamlin read from a well-worn Bible.

"Psalm Forty-six," Mr. Hamlin explained. "It's my favorite.

"God is our refuge and strength, a very present help in trouble. Therefore we will not fear, though the

40

earth be removed, and though the mountains be carried into the midst of the sea; though the waters thereof roar and be troubled" —

The boy Sid absently picked his nose, and Mrs. Hamlin cuffed him briefly, her face grim.

— "and though the mountains be carried into the midst of the sea."

When Hamlin had finished, Emile and the baron let the board and its burden down into the hole. The girl dropped a bouquet of daisies on the dead man's chest. Mrs. Hamlin wept, and Lorenzo Hamlin wiped his eyes with a handkerchief as Emile and the baron shoveled dirt into the hole. Of them all, the girl Lutie showed the least emotion, staring fixedly down the aquiline nose at her dusty shoes.

"You gentleman Catholics?" Mrs. Hamlin asked, seeing Charles and Emile cross themselves as Lorenzo Hamlin and the boy pounded a rude cross of boards into loose dirt at the head of the grave.

"Madame, we are," Emile admitted.

"We're Baptists," Mr. Hamlin said dully.

Saddened by the experience, the two said their farewells and rode away. They did not open the tinned stew. Instead they chewed on pilot crackers and a chunk of cheese.

"They will have a hard time of it," Emile predicted. "They do not seem to me to be the pioneer type."

Charles did not agree. "That woman," he said. "The wife. She will prevail, that one! Inside she is hard like iron. It will take a great deal to defeat her." He lit a cigar. "The husband is weak. Well-meaning, but weak. And while this land is rich, they have settled on an abominably poor part of it." He puffed contentedly, shifting his weight as the horse ambled through a few early daisies. The baron's seat on a horse had always been admired. He rode in the classic style of the cavalryman; reins gathered in the left hand, directing the horse only by the pressure of the leather strap across the animal's neck. The wiry pony had learned quickly, as the baron expected him to.

"Emile?"

"Eh?"

The baron reined up, snapped his fingers. "It has just come to me where I saw that girl!"

Emile had been daydreaming. "What girl?"

"Lutie, the tall daughter, the one with the beautiful hair and that long straight body, the high proud bust!"

"You see girls all the time! Your mind is filled with girls!"

"No, no!" Charles insisted. "She is the one I told you about! You remember — the one who blundered into my California car while I was shaving? I made a little joke with her. At least, I meant it as a joke. I yelled 'Boo!' and she ran like a rabbit!"

"At times, Charles, you can be cruel! The poor child was probably frightened to death!"

"But I did not mean to be cruel! Believe me, it was only a joke!"

42

"I daresay she and her family had ridden all the way on one of those emigrant things — what they call the Zulu cars. Perhaps she wandered too far and came into the first-class cars, and so into the California. She was probably terrified at the sight of a man with his face foaming like that of a mad dog!"

Charles was annoyed. "Do not presume to teach me manners, my friend! I meant well."

They rode on in silence. After a while Emile said, "I beg your pardon, Charles. It was just that I felt very sorry for that poor girl. An attractive young lady, rooted up from her home in Ohio and set down on the lonely prairie."

Charles had forgotten his pique. Seeing a fat antelope on a rise, he pulled up a packhorse by its long tether and snatched out his Belgian hunting rifle. "Tonight," he cried, "we will have fresh meat!" But as he worked the lever and loaded a shell into the chamber, the animal gathered spidery legs under it and sprang away into a draw, bounding like a mechanical toy.

"Damn," Charles grumbled. Regretfully he put the rifle back into the pack.

"There will be other times, other game," Emile soothed.

The baron brightened. "Yes, that is right." Then his face became thoughtful. "Do you know, Emile, I have a wonderful idea! The thought came to me this morning as we were riding."

"And what is your marvelous idea?"

"A — a — I shall call it a hunting wagon."

"A hunting wagon?"

"I will have it made in Chicago and shipped out here on the cars." Against Emile's protests he took the neatly drawn map and scrawled again on its back. "It will be more a great carriage, perhaps, with high wheels so it can surmount any obstacle. I will fit it up with cushioned seats, maybe even a divan. There will be compartments for food and for ice to chill the champagne! Perhaps an observation deck on top fitted with a telescope to look for game and to serve as a shooting platform! With such a vehicle I can invite friends along — Marie de Courcy and the Dessineses and Coline Sevard — to join me for a merry shoot on the prairie!" He showed Emile his sketch. "*Voilà!* What do you think of that?"

Emile did not look at the sketch. Instead he pointed. Ahead, cattle grazed in the deep grass on the baron's side of the river. Two rawboned men lounged on ponies, leaning elbows on their saddlehorns. One, a hawk-faced man, chewed tobacco methodically, and spat into the grass. The other, a lean man in leather pantaloons, watched them through narrowed eyes.

"Hello," the baron said. "What is this, now?"

Emile touched his arm. "I will handle this," he cautioned. Riding forward, he tipped his hat politely. "Gentlemen!"

"You all are on Slash G land!"

"I beg your pardon?"

The baron spurred his horse beside Emile. "Who are these men?" he demanded in French.

44

The tobacco chewer spat. "You heard what Jim said! You're on Slash G land. Get off!"

"Now let us talk this over," Emile offered. He took out his map again. "My client here is Charles, Baron de Fleury. He has bought from the Northern Pacific Railroad all the land on this side of the river, extending" — he consulted the map — "extending all the way to what is called Pigeon Creek. Pigeon Creek, gentlemen, is over four miles yet up the river. So you see —"

"Don't care about no map," the leather-pantalooned man said. He had an air of quiet authority. "We get our orders from Henry Griffin. Ain't no one allowed on this range but Slash G cattle and Slash G folks."

The baron swore, reached for his rifle.

"Charles, wait!" Emile cautioned.

The tobacco chewer had drawn a revolver and was sighting down the barrel. "Put that weapon back where it was!" he instructed.

"Put it back," Emile advised. "The law is on our side, Charles! There is no need to risk confrontation."

Leather Pantaloons spoke in low tones to his companion. "Furriners, too, by God!"

Reluctantly Charles slid the rifle back into the pack.

"That's better," Leather Pantaloons said. "Now get — the both of you — and don't come back!"

The baron stared back at the hard-eyed men. One hand rested uncertainly on the figured butt of the Colt's revolver at his waist. "You are dogs," he said. "Cur dogs! *Chiens — chiens —*"

The tobacco chewer reddened under leathery cheeks. "Don't try our patience, mister!"

Emile seized Charles's reins and turned his own mount back down the river. "Come along, please," he insisted, his voice tight. "Charles — I beg of you —"

When they paused in the shade of a thicket of willows, the two men still sat their horses atop a little rise, watching. Charles was furious. "If you had not stayed my hand —"

"If I had not stayed your hand," Emile said, "we would both have been dead! Those are rough men, Charles! Out here a shooting is common, and often not even pursued in the courts!"

The baron's fingers angrily combed his beard. "But it is my own land! Did I not pay for it?"

"It is a long way back to the California car and the amenities. In the meantime, please compose yourself! Do not let this matter prey on your mind! I am your lawyer, so let me handle the matter properly, in the legal way. Do you not trust me?"

"I could have killed them both!" the baron muttered. "I killed three men in duels who provoked me less!"

That night they made their final camp along the river. Emile, an avid fisherman, caught a string of fat trout and broiled them. They had also a tin of preserved peaches and a bottle of Montrachet, chilled in the icy stream. The baron seethed with resentment.

"It was a mistake to let them drive us off! Out here a man is apt to be judged on his first actions!"

The lawyer caught his arm, pointed northward. In the gathering dusk the heavens were lit with reddish glow. Rising and falling like banners in the wind, streamers of cold rose wavered toward the zenith. The display shimmered and waned, grew stronger and faded — a stage drop for some celestial play.

"*L'aurore!*" Emile exclaimed. "The northern lights, they are called out here! Charles, that is an omen — good luck! Don't be downhearted! Fortune smiles on us! Can you doubt it?"

But Charles was still angry.

CHAPTER
THREE

In June the sun rose early. Lutie lay on a pallet beside the deep-embrasured window of Uncle Milo's sod shanty. The earthen walls were over two feet thick, and in the sunny recess her pot of geraniums made a brave show. Papa and Mama still slept on the rude bed, a wooden frame strung with cords and topped by a ticking bag stuffed with grass. Sidney was burrowed into the board-lined hole dug in the back wall, curled in his nightshirt like a small animal. Papa explained that the hole was probably where Uncle Milo slept during the frigid Dakota winters when the temperature was said to drop to forty below. Sidney had appropriated it for his lair.

Lutie was bone-tired. Her limbs ached, her hands were too sore to play the banjo. Her hair, she was sure, had bleached out in the sun though she always wore the old straw hat she found in the shed that served as stable, barn, and catch-all for the odds and ends Uncle Milo had gathered together.

Through the green spice-smelling leaves of the geranium, a shaft of sunlight reached her face. She closed her eyes against the brilliance, seeing a rosy backdrop to her thoughts. That Frenchman! Again she pictured him in the parlor car bending over that lady, pulling her gown up so he could caress the creamy thigh. What an abandoned way to carry on, even in the confines of a private car! Lutie did not care if he *was* rich. Even rich people should have standards! But Frenchmen had a reputation for licentiousness. She had read all about them in a novel before Mama took it from under her pillow in Columbus.

Sidney stirred, yawned, curled himself tighter. He had found a job working Saturdays at the Mercantile in Little Misery and was tired. Papa breathed heavily, Mama snored in a high-pitched whistle.

Lutie knew the signs. Soon they would rise; the daily toil would start. Under Mama's stern direction they had already planted corn, started a garden patch, sowed wheat and rye and barley in the land Uncle Milo plowed before his tragic death. Mama, more by an imposing manner than any real logic, had secured credit at the Mercantile. Now they had flour, sorghum molasses, and salt pork. They would get along, Mama said.

The bearded Frenchman continued to loom against the glow under her lids. When the Frenchman and the blond man rode by and helped to bury Uncle Milo, Lutie knew he did not recognize her, and was glad for that. He looked formidable: dark eyes, the scar on his cheek, tight-curled black beard. She liked the blond man better. He was gentle, and pleasant. Emil? No, that was German. A lot of Germans lived on the South Side in Columbus, and some of them were named Emil. No, the blond man was Emile. E — meel! Pleasurably, her lips formed the word. Emile sounded much better; not so Dutchy as Emil.

Hearing a faint knock at the glass, she opened her eyes. An alien face, dark and hawk-nosed, stared through the sand-scratched panes. Terrified, she sat up, clutching the ragged quilt around her breasts.

"Papa!"

Mama's whistle stopped, Papa made a strangled noise. Sidney rolled to his knees and stared from his recess like an alert prairie dog.

"Papa, there's a man — a man —" Voice failing, she pointed but the face had vanished.

Mama acted quickly. She grabbed Uncle Milo's old shotgun, thrust it into Papa's hands. "Quick!" she cried. "Go out and see who it is this time of night!"

Papa took the gun. He did not like guns. "It's not night," he murmured, squinting at the sunlit window. "Mattie, it's broad daylight! Lutie, were you dreaming or something?"

"No!" Lutie insisted, trembling. "There *was* a man looking in my window! I saw him, Papa!"

Mama never used profanity but she could make ordinary words sound like swear words. "Give me that gun!" she cried, tearing it from Papa's hands. Bare feet slapped against the earthen floor as she ran across the room. Sidney hurried after her in his drawers to unbar the door. Papa tried to rise, got his feet tangled in the bedclothes, and fell back.

From outside came Mama's stern command. "Halt, there! Halt, I say, or I'll shoot!"

50

Urged by a dread curiosity, Lutie scrambled from bed.

"Don't go out there, child!" Papa warned, trying to get a leg into his pants. "There may be danger!" He hobbled to the door. Lutie followed him, peering over his shoulder.

"Stop!" Mama ordered again. There was a thunderous roar. Mama fell back into Papa's arms. Sidney jumped up and down, crying, "You got one of 'em, Mama! You got one of 'em!"

Lutie looked out into the morning. Three blanket-wrapped figures fled across the sun-washed prairie. One man dropped his wrapper, bent hastily to retrieve it. The recovered blanket streamed in the wind as the fugitives gathered speed and disappeared over a rise.

"Indians!" Mama cried. "Red Indians!"

Lutie remembered the scowling face, the hawklike nose.

"Indians!" Sidney exulted. "Yow-ee! We drove 'em off, like in that Beadle book I bought on the train!"

Papa took the smoking shotgun from Mama's grasp. "Mattie," he protested, "I don't think you ought to have done that. They're harmless. Poor folk — all they can do is wander the country that used to be theirs, and beg. Probably Milo befriended them and they were just coming by for a cup of coffee."

Mama was indignant. "They should knock at a decent hour, like proper humans — not peep into windows!" Seeing Lutie in her nightgown, Mama revolved her by the shoulder, saying, "Girl, put on some clothes! No lady goes about like that." To Papa she said,

"Lorenzo, clean that gun before the barrel gets pitted."
She took Sidney by the ear and twisted till he yelled.
"So that's what you spent that dime for! I told you to
buy something educational. The Lord only knows how
you're going to learn anything out here in the
wilderness!" Getting into her calico, Mama was soon
cutting bread and frying salt pork, making coffee. The
excitement was over. Lutie felt somehow let down, and
ate little that morning.

"I'm just not hungry," she explained.

On the prairie the wind blew ceaselessly. Milo
Hamlin had planted cottonwoods around the sod
shanty to break the wind but the trees were small and
immature. Life was a constant battle against dust that
filtered into everything — beds, pots and pans, food,
clothing. Mama, always a neat housekeeper, was
frustrated. Russian thistles were a plague, growing
everywhere. Dead ones rolled over the land to gather in
spiny clumps against trees, walls, fences. Lutie and
Sidney tired of endless circuits to the river to fetch
water for the cow, the mule, the chickens, but along the
banks grew thickets of wild plums and grapes that
promised soon to ripen.

Gathering cow chips for fuel was the worst. Lutie
hated the petrified droppings. Sidney amused himself
by scaling them into the sky and running to retrieve
them before they came again to earth. Then there were
snakes. Lutie was terrified of them, though Sidney was
braver. He teased rattlers with a stick, jumping back in
pleased fright when they struck. Once, when Lutie was
hoeing in the potato patch, a thick muscular body

52

coiled near her bare feet. Her scream brought Sidney, who chopped the snake with the hoe.

"Don't go near it, Sid!" she begged. He squatted barefoot to poke at the fragments with his finger. "Please, Sid!"

"Aw, it's dead!" he protested.

The body of the ugly thing had been severed by a blow only a few inches behind the triangular head. Sid started to pick up the head, intending to show it to Papa, but the fragment of rattler convulsed in a quick movement and struck at him. White-faced, Sidney scrambled back. "Jesus!" he muttered.

"That'll show you!" Lutie cried in dread and satisfaction. "And don't cuss!"

Somehow they prevailed into the summer. Papa's wheezing grew worse, though he insisted the prairie air was clearing his lungs. Mama grew more hard and brown and adamant. She made lye soap from rendered fat and wood ashes, remembering a recipe from her girlhood on the Virginia farm of Major Edmund Dysart. "Although," she pointed out to Lutie, "when I was a girl, the servants made the soap and did such as that." Lutie shelled corn by drawing the ears over a spade set on a washtub, and learned to ride the mule, which she named Horace, bareback. Mama was scandalized when she insisted on wearing a pair of Uncle Milo's old jeans, but Papa was on Lutie's side.

"We haven't got a sidesaddle," he pointed out. "Let the girl alone! Out here, who's to see?"

They had no neighbors, that was true. Sometimes, when the air was clear of dust, they could see a low sprawling house far up the river on the other side, surrounded by outbuildings and corrals. "Probably the Griffin ranch," Papa said. "That's most likely where those pesky steers come from that get into our fields!"

There were other interlopers, including a coyote that tried to make off with the chickens. There was also a badger living in his den near the sod shanty, a fierce gray hermit whom they learned to leave alone. Prairie chickens abounded, the *boom-boom* mating call sounding loud against the wind. They were good to eat but the family had few shells for the shotgun; Mama wanted to save them against an Indian attack. Sometimes deer came down from the painted bluffs to nibble lettuce and carrot tops in the garden patch. In spite of Lutie's protests Papa killed one for fresh meat, though Mama had to butcher it. "The darkies always did this, too," Mama remarked with bloody hands. "I declare, I don't know how I got involved in this mess!"

On Sunday they rested. Mama read to them from her Bible. Sid and Lutie played Old Sledge with a greasy deck of cards that had belonged to Milo Hamlin. Mama was against cards on a Sunday, preferring Sidney to study the Mitchell's *Geography*, Ray's *Arithmetic*, and the McGuffey reader they had brought from Columbus. But the card game usually did not last long. It always broke up in a quarrel, Sid accusing Lutie of cheating.

"I did not!"

"You did too! I saw you hide that card under your dress!"

54

Lutie hated to lose, and customarily cheated. She was indignant only at being discovered. Papa woke from his nap and Mama scolded them roundly. "He needs his rest," she said.

Angry, Sid decided to go down to the river and fish. In the afternoon heat Lutie followed him into the yard, unhappy at loss of companionship. Sidney, wetting a handful of weeds in the watering trough to stuff in his hat against the sun, refused to be mollified. "You're a cheater!" he said bitterly, and departed.

On sudden impulse Lutie put the hackamore on old Horace. "Mama," she called, "I'm going for a ride along the river!"

Sitting in the gloom of the sod shanty, knitting, Mama looked over her spectacles. "On Sunday? Child, are you crazy?"

"It's such a fine day! Tomorrow it'll be all working and churning and hoeing and things like that! Please, Mama!"

"Well —" Mama hesitated. "If you're careful —"

Lutie was already gone, scrambling on Horace's broad sweaty back. "Mule," she cried, digging bare heels into the animal's ribs, "let's ride out and see the world!"

The air was still with brilliant breathless heat. Convoys of snowy galleons sailed overhead. The buffalo grass swished pleasantly as old Horace ambled. Along the river the leaves of the cottonwoods trembled on their slender stems, buffalo peas lay in pink and purple masses. High in the sky a red-tailed hawk soared. When he came between Lutie and the sun the delicate wings were edged in an aureole of flame. She turned her face to the sun, feeling a great swelling in her breast. To be up there, like that hawk, soaring in the blue on powerful wings!

Riding upland from the river toward the many-colored bluffs, she turned, looking back along the streaked track of the mule's progress through the grass. Was that a horseman, down in the cottonwoods and willows? For a moment she felt apprehension. Then she shrugged, urged Horace forward. It had probably been her imagination. Anyway, it was a fine day for anyone to ride.

Closing her eyes, she gave her body to the easy surging and falling back of the mule's broad barrel. The motion felt pleasant, stirred a delicious tingling in the soft flesh of her inner thigh. *Up, down, up down* — she sang, softly:

> "I won't have none of your weevilly wheat
> And I won't have none of your barley.
> But I'll take a measure of fine white flour
> To make a cake for Charley!"

Lutie wished she had a Charley, her own Charley, to make a cake for. But there was never anyone around but Papa and Mama and Sid. She sang again, softly, thinking of Emile, with his blue eyes and wheat-blond hair, gentle ways. She tried to picture his face, how it would look bending over her, soft flaxen beard tickling her ear. She giggled, and sang more loudly, wishing she had brought the banjo;

"The man who drinks the red red wine
Will never be a beau of mine!
The man who is a whiskey sop
Will never hear my corset pop!"

Was that the dark bulk of a horse in the cottonwoods, paralleling her course? Shading her eyes with a hand she stared down the slope. The shimmer of gold on the river flared into her eyes and made them water. Oh, well, what matter? Someone else was out for a Sunday ride.

Halfway up the slope she slid off Horace, dropping the reins over his broad gray muzzle. There lay an outcropping of gray rock, a granite shelf poking from the green. She sprawled on it, cheek against the hard rock. Deliciously her body drank up the heat. "You just sashay around and graze," she told Horace. "Don't go far away, though — you hear me?"

Eyes closed, she flattened her body again on the warm stone. Perhaps she dreamed; she did not know. When a cloud passed between her and the sun she roused. With legs drawn up, arms locked about her knees, she looked at the country, dappled in sun and shade.

On the far side of the river cattle grazed. There must be hundreds, brown and white spots moving ceaselessly against the green grass. Beyond the ridge she could see the roofline of the ranch house; she did not know she had ridden so far. A lark sang his sweet song in the grass, a squirrel emerged from a fissure in the rocks and looked at her with tiny bright eyes. She made a chirking sound and the squirrel sat erect, tiny paws folded over a silvery belly. Then he flirted his tail and disappeared.

Rolling over, she propped her head on her hands to watch a dung beetle rolling his tiny ball. Mischievously she pulled up a stalk of grass and teased him. Time after time she took the tiny ball of dung away. Time after time the insect came patiently back for it, rolled it on, intent on the task.

Tiring of the game, she stood up, brushing the seat of the old jeans. A few feet away grew a patch of buttercups. She knelt in their midst, gathering blossoms of newly minted gold, *Charley — to make a cake for Charley —*

Reaching for a distant flower, she leaned far over. When she saw the snake coiled among the blossoms, body thick and checkered, small flat triangular head rigid and intent, she congealed in fear. Her hand paused in midair, not a foot from the rattler's tiny forked feeler, playing in and out.

Charley — to make a cake for — Her tongue stuck to the roof of her mouth as the projectile-shaped head drew back, ready to strike.

She screamed, drew her body convulsively backward, but she was not quick enough. The fangs, seeking her outstretched hand, missed; they pierced the coarse stuff of the jeans, stung the soft flesh of her thigh.

She screamed again, feeling the weight heavy on her jeans. Frantically she beat off the snake with her hands. The fangs pulled loose and the thick ugly body fell into the grass. For a moment the rattler lay still, forming a loose W. Then it wriggled quickly away.

"Oh, God!" Horror-struck, she stared at the frayed spot where the fangs had entered, pierced her flesh.

58

Already the wound hurt. The cloth was stained with amber-tinted fluid that must be some portion of the deadly poison.

Swaying on bare feet, nearly swooning, she heard a dull and persistent sound. The pounding of pulse in her ears? Maybe the poison had already reached her heart. She wept, terrified. "Help me, someone!"

The thudding became louder. Breast heaving under the coarse shirt, she gasped for air. Desperately she looked around through eyes already glazed with the fear of death. The insistent thud was not her heart; it was the beat of hooves. Up the grassy rise spurred a horseman. Someone *had* been following her! He was redheaded; in the sunlight, tight curls shone like copper. The pinto was still galloping when he flung himself off and ran toward her. "I heard you yelling!" he announced. "What's wrong?"

Her hands clutched the wounded thigh. "A — a snake! He bit me! I was just gathering flowers —" She pointed to the scattered bouquet. "I was just sitting there, in the flowers, and he —"

"A massasauga?"

She didn't understand.

"A rattler?"

"I guess so. Anyway, I was in the flowers, and when I looked up, there was this snake, and he — he —"

The redheaded man — he was more of a youth, really — was not paying attention to her explanation.

"Lay down," he ordered. He pulled off his short leather jacket and folded it to cushion her head. When she hesitated his voice became sharp. "God damn it, ma'am —"

She sagged to the grass.

"Lay down!" Roughly he pushed her flat. Reaching into his belt, he drew out a long knife. Fearful, Lutie raised her head.

"What are you going to do?"

Big-knuckled hands snatched a fold of the jeans. He began to saw through the cloth.

"What are you doing?" Again she struggled up but he pushed her back. "Those are the only — the only —"

He cut through, laid back a wide flap of cloth. "God damn it — beg your pardon — I'm doing what has to be done! You don't want to die, do you?"

She flung an arm across her eyes. "No."

"Then lay still!"

Her body jerked when she felt a sting in the wound. "It hurts!" The sunny world reeled; darkness pressed in on her. She was afraid she was going to faint.

His voice came from faraway. "Just had to make a little cut to let it bleed!"

He had slashed her with his knife! Did he know what he was doing? Still, she had no choice.

Something soft and warm enveloped the wound, soothed it. Lying obediently flat but lifting her head, she stared. The coppery head was bent over her thigh; the young man's lips sucked softly. Alarmed, she cried, "Here, now! What's going on?"

He paused for a moment, wiping blood from his mouth with a sleeve and spitting. "You *are* a goose!

60

How long have you been around here? Don't you know you've got to slash the wound, suck out the poison?"

"Oh," she murmured. Her body trembled again, not from pain, as his lips worked at the wound. He spat, finally, and wiped his mouth. "Don't move!" He ran to the black horse, grazing near old Horace, and hurried back with a coil of rope. Handling her like a sack of grain, he rolled her over and tied a loop of the rope tightly around her thigh above the wound.

"There!" he said, panting. "That'll keep the venom from getting into your vitals till we can get a doctor!" Cutting off the rest of the coil, he wound it over the horn of his saddle and gathered her in his arms.

"What are you doing?" she demanded, struggling.

He threw her on the saddle of the pinto and vaulted behind her. "Nig will carry double," he said. "You from Milo Hamlin's old place, down below?"

She felt faint. Starting to sway in the saddle, she was glad when a hairy freckled arm clasped her waist, pulling her upright.

"He was my uncle — Milo Hamlin."

"I'm Buck Griffin. From over there!" He pointed toward the ranch house. "Our place is closer. We'll get you to bed and send Jim Peck or Hank or one of the other hands to fetch Doc Cromie from town. Now you just sit easy there, and we'll be home — I mean our place — in no time!"

The world was turning black again. Lutie sagged over the broad arm encircling her waist. "Horace," she murmured. "What — what about Horace?"

He bent to catch the words, ear close to her mouth. "Who the hell is Horace?"

She wanted to sleep. Her leg hurt. The blackness began to overwhelm her. "My" — her lips seemed stiff and wooden — "my — mule!"

He laughed. "Horace'll find his way home, ma'am! Mules are smart!"

The last thing she remembered was the young voice in her ear again, awkward and embarrassed. "I hope you'll excuse my talk, ma'am. I — I ain't used to strange ladies!"

When she woke she was lying in bed — a strange bed, a real bed! Painfully she opened her eyes. Her head ached, her mouth seemed lined with cotton wool. When she moved, a pain lanced her thigh. It was night. The only illumination in the room came from a kerosene lamp that cast flickering shadows on the wall. Squinting, she examined the wall. Wallpaper, real wallpaper! Not since Columbus had she seen wallpaper like this, big pink roses and trellised vines on it. Uncle Milo's old sod shanty had whitewashed earthen walls, the flaky stuff peeling away to show scabrous black patches. Dirty cheesecloth was nailed to the rafters to keep spiders and beetles from falling into their plates.

Rolling her head on the pillow, careful not to move quickly lest her head split, she scanned the room. A polished mahogany bureau on which the lamp glowed softly, a clothes press, a marble-topped table near the window — and lace curtains, stirring in a night breeze. A door stood halfway ajar. On the far wall were crayon portraits of some sort — she could not make them out — and an etching of a lake scene with tall fir trees along the shore, a crescent moon.

Had she died and gone to heaven? Wondering, trying to sit up, she felt bone-deep pain in her thigh and she remembered. *Charley, bake a cake for Charley! Daisies, the snake, the ugly head darting toward her. Won't anyone help me?* Then the red-haired young man —

"Awake?" a pleasant voice asked.

She tried to focus on the countenance looming near as she sank back on the pillow. It was a round face with a neatly trimmed grayish beard; gold-rimmed spectacles glinted in the yellow lamplight.

"I'm Dr. Cromie, from Little Misery. The Griffins called me to tend you. Let's see — Lutie, wasn't that it? Lutie Hamlin, from Milo Hamlin's place down the river?"

"Yes, sir," she said. "Lutecia Hamlin." Even her teeth felt strange. Anxiously she ran her tongue over them. "Oh," she groaned, "my head hurts so! And my leg, where the snake bit!"

Dr. Cromie felt her brow with a practiced hand. "A little fever, but that's normal."

"Am I going to be all right?"

He poured a twist of white powder into a glass of water, stirred it. "Of course you're going to be all right! Here — drink this. It will make you sleep. That's all a healthy young girl needs; plenty of sleep." Gently he pulled back the coverlet, lifted the embroidered hem of her nightgown. Fringing the bottom was fine Swiss lace.

"Where did I get this gown?" Lutie asked, putting the glass down. The milky liquid tasted like mint.

Dr. Cromie adjusted the rimmed spectacles. "Belongs to Carrie, I suppose. Or maybe Mrs. Griffin — I wouldn't know about such things." He touched her thigh with gentle fingers. "Hurt?"

She set her teeth. "Yes."

Her leg looked dreadful. For a hand's breadth around the wound the flesh was puffy, spongy-looking, suffused with dull red. Radial streaks of color surrounded the bite, and the wound itself was crusted and evil in appearance. Dr. Cromie dabbed it gently with a damp medicine-smelling cloth. "Had to put a few stitches in," he apologized. "That fool Buck cut pretty deep. That's Buck, all right! If a peck's good, use a bushel!" He smiled. "Probably saved your life, though. Buck's really a good boy."

Suddenly she uttered a cry of alarm.

"What is it?" Dr. Cromie asked, startled.

She began to cry. "Papa and Mama! When I left, Mama told me not to be gone too long!" She looked wildly at the night outside. "Mama will be mad!"

Dr. Cromie soothed her. "Everything's taken care of, child! The Griffins sent their buckboard to pick up your folks. Right now they're downstairs in the parlor with Henry and Emma Griffin. Now try to sleep."

Her eyelids were becoming heavy, like lead. The minty taste in her mouth was pleasant. Her thigh no longer hurt, and the ache in her head was subsiding.

"Sleep," Dr. Cromie repeated.

"And Horace?"

He chuckled. "The mule?"

"Yes."

"He went home like a good mule," Dr. Cromie said. "Now that's enough talk! Good night." He pulled the coverlet around her and turned down the lamp.

She slept. At least, she thought she slept. Perhaps it was a dream, but it did seem to her that during the night someone was watching. Her eyes were heavy, so heavy. With a great effort she forced them open. In the yellow aura of the lamp she saw a man standing in the open doorway. A clock ticked, the curtains lifted briefly and then fell back. *Something red, something coppery in the lamplight*. Drifting into the blackness again, she remembered the strong arm around her waist as she sagged in the saddle of a big black horse called Nig.

CHAPTER
FOUR

The summer was dry. The late corn they planted rustled sere and stunted, and Mama's garden wilted in the breathless heat. But somehow they got along. Papa finished the plowing and sowing, then managed to get a part-time job bookkeeping at the sawmill in Little Misery, riding the ancient mule to town and back. The mill sold a lot of lumber to Baron de Fleury, the Frenchman, who was building a magnificent house — a "chateau," he called it — on a bluff above the river several miles from Little Misery.

The Hamlins ate a lot of corn cakes and sorghum molasses and got quickly tired of that meager diet. But Mama said corn had a lot of nourishment in it, and that sorghum gave one needed energy. Mama was always busy. With wood ashes and beef tallow she made soap. She hoed in the garden and brought water from the river, insisting that Lutie and Sid remain in the house, studying their books. Almost daily she bent over the staved wooden tub, trying to get the chocolate-colored dirt out of her family's clothes. Hanging them on the line where the whipping wind dried them in minutes, she grumbled, "Clean for brown, I guess, but dirty for white!" Straightening from the washboard only long enough to rub the small of her back, she said, "There's only one way out of this fix your father's got us into! That's *learning!* Lutie, now that you're done with your arithmetic, trade books with Sid so's he can find out that three goes into fifteen five times, no more, no less!"

Over the summer Mama's white skin turned brown and began to look leathery and wrinkled. She lost weight, too, Lutie thought, and her nails were broken, her palms calloused. When she saw Lutie looking curiously at her hands while she was frying a precious bit of side meat, she was annoyed.

"Child, don't sit there and gawk! Put the knives and forks on the table!"

Tired of studying, Lutie and Sid got out the greasy deck of cards one morning and played Old Sledge. Mama was digging in the withered garden, and wouldn't know.

"Instead of wasting time at cards," Lutie said with some asperity and complete lack of logic, "you ought to be out there helping Mama chop weeds!"

"What about you?" Sid protested.

"I'm a girl."

Drawing a card, Sid looked pleased.

"Anyway," Lutie said, "there are other ways."

Sid, arranging his hand, asked, "Other ways for what?"

"I mean — other ways to get ahead besides studying musty old school books. Other ways besides learning."

Sid shrugged.

"For instance, marry a rich man."

Sid hooted. "Ain't many rich men out here! You'd have to go to Denver or San Francisco or someplace like that." His eyes narrowed. "That baron or whatever he was that come by when we were burying Uncle Milo. That Frenchy whatever-his-name-was!" His voice slid into the classic schoolboy taunt, delivered in a singsong. "Lu — tee's — in — love! Lu — tee's — in — love!"

"I am not!" Quickly she looked out the window to see if Mama had heard them. "I am not!" she repeated, laying down her hand. "Anyway, I win!"

Sid stared in disbelief. "Where did you get that ace? It was on the bottom of the deck! I caught a peek when you were dealing!"

"I *drew* it. So you lose. Now you owe me" — rapidly she calculated — "eighty-five cents."

"You cheated again!" Sid wailed. "God damn it, Lutie, you cheat all the time! You'll do *anything* to win!" Frustrated, he threw down his cards and stalked away.

It was not the baron Lutie had been thinking of; it was Emile Durand. Again in her mind's eye she saw the soft brush of his mustache, the softer blue of his eyes. Closing her eyes, she wondered idly how it would feel if that silky mustache were pressed against her lips. Staring at her geranium on the deep-embrasured window — the only thing that seemed to grow on their parched acres — she touched her lips gently with the tip of her tongue. "Emile," she murmured. "Ah, Emile!"

"Well!"

She started, opened her eyes. Mama stood in the doorway, streaked hair tied up in a bandanna; she was holding a dipperful of water from the bucket near the door. "Is this the way you study your fractions, my fine lady?"

"I — I was thinking, Mama."

"Go out and feed the chickens with the corn that's left!" Mama ordered. "You might as well do that as daydream!" Then, seeing the look in Lutie's eyes, she added, grumpily, "Well, I suppose all females daydream at times. I mind I did, when I was a young girl in Bedford County." She set down the rusty dipper and rubbed her hands together. "I wish I still could. It would help against the wind and the drought and all."

Tossing corn to the chickens, Lutie's mind turned to another male — Buck Griffin. Buck was — well, *nice*, but raucous and high-spirited, not cultured like Emile. Since the day of the massasauga the Griffins had become fond of Lutie. Buck often drove her over in his father's trap to the rambling ranch house for supper. In the evenings the Griffins liked for Lutie to play her banjo and sing. Old Pa Griffin was fierce-looking, with sweeping iron-gray mustaches stained by tobacco. At first he frightened her, but Mother Griffin, a sweet and gentle creature, reassured her. "Honey, his bark's worse than his bite! Speak right up to him and he'll come round!"

There was Carrie, too, Buck's "little sister." She was almost as tall as Buck, a slender and willowy girl with huge dark eyes and what Lutie figured to be a kind of spiritual quality about her. Carrie read the Bible a lot and adored Buck. Jim Peck, the foreman, ate with the Griffins. He was a closemouthed man with hard eyes, a distant cousin of Mrs. Griffin. Lutie had never seen him without a pistol on his hip, except at table, and wondered if he took it to bed with him. The rest were hired hands, but they never came into the main house. There was a Chinese cook for the hands but Mrs. Griffin cooked for the family, and she was a good cook. Lutie enjoyed the Sunday dinners with roast pork and fried apples, or maybe flour-dredged steaks with cream gravy. It was a welcome change from corn cakes and side meat, although she wished they would invite Papa and Mama and Sid, too, so they could enjoy the good food.

Mama was not quite sure she liked for Lutie to be with the Griffins so much, but Papa thought it was all right. "They seem neighborly folk," he said, "and everyone in town speaks highly of them. They've got a piano, too, Lutie says. A family that brings a piano all the way out here has got to have some of the finer sensibilities, seems to me."

"That's right," Lutie confirmed. "They're very refined, Mama, with ancestors — just like you."

Buck taught her how to ride, really ride. On a Sunday afternoon he would saddle up a gentle mare for her and his own wild-eyed prancing black, Nig. "Black as night, and his heart's black, too!" he grinned. "Got to *ride* that horse all the time, show him who's boss, or he'd be on *top* of me! Guess he'd jump to the moon if I'd let him."

As they rode away Jim Peck teased Buck. "Best girl, eh, Buck? Going sweet on us after all these years?"

Buck's ears turned red. "Don't mind him," he muttered to Lutie. "He's just got a big mouth, that's all."

Lutie, just to devil Buck, said, "Really, I don't mind. You *are* sweet, Buck!"

The blush deepened. "Aw —" A lock of red hair fell across his freckled brow, and he tossed his head. "Race you down to the meadow!"

He carried her banjo under one arm. When they dismounted in the shade of a huge cottonwood, roots nourished by the lazy flow of the Little Missouri, he squatted beside her in the sun-baked grass, chewing on a seed-tipped stalk. "Pasture's not so good this summer. Too much sun and wind, not enough rain."

Lying on her back, Lutie stared up at the leaves dancing on threadlike stems. "I know. Our garden is purely baked." Casually she adjusted her skirt, pulling it down over her legs, and selected her own blade of grass.

"Play for me." Buck handed her the banjo.

She chewed the grass. "Play what?"

"I don't know. I haven't got any ear for music, but I kind of like to hear it, especially on a nice day like this." Clasping hands around his knees, he stared up at the ranks of white clouds moving grandly across the hot blue sky. " 'Nellie Wildwood,' I like that. Or the one about the bird —"

" 'Bird of the Wilderness'?"

"Guess so." He moved closer. "Whatever *you* like. That's what pleasures me."

She picked up the banjo, twisted keys till it sounded in tune, plucked a chord.

"Sing too, Lutie."

She liked for him to coax. "Buck, you know my voice sounds like a crow!"

"You've got a beautiful voice, Lutie, you know you have" He laid an imploring hand on her knee. "Come on!"

"All right, then." She did have a good voice; she knew it. In a high clear soprano she sang the verse and several choruses of "Nellie Wildwood";

> "She perished in the forest that day
> All covered o'er with leaves —"

Buck's hand slid along the fabric of her good skirt. "Why did she die? I don't remember."

She pushed his hand away. "You do too! As many times as I've sung that song for your father —"

"I forgot. Tell me again."

"For *love*, silly!"

He grinned. "Me, too, Lutie — I'm dying of love, too."

He tried to kiss her but she fended him off. "You look pretty healthy to me! Now you just stop that or I'll not sing another note!" She took up where she thought she had left off:

"Her body fair was never found
And there are those that say
The angels took her high above
To wait for Judgment Day."

Half pleased, half angry, she dropped the banjo and
pushed at his chest. "Buck, stop that!" Remembrances
of Mama's warnings flooded into her mind. "What's
got into you? I declare, this is no way to treat a — a" —
she tried to think of words — "to treat a — well, a guest
— in your father's house!"

"We're not in the house." His face pressed against
her bosom; she smelled the pomade he used to plaster
down the unruly red hair. "Nellie Wildwood hasn't got
the only body fair around here, Lutie!"

Feeling his hand grope upward on the soft inner
curve of her thigh, she cried out in warning. "I'll
scream!"

His voice was thick with passion.

"Nobody'll hear you."

For a moment, feeling her will to resist weaken, she
lay quietly, wondering what to do. She did not like for a
man to have this power over her. Buck's breath was
moist and sweet in her face. She tried to focus her eyes
on his, but they lay too close together.

"Buck — no —" she whispered. "Please —"

His hand pulled hard at her skirt.

"What are you doing?"

"Where the snake bit you, Lutie." He grinned. "I just
want to see if it healed all right!"

She was frightened by the hot light in his eyes, and twisted violently under him.

"God damn it!" he complained. "Stop bucking like a damned jughead, Lutie! You know you like it as well as I do!"

Clenching her fist, she struck out wildly, hitting him in the nose. As with most fair-skinned people, Buck's flesh was tender; blood spurted. "Ow!" he blurted.

Smoothing her skirt, she sat up quickly. "Well, you deserved it, you great lout! Trying to undress me, that's what you were doing! You tore my shirtwaist, too — I hope no one notices till I can get home and fix it!"

Not looking at her, Buck squatted, holding a handkerchief to his bleeding nose.

"Did I hurt you?" she asked, holding the neck of her blouse modestly together.

"Hell, no! How can you hurt someone by hitting them in the nose with your fist?"

"I'm sorry." Taking the handkerchief, she dabbed at the blood, then giggled. "Lord, your nose looks like a beet!"

When he reached for her again, she quickly drew away. "Want me to do it to you again?"

He sighed, looked at the bloodstained cloth. "I guess I apologize! It was just the sun and the grass and the river talking and the nice day and all."

Her voice took on an edge. "I guess *I* didn't have anything to do with it, then!"

He looked at her, uncertainly. "Of course! I mean — well —"

She knew what he meant, and felt magnanimous. Sure of herself now, she stroked his bronze curls, wet with sweat; they shone richly in the sunlight that had crept under the cottonwood tree. "It's all right, Buck. I forgive you." Rising, she planted her booted foot wickedly in his back, bowling him over so he almost fell into the shallow weed-grown eddies of the river. Laughing, she raced to the mare and flung herself on, spurring toward the distant ranch house. When she reined up to look over her shoulder Buck was stolidly clambering up on Nig, her banjo in his hand. Feeling good, she waved. It was nice to control a man so, to dance on the edge of danger and then draw back, leaving him tantalized and frustrated. For a while, she was afraid. Now she knew she could handle men. It was — power. Yes, that was it. Power over them; perhaps, she thought, it might be as good as — how had Mama put it? — as good as letting a man "have" her.

The summer continued parched and dusty. It seemed to Lutie the hot dry wind blew constantly. Feeding the scrawny chickens, she squinched her eyes shut as the wind tore at her skirt, blew her hair into tangles. Even the chickens, scrabbling for the few grains of corn, looked ruffled and frowsy. She had to breathe, but even with her lips pressed tight together the talcum-fine dust came through her nose and settled dry and gritty on the inside of her teeth. Mama, grim and touchy, railed at her when she came into the soddy.

"For the Lord's sake, Lutie, shut that door, quick!" Ineffectually dusting the rude furniture, Mama spoke through tight lips. "Now I can surely guess why poor mad Milo hanged himself! He was driven wild by this cursed country! Sometimes I'm tempted myself, if there wasn't so much washing and cooking and sewing to do!"

Lutie was shocked. "Mama, you shouldn't say things like that, not even joking!"

"I'm not joking." Mama stared out the window at a boiling dust cloud on the horizon, a miniature cyclone that spiraled dizzily along the edge of the bluffs. "In Virginia I had a slave to do this dusting. Well —" She sighed, shook out the dustrag, went back to dusting.

Up the river, atop the high bluffs, the baron's chateau was growing. Lutie and Buck, riding along the river, watched it in fascination. Buck swore.

"Ain't that a caution, though, that big pile. That Frenchy has lost his mind!"

From dawn to twilight workmen labored; sawing, hammering, laying up stones in walls and paving long curving promenades. At Little Missouri freight cars unloaded marble washbasins, mirrors, a huge ebony piano, sofas, carefully crated paintings, roll after roll of thick-piled Wilton carpeting all the way from England. Masons came from Italy to build mantels. A Swiss workman laid up chimney after tall chimney, some in massive vertical towers, others spiraling around and around in intricate brickwork as if a mischievous giant had grabbed them by the top and twisted hard. Roll after roll of wire came too, Papa reported, the shiny spools ticketed "Barb Wire Fence Co., DeKalb, Illinois

— ship to Baron Charles de Fleury, Little Missouri, D.T."

Mama was curious. "Wire?" she asked. "What kind of wire?"

"It's a new patent," Papa explained. "They take iron wire and twist sharp barbs into it to keep things out — or in. It's a new thing, to fence off the land." He ate some of the beans Mama put on his plate, chewed a bit of the fried pork dipped in flour, and then laid down the fork. "Seems I haven't got much appetite lately, Mattie."

Sid smacked greasy lips. "Mama, I'm holler as a beech log! Can I have his beans?"

Mama rapped him on the head with her spoon. "No, you can't! He needs his food, working the way he does at that sawmill! And besides, wherever did you learn to say rube things like that? Land sakes, you and Lutie are getting to be regular hayseeds! No one would ever suspect you two had Dysart blood in your veins!"

"Buck talks like that!" Sid protested, rubbing his crown. "I heard him when he and Lutie were back behind the —"

"You be quiet, you little sneak!" Lutie snapped.

"Children, children!" Papa ate a few more beans, pressed a hand to his breastbone, swallowed hard. "A touch of dyspepsia, I guess. Nothing serious."

"The wire, Papa," Lutie inquired. "Is it allowed to put up wire around here? I thought everything was — well, open, except for corner markers like Uncle Milo put in."

"It's legal, I guess, if you own the land. But there's a lot of grazing land around here seems no one's got a clear title to. People just use it for their cattle, like that patch up the river the Griffins graze their stock on. Fencing is apt to cause a lot of hard feelings."

"Mr. Griffin says if anyone ever tries to fence in the land he won't stand for it. That's what he said!" Lutie was very firm.

"Buck would shoot 'em!" Sid grinned.

"Now that's enough talk about shooting," Mama warned. "Lord knows there's enough heartbreak and despair out here without anyone looking for more!"

"That's right," Papa sighed. Lutie noticed with a pang how gray he seemed to have gotten since they came to Dakota. She decided this was a good time to spring her surprise to cheer him up.

"Next month is Buck's birthday!"

"That's nice," Papa said. Mama said nothing. She didn't actually approve of Buck Griffin — too forward, she said.

"And we're all invited."

Mama was wiping her unused spoon with a napkin. Though the few good linens she had brought from Columbus were now threadbare, and gray from washing in the river water, she insisted on proper napkins at their meals. She even packed a napkin with Papa's lunch when he went each morning to the sawmill. "Invited?" she asked. "To what, pray?"

"Why, to Buck's party, of course! He'll be twenty-one, and they're planning a big celebration! An ox roast, horse races, a shooting contest, dancing — oh,

78

everything! Mr. Griffin is inviting Mr. Sam Oates from the newspaper and Mr. Larson at the sawmill and Jake Sigafoos and his family and all the big ranchers from as far away as Dickinson and Chama and Wibaux. There's to be dozens and dozens of guests!"

"Will there be wrastling?" Sid demanded. "Since I been helping out at the Mercantile, throwing those big feed sacks around, I got muscles like iron!" He rolled up his sleeve, tightened biceps. "There — feel that, Lutie!"

She ignored him. "There's going to be such fun! And we'll get to meet so many people! It's not like here. I mean —" She stopped, seeing the look on her father's face. "You'll enjoy it, Mama, really you will! You can dress up in that ruffled silk dress that's been in the bottom of the trunk for such a long time!"

Mama pursed her lips, drummed lean fingers on the table. "Dancing, eh? It's been a long time since I danced."

"When is this party?" Papa asked.

"Next month. The twentieth of September." Lutie got to her feet, ran around the table, kissed them both. Mama's cheek felt dry and dusty, and Papa hadn't shaved today. But she loved them both. If only they had the spark of life *she* had! You could *make* happiness, even in this desolate country, if you really wanted to. But Papa and Mama had never learned how. She was sorry for them, but she would never let that happen to her. She would grab life, twist it, make it holler uncle; no need ever to be glum.

The change of seasons was already beginning. The winds slackened, the nights grew still and cold, the days were noticeably shorter. Ice rimmed the trough where the chickens and their new heifer drank. In its daily travels the sun spanned a shorter and shorter portion of a sky that hurt the eyes with its intense blue. The willows along the river rustled dryly, their leaves like brown wrapping paper. In the morning Mama's squaw bread — dough fried brown in bacon grease — tasted good to Lutie, drowned in syrup, although she was afraid she would get fat and then Buck wouldn't like her anymore.

Overhead, skeins of Canada geese formed for the long journey south. Gophers worked frantically to gather seeds and grasses against the coming winter. Still, the days were warm and sunny. The land seemed for a while to have come to a standstill, basking in the sun to rest after the growing season.

Buck rode over to bring the Hamlins a personal invitation. Papa said, "Why, Buck, thank you. It's not every day a handsome young fellow turns twenty-one!" Mama smiled uncertainly. "Can I bring something?"

Under his sunburned cheeks Buck seemed to blush, not meeting Mama's eye. "Only —" He swallowed, started again. "Only Lutie, ma'am!"

Sid giggled, but Mama quelled him with a look heavy as a sadiron. "Of course we'll bring Lutie, Buck! And it's gracious of you to ask us."

Walking with him down to the river, Buck riding Nig, Lutie felt warm and pleasant in the slanting sun. A few late bees buzzed, and a lost butterfly darted among the crisp-leaved willows.

"I'll make a present for you," Lutie offered.

"What?"

"That's a secret, mister!"

Out of sight of the soddy, Buck scooped her up with one fence-post of an arm and sat her on the saddle before him. He laughed, squeezed her when she struggled, and let her down again. "I hope your present is what I think it is!"

She hadn't yet decided herself what it was to be. Standing in the lacy shadow of the willows, she pulled off a leaf and crumbled it in her fingers. "What do you want, then?"

"Well," he said, "it ain't something you *make*."

"Oh, you silly goose!"

Bending from the saddle, he snatched a kiss and spurred away. She watched Nig top the rise, hooves drumming, Buck whooping like an idiot and slapping the black's powerful haunches with his hat.

She didn't see him again until the party. She and Papa and Mama dressed in their best, clothes put away and smelling of the perfumed soap Mama had packed them in to discourage moths. Lutie wore her prized hat with the cherries and Sid had polished his copper-toed boots till the metal caps shone like twin suns. Lutie took along her banjo, of course, and the pair of socks she had knitted for Buck. They did not seem exactly the same size, but Mama said that girls nowadays couldn't knit anyway, and besides it was the intention that counted. Mama baked three raisin pies, and from their scanty funds Papa had bought Buck a nice barlow knife from the Mercantile.

They had to cross the bridge at Little Misery and then double back on the other side of the river. Except for a few lounging blanket-wrapped Indians dozing in the sun, the town looked deserted. Jake Sigafoos, the livery-stable man, was just pulling away with his wife and family in his piano-box buggy, all shined up for the occasion. "See you at the shivaree!" he called, waving his whip. Swiftly the piano box rolled away, wheels raising pencil-thin streamers of dust that hovered a moment above the bays and then were blown away by the wind.

They followed more slowly, old Horace shambling along at his measured pace. "Ow!" Sidney yelled, and Mama turned swiftly. "Lutie, are you plaguing that boy again?"

"No, I'm not!" Lutie protested. "He's always howling about something, Mama, you know that!"

"I got a bug in my eye!" Sidney complained. "It hurts!"

"Let me see." Mama inspected the eye. With dexterity born of long practice, she drew Sid's face to hers, stuck out her tongue, and deftly touched the eyeball. "There!" She spat, delicately. "Now you two sit there and don't let me hear a word out of you till we get to the Griffins'!"

Lutie closed her eyes, swaying gently to the motion of the wagon. *Emile* — She saw again his gentle smile, the handsome face and the understanding eyes, the soft brush of the golden mustache. He would get something in *his* eye, and she would put her hands ever so softly on his cheeks and draw his face to hers —

"Listen!" Papa said.

Unwilling, Lutie roused herself, opened her eyes.

"What?" Mama asked.

"The music! Can't you hear it?"

They were laboring up a windburned hill, Horace blowing and whuffling, but against the rush of the wind and the distant murmur of the river she could hear the sawing of a fiddle and the chant of the caller:

"Gents bow out and ladies bow under!
Hug 'em up tight and swing like thunder!"

Mama wrinkled her nose. "Lutie, you said there would be dancing!"

"That's dancing, Mattie," Papa said.

"I'd hoped to waltz a little, or maybe schottische."

"This is the West, Mattie, and not Bedford County in Virginia," said Papa. "They're frontier folk and do things different. You ought to try it. Now don't be stuffy, please."

The hollow next to the river where the Slash G buildings lay was bordered with cottonwoods. They slowed the wind, somewhat, but Lutie's skirt was plastered flat against her legs when she got down. She was embarrassed, fumbling at the gingham material and trying to pull it loose; she should have worn all the petticoats Mama ordered. Still, she liked her legs — her limbs — to feel free and unhampered. Buck picked her

83

up in his arms and swung her high, laughing. Mama looked on with pursed lips.

"Lutie! My girl!" The sun behind him lit the red hair, making a coppery aureole. Suddenly remembering his manners, he put down his prize and turned to the Hamlins. "Sir, Mr. Hamlin, sir, and ma'am — I'm glad — we're *all* glad you could come." He rumpled Sid's cowlick. "Hi there, Sid!"

Mr. and Mrs. Griffin hurried over also, to greet them. Carrie, Buck's sister, hovered behind them. Shyly she curtsied, eyes downcast.

Lutie had not seen so many people since the crowded Chicago station. Like a multicolored liquid they filled the grassy bowl, washing here and there, up the hill and down, as the widespread activities flourished. Lean men in best shirts and scrabbling boots were trying to climb a greased pole atop which was tied a jug of whiskey plugged with a corncob. On an elevated platform of raw new lumber dancers kept up a steady tattoo of bootheels, accompanied by feminine shrieks of pleasure. Small children lurched across the meadow in a three-legged race, the prize a sack of jawbreakers. Under the shade of the cottonwoods a few ladies had volunteered to watch the swaddled infants lying about on the grass. A crowd gathered around the long tables supporting iced barrels of beer, the bartender from the Empire Saloon in town trying in vain to keep up with the demand.

"Mrs. Hamlin, you just bring them raisin pies right into the summer kitchen," Ma Griffin said. "I and some of the other ladies are starting to lay out the victuals."

Pa Griffin clapped Papa on the back. "Come along, sir, and —"

"You can call me Lorenzo."

"Lorenzo, then. I got to get over to that roasting beef and baste it proper! Seems like no one can do it right but me!"

From a distant knoll a sprinkling of blanket-wrapped Indians watched the merrymakers. Sid narrowed his eyes and drew an imaginary bead on them. "Wisht I had my good old rifle!"

Drawing Lutie away with him, Buck laughed. "God, you're bloodthirsty, Sid! They ain't going to harm no one. Old Custer took all the fight out of 'em before he lost his own hair." He pulled her after him. "After we eat, we're going to have horse races and such. I got Nig all primed. That black devil can outrun a bolt of lightning if he's of a mind to!"

Carrying her banjo in one hand, she drew the other from his grasp. "Where are we going?"

"Just in here, in the barn. Pa's Morgan has got a colt that's the cutest thing you ever saw. Wait till you see him!"

After the dazzling September sun the barn was dark, fragrant with the smell of oats, hay, and saddle-soaped leather. A beam of light pierced the gloom; motes drifted diamondlike across the sunny shaft. As from a great distance Lutie could hear the thump of bootheels and the muted fiddle scraping out "Money Musk."

The half-grown colt, standing awkwardly beside the mother, looked at her with wide brown eyes. She stroked the sleek muzzle while Lady Evelyn, the

85

Morgan mare, looked at her benignly. "Oh, he is a champion, Buck! Whatever do you call him?"

"It's up to you," Buck grinned.

"Up to me?"

"I've been working on Pa to let me give him to you — when he's put on a little more weight, that is. I almost got him convinced."

Dropping the banjo into the hay, she threw her arms about him in purest delight. "Oh, Buck, not really! That's just about the nicest thing that ever happened to me! My own horse!"

Before she was aware of what was happening, he clasped her in his arms. They fell into the hay together. "Now, Buck!" she warned. "Don't spoil it!" But then, grateful for the generous present, she tempered her protests. "Oh, it was so *lovely* of you!"

Eagerly he buried his hot face in the little hollow between her shoulder and neck. "God, you smell good, Lutie!"

Finally, exasperated, she slapped him. "I don't know what I'm going to do with you anymore!"

Sullenly he let her go and sat cross-legged in the hay like an angry Buddha. She had seen a Buddha once, in Papa's books, only they were usually peaceful-looking. Buck was frustrated.

"You never want to have any fun!" He took a flat black bottle from his hip pocket and drank from it, wiping his mouth with a red-furred forearm. "Nicey-nice!" he jeered. "Maybe you're *too* nice for a plain old ranch hand like me!"

Instantly she was contrite. "I'm not either! It's just that — that —"

"Just what, missy?"

She smoothed her dress primly. "Nice girls — I mean proper girls, proper ladies — they don't roll around in the hay with men!"

Unconvinced, he only grunted and sampled the bottle again.

"Buck, I *do* love you!" She put a hand on his arm, feeling a little tingle at the warm solidness of his flesh.

"Show me, then."

"What do you mean?"

"Well, you might start by having a little drink with me."

She had never known liquor, and thought immediately of an appropriate song:

> "I love my mammy and pappy
> But take a warning from me!
> Oh, never waste your affections
> On any young man so free!
> He'll hug you and he'll kiss you
> And he'll tell you more lies
> Than the cross-ties on the railroad
> Or the stars in the sky!"

Only fourteen, she had heard a colored girl sing it, and figured out the chords on her banjo. Mama, overhearing her, made her go to bed without her supper.

"What's in the bottle?" she demurred, knowing full well what it was. Buck, she knew, frequently pilfered his pa's whiskey, pouring water back in to bring the liquid back to the previous level. Pa Griffin sometimes complained that whiskey didn't have the kick it used to have.

"Just a little mild tonic. Doctors give it to old folks when they need something to spark up their livers. Pa takes it regular!"

She wavered, not wanting Buck to think her nicey-nice.

"Just a sip, then."

He leaned forward, insisting on keeping his hold on the bottle.

"Why? I can hold it myself. I'm not an infant!"

He giggled. "Don't want you to spill none! This is Mose Hopkins' Old Original. Pa gets it sent in all the way from Frankfort, in Kentucky. Costs like blazes; three dollars a bottle."

Gingerly she tasted, and made a face.

"Aw, go on! That wasn't but a drop!"

She tried again. The stuff was warm and tingly on her tongue, and burned when it went down. She spluttered, coughed. "Oh, my!"

"Go on!" Laughing, Buck bore her down and tipped the bottle high. She had to swallow, but squirmed angrily, trying to protest.

"Buck —"

"Just another little dram, now! That's to make you nice and friendly, Lutie!"

Though slight, she was strong and wiry. Getting her knees against his chest, she kicked him away and sat up, gasping. He looked in mock dismay at the bottle.

"God, Lutie, you drank most all of it! Now I'll have to sneak into the bedroom and fill it again!"

Shaking her head, blinking, she rubbed her throat. "You *made* me! Oh, lord, that stuff burns like fire! I can hardly catch my breath!"

"Ain't it pleasant, though? Like a nice warm fireplace after a snowy day!"

Gradually she did begin to feel nice and warm inside. But she was still angry at the way he had overwhelmed her; she did not like to be overwhelmed. "That wasn't nice to do that to me, Buck Griffin! Don't you ever try that again or I'll scratch your eyes out!"

Contented, he lay down, head in her lap, one booted leg cocked over the other. The feel of his tousled head in her lap stirred feelings in her she did not like. Then she decided the best way was just to show him she did not care one way or the other. They remained that way for a long time, Lutie listening drowsily to the tune of the fiddle, the thump of distant boots, the shouts and cries and hubbub that came through only softly in the fragrant barn. She licked her lips, tasting the liquor again. It wasn't as bad as it had at first seemed.

"Lutie?"

She roused herself, opened her eyes. The fire in her bosom was warm and pleasant.

"I love you. You know that. I'm sorry for what I did. I — I just thought it would loosen you up a little, make you not so prim."

She nodded. "Mmmmmm."

When his finger touched her breast, she stiffened. "Now, Buck —"

"Well, it ain't wrong when two people love each other, and plan to get married, is it?"

She could not move to avoid him. It was pleasure; the incandescent glow of Mose Hopkins' Old Original, all the way from Frankfort, Kentucky, the drowsy feeling, the touch of his fingers —

"I gave *you* a present," he murmured. "The Morgan colt. You know it's my birthday, though, Lutie. It's time for you to give *me* something."

She thought of the socks she had knitted for him. In this warm drowsy bower, this lovely sweet place with Buck beside her, the thought of socks seemed horribly gross, simply out of place. She would get them for him, though. After a while.

"Lutie —" He rolled over, put his arms about her neck, pulled her face down to his. "Lutie —"

She struggled weakly, uncomfortable at the thought that her will was flagging. Somehow her limbs seemed to have turned to water. Closing her eyes again, not willing to witness capitulation, she felt the sandpapery bristles of his cheek against hers. He smelled good, too, she thought, helpless at the warm tide rising within her.

"Buck, please don't! I — I can't —"

Kissing her, he fumbled at her clothing, pressing his hard flat body against her. Dimly she speculated that her mistake had been in daydreaming about M. Emile while they were riding in Papa's wagon. The daydream,

90

most likely, had excited her in an unmaidenly way, weakening her defenses against this — this —

"Buck, please —"

At least, daydreaming of Emile was as reasonable an explanation as anything else.

"I — I don't know anything about this, Buck!" There was panic in her voice. "I never — I never —"

What was he doing to her? She began to cry, but Buck paid no attention to her muffled weeping. The sun-splashed barn reeled dizzily.

"Buck!"

His voice was thick and breathless in her ear. "Lutie, I do love you so! You're so sweet — *my* sweet!"

Feebly she struggled, but there was no use. After a while her body went limp and she sighed, a deep shuddering breath. A great lassitude enveloped her; she lay with eyes closed, hair in disarray, bosom rising and falling slowly.

"Buck." Eyes still closed, she raised a hand and touched the beloved cheek. "Oh, Buck!"

Opening her eyes, she saw him propped on brawny freckled arms, looking at her soberly.

"What did we do?" she asked, beginning to be worried. "Buck, what —"

He touched her lips with a finger. "Don't talk. Just lay there, honey, and let me look at you."

She struggled to rise, adjust her clothing, suddenly very frightened. "What if —"

"Who cares about 'ifs'? I love you so! Lutie, I'm going to marry you, so don't worry about anything. You hear me?"

Confused, distraught, she did not know what to say. Mama! If Mama ever found out! She had been wicked. Good girls did not let men do — things — to them before they were married. Still, she felt a perverse tenderness for him. Gently she touched the red curls, smiled up at him; the silky feeling pleasured her anew. He must just have washed his hair. Satisfaction suffused her. In spite of the guilt, she had enjoyed it. Was it — could it be — really wrong, yet so filled with pleasure?

"I love you too," she said in a husky whisper. But he suddenly scrambled up, peering toward the almost-closed barn door.

"What is it?" she asked in alarm, sitting up.

He shook his head, puzzled. Then, rising, he walked toward the bar of sunshine. Peering out, he watched in silence. The fiddle music had stopped.

"Buck, what is it?"

A stalk of timothy hay dangling from his lip, he sauntered back. "You'd never guess, Lutie!"

She had regained some of her composure. Picking up the cherried hat, she tied the ribbons under her chin. "Riddle me no riddles, please."

"That baron galoot, de Fleury, he just drove in, and he ain't even been invited to the party." Buck grinned, wickedly. "I just don't guess there's going to be *some* fun! Oh, no!"

CHAPTER
FIVE

"Come on!" Sid urged. "Let's get the hell out of here!"

Clarence Sigafoos, the liveryman's son, held a finger over his lip. The dust in the mow had tickled his nose.

"Jesus, you better *not* sneeze!"

The towheaded Clarence blinked, withdrew his finger. "Why do we have to get out?"

Sid was shaken. He was not sure what had gone on between Lutie and Buck, being a quite innocent boy. But Clarence was more knowledgeable.

"Them two!" he giggled. "Boy, when I tell what —"

Sid seized him by the throat. The words broke off in a gurgle. Clarence's face turned red. His blue eyes started to pop, and Sid relaxed his grip.

"If you ever open your trap to anyone, I'll kill you!"

Clarence was bigger than Sid, and strong, but the fire in his companion's eyes made him quail. "What you think I am — some kind of a sneak?"

Together they went silently down the wooden ladder at the back of the barn. "I don't know what you are," Sid muttered, "but what I said still goes: I'll *kill* you!"

Before the Griffin ranch house, the baron sat easily on his long-maned coffee-and-cream mount. Behind him was a team of mules hitched to a fancy wagon loaded with boxes, and driven by a dour-faced man dressed in sober black. The Hamlins' wagon was a creaky contraption with leaning wheels and floorboards of weathered gray oak gouged and split; the iron fittings were red with rust. The Griffins owned a lot of wagons, all worn and shabby, though serviceable. But this wagon was like something out of a county fair. The wheels were green, with orange spokes, and the hubs brightly polished brass. The body was brown, with orange striping, and the driver sat on a leather-upholstered seat; he was in sober black, with a kind of plug hat. On the side was blazoned a coat of arms, and below it a painted representation of what appeared to be a brand — a script F in a kind of rosette. Gradually the sounds of revelry died, starting first at the confrontation and then spreading to activities scattered throughout the meadow. The bartender stopped drawing beer. Horseshoes ceased their metallic ring. Two wrestlers paused in their tugging and stared, hands shading eyes. "Money Musk" trailed off as a fiddler's bow stopped in midair.

"That so?" Pa Griffin was asking. He stood under the roof at the ranch-house door, arms crossed, stained mustaches working.

The baron twitched at the reins. The caracoling Arabian stopped its prancing.

"*Oui, monsieur.* I hope you pardon my *mal anglais* — my bad English. But I come to join the party." He waved toward the wagon and the gaunt-faced driver. "Here is what we drink in my country when we are happy — champagne! Cold, too, in ice we buy from another neighbor — Mr. Liveryman Sigafoos!"

Anticipating violence, the two boys pressed close. Buck, glowering beside his father, muttered, "Tell him to get the hell out of here with his fancy wine! We don't need none of it, nor him!"

The baron must have heard. He smiled. "I come in good faith! I want to be *amis* — friends — with the — the" — the labored English failed, and he frowned — "*avec tout le monde*." Suddenly he brightened. "With everybody, I mean to say!"

Buck was insistent, muttering again in his father's ear. "Tell him to get out, Pa. How do we know what he's saying in that frog language? If you don't run him off, I will!"

At Buck's side, Lutie stared at the insolent nobleman, remembering her fright and shame when this imperious man had shouted "Boo!" in the varnish of the Pacific Express. She saw again the wicked glint in his eyes, remembered the soap-foamed cheeks, grinning mouth, flourished razor. "Make him go!" she whispered, and loosened her grip on Buck's arm.

Buck stepped forward but Pa Griffin grabbed his shirttail and hauled him back.

"This is my business!" The old man swallowed; the knobby adam's apple bobbed up and down between the tight cords in his neck. A stranger in his house was a guest, he always said. He heaved a kind of whuffling breath, and the grizzled mustaches flew out and back.

"You're welcome," he said, stepping off the veranda to offer his hand, "Mr. —"

"Call me Charles." Nimbly the baron dismounted, to shake Pa Griffin's hand. "And you must be Buck."

In response to his father's heavy look, Buck dumbly held out his hand.

"This young lady —" The baron's dark eyes lit. "Do I, perhaps, know you from something — I mean — somewhere?"

Lutie, embarrassed, shook her head.

The community seemed to take a relieved breath. Horseshoes started to clang again, the wrestlers took new "holts" on each other, the lager started to flow. Men took cases of the strange French wine from the wagon, and watched in astonishment as it popped and foamed. Ice broken, others came forward to shake the baron's hand. Dr. Cromie, who had studied in France, made small talk with the baron in the nasal language which Lutie thought ridiculous. Jake Sigafoos pressed the baron's hand warmly; Lutie remembered the baron bought a lot of stuff from the liveryman. Mr. Oates from the Little Misery *Gazette* followed the baron with his notebook and pencil, asking for his opinions of the West. Sheriff Holland, fat belly swinging pendulously, was reserved, but shook hands also. He had already had complaints about the "bob wire."

"I hate that man!" Lutie murmured.

Buck drew her toward the groaning trestle tables where the ladies were laying out the food. The Griffins' Chinese cook hacked slabs of pink-edged beef from the spitted ox; a helper plopped the meat onto a plate and poured mahogany-red sauce over it. "I'm hungry as a spring bear!"

96

Lutie's stomach churned. "You shouldn't have given me that stuff to drink, Buck. It was awful strong."

"Pshaw!" he grinned, handing her a plate. "Fill 'er up! What you need is some good old ranch grub."

There were fried potatoes and onions, squash baked with pork, fresh corn stewed with tomatoes, carrots glazed in brown sugar and butter, piccalilli, doughnuts, a great tin pan of blackberry duff, pies, jars of jelly and jam, hot biscuits, an urn of strong bitter coffee, and iced lemonade for the children or those who preferred to cool off after their exertions. Lutie and Buck sat on the porch swing with their plates. He devoured everything on his plate; Lutie only played with her food.

"You gonna eat that beef?"

She shook her head. Deftly Buck speared the slab with his fork, gnawed the edges. Watching him, Lutie felt faint.

"Don't swing so hard!" she protested, closing her eyes and gripping the chain.

"You sick? God, you ain't supposed to get sick for another two or three months!"

She didn't know what he meant, but the morning had been too much. The excitement, the foul whiskey, the unnerving thing that happened in the barn . . . She put a hand over her mouth and stopped the swing by scraping her shoes on the floor.

"Buck, I've got to —"

Drawing his new boots out of the way, Buck set down his plate. "Out back, quick!" Taking her arm, he dragged her through the parlor, past the curious ladies who were frying potatoes and cutting up pies. Vaguely she remembered the outhouse, but never reached it. Tottering away from Buck, she heaved into Mrs. Griffin's marigolds bordering the walk. Buck held her by the shoulders. "Again!" he commanded. "Get it all up!"

Finally, pale and shaken, she straightened. Buck wiped her face with his bandanna. "Christ, you *were* sick! Why didn't you say something?"

Ladies were watching from the kitchen window. Mama banged open the door and marched down the graveled walk. "Whatever in —"

"Lutie got a little upset to her stomach," Buck explained. "I guess it was the excitement and all."

Mama took Lutie by the arm and looked suspiciously at Buck. "Excitement never bothered her before!"

"Well —" Buck dug a toe into the gravel, avoided her eye.

"Are you all right now, daughter?"

Miserably Lutie nodded. She *did* feel better, though.

"Some of the folks want you to play your banjo. Come into the parlor."

Buck disappeared. Obediently Lutie followed Mama. A heavy plush carpet lay on the floor, alive with roses as big as cabbages. On the walls hung framed crayon portraits of old Griffins, she guessed, and a pair of chromos Lutie remembered from back home, "Wide Awake" and "Fast Asleep." One showed two cherubs, fat and contented, watching with marveling eyes a bluebird singing in a tree. In the other they had fallen asleep in each other's arms. Someday soon, Lutie supposed, she and Buck would lie like that, in each other's arms, man and wife. Suddenly she was angry. She should never have let him do that to her! She had lost something, something integral to herself, something more precious than Buck! She had lost — power. Yes, that was it. She was Buck's now: *he* had the power!

"What are you scowling like that for?" Mama hissed in her ear. "Smile, child!"

The ladies had separated themselves from the male foolishness going on outside. Some played euchre in the big parlor, others chatted languidly, waving palm-leaf fans. Mrs. Griffin, beaming and rosy-faced, tapped her iced-tea glass with a spoon.

"Ladies, this here is Miss Lutecia Hamlin, from down the river. A lot of you know her pa, Mr. Hamlin over there, who keeps books at the sawmill. Now this pretty young lady is going to favor us with a few songs, accompanying herself on the banjo."

Papa, eschewing the rowdiness outside, led the applause. Mama nudged Lutie. "Go *ahead!*"

Still a little faint, she plucked a chord. Tomorrow was Sunday, so she sang "Jordan Am a Hard Road to Trabbel." There was polite applause. "How about 'Lily Dale'?" someone asked. "My poor dead sister was named Lily, and I always think of her when I hear that sad sweet song."

Sadness fit Lutie's mood, sadness mingled with resentment. Mournfully she sang of poor Lily Dale. Someone asked for "Bird of the Wilderness." She sang that, too, and then laid down her banjo and begged off. She had to go someplace to think.

Spiritualism was popular on the frontier also. A fat lady in taffeta — Lutie remembered her from the emigrant train — formed a circle and had everybody hold hands. "You, too," she urged Lutie. "Dear, the spirit guides have ever so much to say to you!" Lutie pretended not to hear. When they drew the shades, leaving the parlor in a musty gloom, she fled. *Old fools!*

Outside, the beer was gone but there was plenty of champagne. Now that most of the females were inside, the men really whooped it up. Jim Peck, the Slash G foreman, was having trouble keeping the celebration within bounds. For lack of partners the square dance had ceased, but on the wooden platform boots thumped as a gaggle of ranch hands hopped about in heel-and-toe. A wrestling match grew out of hand and the more sober spectators had to pull the bloody contestants apart. "Damn fools!" old Pa Griffin snorted, pinioning one himself. "This here is a birthday party, you yahoos, not a saloon brawl!"

As the marksmen's aim faltered from repeated drafts of champagne, the shooting contest degenerated. After a while some wags began to deliver wild shots in the general direction of old Yellow Hat and his blanketed Indians on the ridge. The Sioux fled while the shooters grinned slyly and apologized for poor aim. Under the cottonwoods, horsemen were preparing for a race to the river. Lutie, seeking Buck, found him there with the black bottle, leaning against Nig. The big horse was uneasy, caracoling sidewise as she approached, though

Nig knew her well. She took the bottle away from Buck. "You filled that up again from your pa's jug! Look at your eyes — all glassy and silly-looking!"

He reached for the bottle but she threw it into the tall grass.

"Aw, Lutie —"

Primly she stepped away from his embrace, aware of the grinning faces. "You listen to me, Buck Griffin! Even if it is your birthday, you ought not to —"

A sudden gust of wind caught her skirt and blew it around her knees. "Oh!" In panic she caught at it, pulled it quickly down while the men guffawed. Stirred by the wind, a shower of leaves came down; a cloud passed over the sun and the golden afternoon became quickly chill. Weather was making up. Nearby, a group of merrymakers throwing a maul for silver dollars glanced at the dark clouds, and someone declared he felt a spatter of rain. The baron, too, had been competing. He shrugged, rolled down his sleeves.

"One more time!" the burly Jake Sigafoos urged. "One more time, Charlie! This'll blow over quick, you'll see!" Apparently the baron had made some friends, or perhaps, Lutie thought waspishly, his silver dollars had.

"I know what makes *you* so mean!" Buck grumbled in her ear.

She turned.

"That baron feller!" He pointed. "I guess you think he's some punkins, eh?"

"I'm *not* mean! It's just I don't want you to make a fool of yourself on your birthday, that's all."

The rest were mounted, urging Buck to get up himself. Mr. Oates took out his silver watch. "Better hurry, Buck. It's clabbering up to rain."

Buck swung up on Nig, fumbled toes into the stirrups. "You wait right here, Lutie, till I win this race. Hear?"

"If big talk could win," she said acidly, "you'd have the race won already!" She was angry at his foolishness, angry at the way he had grinned when her skirt flew up, tolerating the coarse laughter. If that was all he thought of her —

"Yiii — ii — ii!" Away the riders spurred, hooves drumming in a wild tattoo. It began to rain. At first it was only a slight drizzle, but Lutie finally took shelter under the trees with Mr. Oates, watching the mounted figures become smaller and smaller.

"Now I remember," a deep voice beside her announced.

Quickly she wheeled. The baron's bearded face was close to hers. His eyes, deep-set under the shaggy brows, twinkled.

"You are the girl — that girl — on the Pacific Express. The one" — he laughed, his lips twitching in the dark bush of hair — "the one that flooed — flid — *fled*, that is it — when I say 'Boo' while I shave. *Oui?*"

She colored, lowered her eyes. "I don't remember."

Mr. Oates took his notebook out. "Baron, you and Miss Lutie know each other?"

The baron was amused. "Yes, a person might say that." It was more like *zat*.

Lutie tossed her head. "Maybe it happened and maybe it didn't. There were so many people on the train."

"That is true," the baron said. "But not many like you, mademoiselle. So young, so beautiful! You could almost be French."

Editor Oates laughed. "Oh, we've got our share of local beauties." He watched the racers returning. "But I have to give you that Miss Lutie is a real looker!"

Looking dourer than usual, the baron's driver led the coffee-and-cream mount nearby. Respectfully he coughed, waited. When the baron turned, he said in a rich Scots burr, "It's getting late, sir. The weather is not too promising. Too, you told the ladies at the chateau you would return early."

"Yes, we must never disappoint the ladies!" Bowing to Lutie, the baron took the reins. "Mademoiselle, a great *plaisir*." To Mr. Oates he bowed also, with his free hand shook hands. "Now I must go to the Griffins and thank them, no? for such a nice *soirée*."

Rapidly the riders grew larger, and Lutie could hear shouts. Many of the contestants had gone to the whip but Buck, riding upright, long hair flying in the wind, led by several lengths. Lutie, cheering him on, drew back as he thundered up on Nig, sawing on the reins so hard the black horse whinnied in pain and sat back on powerful haunches.

"You win by a mile, Buck!" Mr. Oates called. Buck's triumphant face quickly tightened as he saw Lutie standing near the baron. Sliding down from Nig, he threw the reins over the horse's ears and sauntered over, thumbs hooked in his belt. "Who's your friend, Lutie?"

Editor Oates sensed a quarrel. Quickly he said, "Why, Buck, you know the baron here!" He turned. "Buck Griffin rides like one of those centaurs they speak about in mythology. He —"

"I don't know about that," Buck growled. "I don't know about no mythologies, either! But I do know I can beat anybody around here, including any maverick froggies that might have strayed off their own range!"

Lutie, standing near Buck, smelled whiskey on the moist breath. For a moment she vacillated, thinking to dissuade Buck from a scene. But when she saw the baron's annoying smile, she changed her mind.

"I bet you can too, Buck!" She put her hand in his. "You ride American style, and everybody knows that's the best way!" Actually, she didn't know anything but the rudiments of riding. But the way the baron sat his mare looked somehow decadent and foreign.

"You, *monsieur*, are a fine horseman!" The baron smiled, turned away. But Buck snatched his arm.

"What did you call me?"

"Now, Buck!" Mr. Oates cautioned. "That just means 'sir' in the French language. Don't carry on so, son!"

The riders, smelling a fight, crowded around. Lutie saw other people ambling near to find out what was going on under the cottonwoods. It was raining harder now. Drops rustled the leaves and began to pelt the hard-baked earth. Pa Griffin stood near the well sweep, one hand over his eyes against the rain, watching. Some of the women came out onto the veranda and talked among themselves.

"I can beat you!" Buck insisted.

The baron shrugged. "This horse, my blooded horse, is not a racehorse, Mr. Buck. She is a jumper. I do not — how you say? — I do not risk her in a race."

"Nig can jump higher 'n any foreigner horse!"

Pa Griffin pushed through the crowd. "What the hell's going on here?"

Buck stared truculently at the baron. "This here coward won't race me! Wants to jump instead, he says!"

The baron shook his head. "Sir, I do not want to — to go against your son in anything. I have a good time here with you all" — he swept out his arm — "all these fine people, but now I must go. I — I" — he stammered a little, forgetting some of his English — "I — what you say — I thank you all, and —"

"You're a coward!" Lutie snapped. "You're afraid!"

Pa Griffin grabbed Buck's arm, pulled him back. "Lutie, you stay out of this! It's none of your business!" He sniffed. "God, Buck, you smell like a distillery! You never could hold your liquor!"

Buck shook his father off, repeating Lutie's charge. "That's right! You're a coward!"

Alarmed, Mrs. Griffin and Carrie joined the group, trying to dissuade Buck. Papa and Mama Hamlin came too, attracted by the commotion. "Lutie," Papa urged, "come away! This is none of our affair!"

Lutie would not be separated from Buck. After all, Buck said he was going to marry her; it was her duty to stand by him. Mama had stood by Papa in hard times.

Could she do less? She held Buck's arm tighter. "Papa, he insulted Buck!"

The baron's eyes widened. "I? Insult?"

"That's right! You — you insulted him!"

"Lutie!" Mama protested. "Can't you do anything with her, Lorenzo?"

Papa tried to take Lutie's arm but she clung stubbornly to Buck.

Mr. Oates cleared his throat. "Now, gentlemen, there's no need to quarrel over a silly thing like this!" But Sheriff Holland broke in, grinning fatly.

"Take him on, Buck. I seen that Nig go over six foot once! No disrespect, Baron, but that black horse flies like a red-tailed hawk!" Others took up the cry; "Go fer it, Buck! That black bastard can jump over the moon!" Someone started to pass around a sweat-stained hat, beseeching bets, giving odds.

"You game?" Buck demanded.

The baron took a deep breath. His face was flushed, and he chewed at a corner of his mustaches. Finally he said deliberately, choosing his words with care, "*Bien.* All right. Let's go, eh?"

The crowd surged away to the meadow. Buck and the baron followed, leading their mounts, but walking widely separated. The baron's man sauntered behind his master, eyes narrowed against the crowd. Jim Peck, in response to a glance from Pa Griffin, moved after Buck, wary-eyed also.

"Pa, can't you do anything?" Carrie wailed, watching them go. "Buck can be *such* a fool!"

"He is not!" Lutie protested.

The old man shook his head. "When Buck's got a snootful, there's no arguing with him — you know that. No, let 'em get it out of their craws!"

Before Papa could stop her, Lutie ran out into the rain. The drops were heavier now, fat gobbets, and the wind blew harder. The sun had gone and the sky was dark, laced with lightning like brilliant embroidery on the black fabric of the storm. Her boots were wet and windblown grass soaked the hem of her skirt. "Buck!" she called. "Wait for me!"

Gleefully men dragged hay from the great barn, piling the bales high to form a makeshift barrier. Jake Sigafoos yelled down from the summit.

"High enough, Buck?"

It was the baron who spoke. "Another course, please. That is, Monsieur Buck, if you do not mind the spoilage — spoiling — of the hay in the rain. I do not know much about the farming yet, but there is, you see, the mold, I think you call it."

"Hang the mold!" Buck glowered. "It ain't your hay anyway."

The baron shrugged again, smiling.

"Ready?" Buck demanded.

"*Oui, monsieur.*"

"Talk English!"

"I am ready."

"You go first, then."

The baron's man led the handsome mare to a fence that had been chosen as the starting point. Lutie bit her lip, clenched her hands. *I hope he falls.* Seeing him gather the reins in a complicated pattern, she said to Buck, "Look at the silly way he holds the ribbons!"

"That's French," Buck sniffed. "Don't no real man ever hold leather *that* way!"

Leaning forward, the baron patted the sleek creamy neck. Taking her cue only from his pressed knees, the mare trotted forward. Suddenly she gathered haunches under her, sailed into the air. The baron leaned forward; horse and rider were almost one as the graceful Arab soared high. He was still far forward as the mare's front hooves struck solid ground again, gradually straightening his seat as he wheeled the horse and trotted back toward the judges.

"Good jump, Charlie," Jake Sigafoos announced.

"That ain't so much!" Buck muttered to Lutie.

"Nig can go ever so much higher," she whispered. "I've seen him! Buck, show that — that *fop!*"

Buck led Nig to the fence. For a moment he reined in the skittish black, staring toward the barrier. Then, with a wild whoop, he clapped his spurs to the ribs. Nig sprang forward, sleek haunches churning. Lutie thought of the great black engine in the Chicago station. *Power!*

"Yiii — ii — ii!" Nig floated over the barrier like a wild black bird, stumbling a little as his forehooves sank into soft earth again. Buck trotted proudly back. He and Nig were wet and dripping. Buck's red hair curled softly from the rain.

"How was that?"

"Good as Charlie's!" Jake decided. "Someone pile a few of the loose fenceposts on top. Make 'er about a foot higher!"

Lutie reached up to pat Buck's hand. "You and Nig are champions!" She looked triumphantly at the baron. He did not seem to notice, instead pointing out to his man the clotted mud on the mare's hooves. The servant dutifully cleaned them with a stick. Looking at the high-piled posts atop the bales of hay, the baron stroked his beard. "*Très haut.*"

"What did you say?" Buck grumbled.

"I say — very high."

"Scared to try it?"

The baron put a foot in the stirrup, pulled himself up slowly, almost unwillingly. He did not answer Buck; instead, he gathered the mare with his knees and together they soared again over the barrier. This time they seemed to leave even more space beneath them. Cantering back to the fence, he nodded to Buck, still sitting the mare easily.

"Watch *me!*" Buck muttered through tight lips. His face was flushed, whether from liquor or anger Lutie did not know; perhaps both. "I'll show up that fancy dan and his foreign horse!"

She caught at his hand. "Buck, be careful!" But he was already gone, whooping like a wild Indian, roweled spurs digging at Nig's flanks. At the barrier the big horse seemed for an instant to pause, almost as if calculating. Then the long cordlike muscles bunched. Nig leaped awkwardly, as if not quite sure he wanted to take the jump. To Lutie the scene seemed played slowly, a dreadful molasseslike sequence. Nig went up, up, up, mane and tail streaming against the gray sky. At the zenith of the leap a front hoof seemed to catch on the fenceposts piled atop the hay. The powerful body twisted, dragged to one side. Buck's hat flew into the air as he fought to control the writhing body under him. Nig tried to straighten out his jump but the big barrel rolled, the legs beat desperately for purchase. Down, then — down, down, down came horse and rider, Nig twisting like a cat in the attempt to land on his feet. Horse and rider landed in the loose earth, Buck underneath. Wildly Nig kicked out, body contorted and eyes rolling, and finally clambered to his feet.

Buck lay flat in the wet earth. Stunned, Lutie thought. She ran to him. "Buck! Are you all right?"

Nig, reins drooping, flanks heaving, trotted back to shoulder her aside, nosing his master.

"Buck!" His eyes were closed. Lutie raised his head, the wet-plastered red curls, to her breast. "Buck! Say something!"

Dr. Cromie quickly pulled her away. "Let me look at him." He slapped Buck's face. Lutie felt a sudden chill, like cold iron, in her chest.

"Buck!" Dr. Cromie urged. He relaxed his hold on Buck and the head lolled sidewise.

Pa Griffin knelt beside Dr. Cromie. "Buck, speak, damn it! Say something!" Behind him was a sea of white and frightened faces. The fat spiritualist lady in taffeta raised fat hands above her head, puffy eyes wide. "I felt it!" she screamed. "Oh, Lord, I felt it — his spirit! It just brushed by me as it went up to heaven! Oh, I felt it!"

110

Sheriff Holland bustled to the scene. "Stand back, all of you!"

"Oh, Lord, I felt it!" the spiritualist lady insisted.

"Shut up, ma'am," Dr. Cromie said. "Someone take her away from here, please."

Buck lay quietly in the wet grass, as if sleeping, face pale and serene.

"He's dead," Dr. Cromie murmured.

"Dead?" Pa Griffin's voice cracked in disbelief. "There's not a mark on him, Doc!"

"Broken neck. If it's any comfort, he died quick. Didn't feel any pain." Someone behind Lutie began to scream, a regular and rhythmic wailing. She felt someone near her and turned. It was the baron. His face was pale against the black brush of beard. "Are you sure?" he asked Dr. Cromie. "I have a famous Eastern physician at my house up there." He nodded toward the ridge. "He has come for the hunting. Perhaps if I rode to get him —"

Dr. Cromie shook his head. "Too late for that!"

The shrill voice was still keening. Someone grabbed Lutie's sleeve, whirled her about, tearing her good dress. It was Carrie, Buck's sister. "You!" She pointed a finger. "You! Damn you! You started it, Lutie Hamlin! You egged Buck on! He wouldn't have done it if he hadn't wanted to show off for you!"

Lutie, eyes brimming with fear and shock, could only stare, fumbling wordlessly at her torn sleeve.

"That's right!" Rain streamed down Pa Griffin's face. He raised fists high over his head, an Old Testament prophet in the woodcuts illustrating the

Dysart family Bible. "You God damned Hamlins! Buck never give anyone any trouble till you Hamlins come along to trouble us!"

Mrs. Griffin caught at his arm. "Pa, don't! It wasn't nobody's fault, can't you see? It was just —"

Taut with grief and rage, Pa Griffin seemed about to strike Lutie but someone pulled him back. It was raining hard now, pelting drops. A rivulet of clear water ran down Buck's pale cheek; it looked as if he were weeping. Lutie stared down at the cold face, feeling the lump of iron in her breast grow insupportable. She shook her head; it couldn't be. It just *couldn't!* Hadn't he — hadn't they — in the barn, just a little while ago —

"Get out!" Pa Griffin shouted. Blindly he waved his arms. "You Hamlins, you damned strangers — get out!" To the baron, standing at his elbow, he said, "You too, you cussed foreigner! Get off this property! If I ever see you again, I'll — I'll shoot you dead! Get out!"

CHAPTER
SIX

The unseasonable rain was only the beginning of bad weather. From a sun-scorched summer, the seasons plunged into icy rains that numbed both body and spirit. The barnyard was a frigid quagmire, the chickens sad and bedraggled as they searched for grains of corn. Papa rose early and came home late from the sawmill, spattered with mud and boots caked with gumbo. His cough worsened. Sometimes he was too tired to take care of the equally spattered and weary mule. Sid, worried about Papa, put Horace away and grained him from their meager store.

Food for the family was scanty too. Coyotes got some of the chickens, and for coffee Papa and Mama were reduced to roasted rye. Lutie tried some and it was awful. But it seemed to her that many familiar things tasted awful. In so many ways, life without Buck and the Griffins had become insupportable and the world a dreary place. Actually, however, she had to admit that she missed the world of the Griffins more than she missed Buck himself. She had not really loved him, and the happening in the barn had been too quick, too ephemeral, to leave a mark on her. Looking out at the leaden skies, she shuddered. Was that all there was, between a man and a woman? It had been so quick, almost — brutal. Still, the time with the Griffins had been pleasant. They had money, and stock, a fine house, a *real* house with hand-painted pictures and wool rugs and brass lamps so highly polished they looked like gold. At Mama's command Lutie rose, wearily, and put a chunk of brown coal in the iron stove that had a piece of firewood serving as a missing leg. The Griffins had power, too, that was it. That was what she liked.

"Whatever are you dreaming about?" Sid wanted to know. He had burrowed into his nest, the hole dug in the back wall of the soddy, making a great pretense of studying Ray's *Arithmetic* while Mama rocked and mended. Papa had not yet come home.

"I'm not dreaming of anything."

Sid was in a teasing mood. "I know something you don't!"

She made a face at him. "What do I care, Mr. Smarty?"

Hearing Horace's homecoming bray, Sid rolled out to help. Hurriedly Mama rolled and cut biscuits while Lutie set the table. At supper Papa was quiet, almost withdrawn, but Lutie was eager to know the news.

"Not much," Papa said. "Oh, the baron was in today to buy some odds and ends of millwork. Talk is he's having some kind of hunting wagon built to take his fancy friends along with him after antelope and elk and such. Old Mr. Griffin came in, too, but wouldn't talk to me." Papa shook his head. "I'm sorry things turned out the way they did. I can understand how he feels."

Lutie did not care how Pa Griffin felt. "Was Mr. Emile Durand with him? The baron, I mean."

"Who?"

"*Monsieur*" — It sounded silly, but she tried again — "*Monsieur* Durand — you know, the blond handsome man that stopped with the baron the day we buried Uncle Milo!" Sid giggled, and Lutie turned a stern eye on him. "That's how they say 'mister'!"

"Eat your biscuits, Lutie," Mama interrupted, "and stop talking foolishness! Can't you see your father's tired?"

Papa touched his lips with the ragged but stiffly starched napkin Mama had placed at his plate. "No, child. I don't remember any *Monsieur* Durand."

For a while the rains stopped. The sky turned blue again, but there was a chill in the air. At night the barnyard puddles froze. The trees turned gold and brown and scarlet. Sid, returning from the river with a bucket of water, reported that in the shallows a thin crust of ice had formed. "There were fish all under the ice!" he reported. "Looked like a million of 'em — pickerels, suckers, sunfish, all kinds!" The cottonwoods poor Uncle Milo had planted around the soddy were iced with silver when Lutie woke.

"Jake Sigafoos says there's weather making up," Papa told them one night. "Feels it in his bad knee, where a horse kicked him. Says it'll snow before Sunday." He had other news. "Baron's big house is nearly finished. Dr. Cromie says there's big doings planned. The baron's bringing out a whole slew of servants from the East — cooks, butler, parlormaids, grooms — all kinds.

He's building a big slaughterhouse, too. Plans to butcher beef right here and send it East in ice for a better price."

Lutie kept her silence. She did not want to be laughed at again for asking about M. Durand. Ridicule was something she couldn't stand, even from that insufferable snotnose Sid. Sid, however, was eager.

"Clarence Sigafoos said there's been fighting already about the fences! Guns and night riders and everything!" His eyes shone. "Is there gunfighting, Papa?"

Papa sipped at the roasted-rye coffee, made a face, put it down again. "I'm afraid there's been some — some unpleasantness. Mr. Griffin's Slash G riders have already cut the baron's new barbed wire along the river, and the baron swears he'll have Griffin to court at Bismarck. Dr. Cromie says he's treated some gunshot wounds on both sides."

"Both sides?" Mama asked.

"The baron's hired some hardcases himself, and says he'll fight back."

Mama shook her head. "I hope it doesn't go any further! Didn't this country get its fill of misery and killing in the War?"

Snow coming, time passing . . . In that passing of time, the season changing, the seasons of Lutie's emotions changed also. Suddenly she came to feel that something was wrong, very wrong. Mama had never told her anything about her body, but she began to realize she was going to have a baby. A *baby?* Good Lord, she was

116

only nineteen! Did *every* experience in a barn result in a baby? With a sinking heart she remembered what Buck had said that awful day, the day of mingled pleasure and dread: "God, you ain't supposed to get sick for another two or three months!" But she was already coming to feel queasy in the mornings, and only pecked at her breakfast of fried bread and sorghum and rye coffee.

Buck — that damned Buck! He had misused her. And now *he* had the power, the power over her, even beyond the grave! She swore, and gnawed her knuckles. What to do? The thought of Mama's finding out threw her into panic. But with them all so close together in the soddy — Papa and Mama and Sid and herself — it would be hard to hide her condition. She clasped her fists so tight the nails dug into her flesh. If she could only *tell* Mama, or anyone, and get help! Surely there were ways to deal with this! If you planted a seed and didn't like the flower that sprang up, you surely could wrench it out. Maybe Dr. Cromie —

"Lutie?" Papa looked up from his reading of the Little Misery *Gazette*.

"Yes, Papa?"

"Is something wrong?"

She shook her head. "No."

As winter, the real and hard winter, set in, Papa's health failed. He coughed a lot, and missed days at the sawmill. The mountain of lignite and firewood laid in against the cold dwindled to a small snow-covered mound. Bread left on the windowsill overnight had to be thawed near the stove before it could be cut. Papa, muffler wrapped around a sore throat, scraped ice from the windowpane and looked out. "Must be ten or fifteen below. Too cold to snow today."

Before Papa left for the sawmill, Dr. Cromie came riding by on his steam-puffing claybank. Sid put the doctor's mare in the barn with old Horace and gave her some of the scanty feed that was left. Dr. Cromie bustled in, red-faced and cheery, slapping his gloved hands together.

"I'm worried about you, Lorenzo. Mr. Larson at the mill says you've missed a lot of time lately. That cough bothering you still?"

Papa shrugged. "There's nothing wrong with me. Oh, a touch of catarrh, maybe, but tomorrow I'll go in. The books must be getting behind."

In spite of protests, Dr. Cromie opened Papa's shirtfront. He put his ear to the pale chest. "Cough for me, please."

Papa coughed, a small dismal sound.

"Harder!"

Papa tried valiantly, but could manage only a small bark.

"Congestion." Dr. Cromie took the stethoscope from his bag and listened again. Finally he straightened, folded the instrument, put it back in his bag.

"Miz Hamlin, he's not to try going in to the mill till that chest clears up. A chest that sounds like that can lead to consumption." He rummaged in the scuffed black satchel and poured powders into a twist of paper. "Make a strong tea with this every night before he goes to bed, and in the morning. See that he drinks it, too.

I'll stop by tomorrow or the next day." He turned to Lutie. "And how is my Lutecia this morning?"

He was the only one who ever called her Lutecia. Papa and Mama had long ago adopted the simpler Lutie. But Dr. Cromie said he liked the full name. It reminded him of what he called his "salad days," when he was a student in Paris. Lutie had never figured out what studying medicine had to do with salads.

"I'm fine," she lied.

Oh, how she wanted to get him to one side, ask him what to do! But with Papa and Mama there, what could she do? Helplessly she watched as he put on his fur coat, reached for the bulky felt cap with the earflaps. *Doctor! Dr. Cromie! Help me! I don't know what to do!* But Mama had the doctor's attention now.

"That sack there, on the floor, Doctor. Are you forgetting something?"

Dr. Cromie looked at the burlap bag as if he didn't recognize it. "Oh, that!" Picking it up, he laid it on the worn kitchen table. "Just a few things I brought along, Miz Hamlin. My patients — they don't have much cash, and they bring me so much truck to pay their bills that I don't have room to store it. Anyway, I have more than I need. An old man don't eat that much."

Risking Mama's frown, Sid opened the sack. There were sugar, flour, salt fish, a slab of bacon, a jug of molasses, and a quart jar of jam.

"We don't take charity," Mama said frostily.

"Now, Mama!" Papa protested. "It was nice of the doctor to remember us. After all, times haven't been flush with us, I must admit."

119

"We surely don't want to be remembered *that* way," Mama said, hands tightly folded at her waist. When Sid, fondly holding the jar of jam, protested, she rapped him smartly on the skull with her knuckles. "You put that down, boy, hear me?"

Lutie found courage to speak — anything to delay Dr. Cromie's departure. There might still be a chance. "Mama," she said, "I think it's silly to act like this!"

Mama was fierce. "Silly? Are you calling your mother silly, girl?"

"I think *it's* silly, not you. I mean, it's silly to refuse good food when everyone in Dakota must know we're having a bad time of it. Do you want your children to starve?" They were not actually starving — yet — but Lutie realized it was a good rhetorical point. She had always done well at school in Columbus when the Girls' Socratic Society met.

"That's right, Mattie," Papa agreed. "If Dr. Cromie was in the same fix, he knows we'd help him. It's only right for folks to help each other."

Mama wavered. Sid joined the argument, holding up the glass jar so light glinted through the ruby contents. "Blackberry, I bet!"

Dr. Cromie nodded. "Blackberry. Ella Sigafoos put it up."

"Oh, all right." Mama's shoulders sagged. She sat down, quickly. "I suppose we should thank you, Doctor!"

Dr. Cromie put on his cap, pulled on gloves, and opened the door. "No need, ma'am. We're neighbors."

120

Desperately Lutie followed him into the snow-swept yard. Standing by the patient claybank, he looked at her kindly through the gold-rimmed spectacles. "Well, Lutecia?"

She couldn't find her voice. There was so much she wanted to tell him, so many questions she wanted to ask, but a dry hard lump had formed in her throat. *Ask me,* she pleaded silently. *Make it easier for me! I've got to talk to someone, tell them how it was.* But no words came; she only stared at the ground, digging the toe of her shoe into the snow.

"It's Buck, isn't it?"

She looked up, hope rising in her bosom. But his next words sent her hope crashing down again.

"You're grieving for Buck."

Silently she nodded, not knowing what else to do. *Keep on, please, Dr. Cromie! Keep talking, keep asking! Maybe I'll be able to get up enough courage to tell you!*

"Well, it was a tragedy. Buck was always headstrong, and this time it undid him, I guess you could say. But there'll be other fine young men for you to know, Lutie. Believe me, it's not the end of the world."

But it is! If you only knew —

Taking her chill hand in his own warm one, he patted it. "Next time I come I'll bring you a tonic. It'll make you feel better."

Feel better? She would never feel good again!

"Goodbye, Lutecia. You hurry in now, girl, or I'll be treating you for frostbit lungs!"

Waving a listless goodbye, she watched the old mare bear Dr. Cromie away toward town. Feet like blocks of wood, her whole body chill — not with cold but from apprehension — she went back into the house. Rocking hard, face wet with tears, Mama clasped the worn arms of the old rocker.

"Humiliation, that's what it is! Humiliation! We're pitiful objects of charity! Now where's your damned railroad pamphlets, Lorenzo Hamlin? 'Stick a crowbar into the rich earth and harvest a crop of tenpenny nails in the spring'! You're as crazy as your brother Milo, rest his soul, and we'll all come to a bad end for your craziness!" Bitterly she blew her nose.

It was the first time Lutie ever remembered Mama swearing. To Lutie it was frightening, an indication of the depth of grief in Mama's breast since the ill-fated move to the Dakotas. And if Mama ever were to learn of Lutie's condition, if that were added to her burdens . . . Now it was not imagination; Lutie was really sick in the morning. She fled back into the snow, and behind the barn she vomited.

The Hamlins were familiar with snow, heavy snow, in Columbus, with winds that blew people along icy sidewalks, unwilling skaters. Horses fell down and broke their legs and had to be destroyed. Houses burned, too, from overheated stoves and from soot catching fire in chimneys. But there had never been anything back there like a Dakota blizzard. When they awoke one morning in the depths of winter a great cloud had risen in the northwest, blotting out the moon

122

and stars. As the light grew they saw a great seamless dome, colored slate gray, like the old roofs in Columbus. There the resemblance ended. Winds came, roaring like a whole den of angry lions. Fine powdery snow, driven by the gale, sifted through all the chinks and lay on the floor as if they were in a fragile boat and the pounding seas were leaking in. Frost on the windows was a half inch thick; even Sid's busy scraping with a table knife could not break through. There was frost in a lacy border along every crack where the cold sneaked in. Together they huddled around the stove, wrapped in blankets, husbanding their tiny supply of fuel. Papa said he hoped the animals were all right in the barn. With the driving snow in the air like a dense fog, it was too dangerous to go out and attempt the hundred yards or so. Papa said a person could get lost and never be found again, at least till spring thaw.

After supper Papa and Mama dozed, sitting near the stove. Lutie climbed into Sid's den to get warm.

"Why are you coming in here?" he demanded. His ear hurt, and he was irritable. Lutie checked an angry reply.

"I'm cold! Anyway, this isn't your private property. This house belongs to Papa and Mama, even if it is only an old soddy." Carefully she wriggled under Sid's blanket, aware of a heaviness, an awkwardness, that was becoming increasingly familiar and unwelcome.

Sid continued to pore over the Beadle dime novel *Old Sleuth* by the guttering light of a candle, but Lutie kept blocking the light as she moved restlessly about, seeking a more comfortable position.

"God damn it!" Sid hissed. "Stop moving around, will you?"

"Shut your mouth," Lutie advised, "or you'll wake Papa. You know Dr. Cromie said he needs a lot of rest."

"I don't care!" Sid *did* care, she knew, but was uncomfortable at the idea of a girl — any girl — in his private lair. "Get out, will you?"

"I won't!"

Balked, he became malicious. "If you don't, I'll tell Mama!"

She sniffed. "Tell Mama what?"

"What I know."

"And what do you know, Mr. Snotnose?"

"About you and Buck."

Her body stiffened; for a horrible moment she feared she was paralyzed. When she spoke her voice was strained, incredulous.

"What did you say?"

He did not speak. She could hear him swallow, hard. She put her face close to his, stared into his frightened eyes.

"What — do — you — know?"

"I don't know anything."

He attempted, nervously, to return to his book but she grasped his shoulder hard and forced him to look into her eyes.

"You — you spied on me — and Buck — that day?"

Sid could not face the terrible stare. He wet his lips, trembled under the clawlike grip. "I — I couldn't help it, Lutie! Honest, I couldn't! Me and Clarence — Clarence Sigafoos — were in the barn, climbing around

124

the hay mow, jumping down into the hay. We didn't mean no harm. Honest, Lutie!" Reluctantly he turned his pale face toward her, eyes frightened in the candle shine. "I saw what he — did to you. I didn't really understand. At first I thought he was hurting you, and I wanted to jump down and hit him. But Clarence told me what you — what you and Buck were doing." Seeing Lutie's stricken face, he became bolder. "I know now, Lutie, why you get sick in the morning and won't eat. And you're — you're getting a big stomach. It's a wonder Mama don't notice." When her grasp on his shoulder sagged, he put a timid hand in hers. "Lutie, I do so want to help you, only I don't know how."

Feeling spent, she lay quietly beside him, all the starch gone out of her. If Sid had noticed her condition, Mama soon would too. And Papa! She made up her mind. Somehow, she would have to go away. But where? Trembling, she rolled heavily to her knees and watched Papa and Mama, dozing by the three-legged stove, hoping they would not be roused by the crackling of the dry cottonwood leaves that filled Sid's pallet. "All right," she whispered. "But the only way you can help me now is to keep your mouth shut. And if you don't —"

Again Sid shrank from the hypnotic stare. "I ain't going to say nothing!"

"You *aren't!*" Lutie corrected. "You damned well aren't or I'll cut out your guts with Mama's carving knife! You know I would, too!"

It was sacrilege to speak ill of the dead, she knew, but she damned Buck Griffin with all the intensity she could muster. Never again would she let a man have sway over her! But Mama would somehow find her out, she knew, miserably; there was no remedy unless she ran away.

She did not, of course, know how or where to run, but the matter was taken out of her hands. When the roads cleared, Sid helped Papa hitch old Horace to the wheel-sprung wagon. The winter had been hard on the mule. Horace was gaunt, ribs sticking out, and his usually alert gaze and feisty ways were subdued. If she had only gotten the colt Buck had promised her, the Morgan colt! By this time he might be big enough to pull in harness beside poor old Horace.

Papa was going in to Little Misery to catch up on the sawmill books and Mama had to buy thread and attend a meeting of the Ladies' Aid at the church. Sid was beginning to get what Dr. Cromie called "cabin fever" and wanted to play with Clarence Sigafoos.

"Remember!" Lutie whispered fiercely. "That goes for Clarence Sigafoos too!"

Sid reassured her. "Clarence won't talk. I told him if he did I'd kill him." Purposefully he drew on his mittens. "He's scared of me, all right!"

When they had gone Lutie drew a sigh of relief. Feeling grimy and unclean from long weeks without a good bath, she heated water on the stove but fell into a reverie and forgot it. At noon she ate a slice of bread with jam from the jar Dr. Cromie had brought, but was not really hungry. Though it was still well below freezing, sunlight streamed in the window casting mellow rays on her geranium. The sod hut was warm

126

and comfortable for the first time in weeks. Late in the afternoon she roused herself, alarmed. If she was going to take her bath she would have to hurry. The water on the stove was still lukewarm. With a pitcher she poured some in the washtub, took off her clothes, and curled cross-legged in the tub, Mama's homemade soap and a washrag to hand. She fitted only bulkily into the tub and her legs were cramped, but the warm water felt good.

Drowsily she soaped herself, not hearing the mule and wagon until it was too late. Horace's homecoming bray chilled her to the bone. Awkwardly jumping to her feet, she stood frozen, spreading the washrag over as much of her as she could manage, looking wildly about for a place to hide.

"Well!"

Mattie Hamlin stood motionless in the doorway, paper sack in one hand, the other groping at her throat as if trying to find her breath.

"Lutie! It's true! Oh, my God!"

Trying to reduce her ample body to maidenly proportions, Lutie cowered. She had feared Mama was becoming suspicious. Now her growing belly must have betrayed her.

"You — you're going to have a — a baby!" Mama's face blanched, and her voice quavered. Dropping the paper sack, she spread a hand over her eyes. Sidney crowded behind her, peering. Papa must still be unharnessing the mule.

"What's wrong, Mama?" Sidney asked.

Mama blocked his view with her spread skirt. "Get some clothes on!" Her voice was bleak, cold. "You — you slut! Sidney, go out and help your father!"

"But —"

"Go, I say! Quick, now!"

No more was said. They ate supper in silence. Lutie, fearful and distraught on her pallet behind the flour-sack curtain, heard Papa and Mama talking until late at night. They talked so quietly she could not make out the words, strain as she would. When they had finally blown out the lamp and gone to bed she waited for a while, then rolled a few things in a blanket, dressed, and crept toward the door. Sid, however, was still awake.

"Lutie?"

Pausing, she shifted the blanket roll from one hand to the other. Already it was heavy.

"Where are you going?"

"None of your business."

"Lutie, please don't go away! I — I'll be all alone!"

He sounded like a frightened child. Actually, Sid *was* a child. She felt a great tenderness toward him; he was now the only person she could trust. Risking discovery, she leaned into his lair and kissed his cheek.

"Lutie —"

In the half-light from the moon reflecting on the snow, she put a finger to her lips. Then she went out into the moonlit Dakota night, pulling her scanty coat tightly about her.

CHAPTER
SEVEN

When the snow from the latest storm hardened enough to bear the huge weight, Emile took the whole party out in the gaily painted hunting wagon: Valerie, Marie de Courcy, M. and Mme. Dessines, and L'Anglaise — Emma, the English girl. Bundled in furs, chatting like magpies, they clambered into the high-wheeled vehicle.

"But there is no Charles!" Valerie pouted. "I come here all the way from San Francisco, and there is no Charles!"

Emile, handing her up to Marc Dessines, fondled his blond mustaches. "As you know, Charles is a very busy man these days. He has had to hurry to St. Louis to sign contracts for the new refrigerator cars he has ordered. But I assure, *mesdames*, I can do anything Charles can do!"

Valerie, the dark one, was quick to protest. "You are married, Emile, with a wife and four children! What fun is that, to snuggle in this hay with a married man?"

Roguishly Mme. Dessines eyed Emile Durand. "But his wife and his little ones — they are now in Chicago, visiting relatives, no?" She winked at her husband. "And what I could tell you about married men!"

Marc Dessines fumbled uncomfortably with the magazine of his Holland and Holland fowling piece. "Emile, what are we going to shoot this morning, if you please?"

Emile climbed cheerily into the front seat beside Murdoch. "Whatever suits your fancy, but I understand it is not allowed to shoot red Indians! Anything else — woodcock, antelope, wolves, a bear if one is seen. But do be careful with that expensive gun and keep it pointed away from us! We do not want to bring the good Murdoch home tied to a pole carried between our shoulders."

Murdoch did not laugh. In response to Emile's nod he slapped the reins over the backs of the mules and the great wagon creaked off into a sunlit dazzle of snow, heading for the river. They all sang, drank hot coffee laced with brandy, and had a marvelous time.

Late in the morning the sun withdrew behind a veil of clouds and the temperature dropped precipitously. At lunch they lay in fur robes in a sheltered draw, warmed by the huge fire Murdoch built. Ravenously they devoured a good *terrine*, hot soup prepared by M. Guillaume, the baron's chef, and crusty bread and cheeses, washed down with champagne cooled in a snow bank. Marc Dessines had bagged three prairie hens and was jubilant, pinching all the girls. Mme. Dessines, head against Emile's shoulder, watched him suspiciously. Murdoch, a respectable distance apart, sat on a boulder and munched a sausage.

"Really," Emma said, "this country is fabulous!" Her bosom lifting, she breathed deep. "After the soot and

130

smoke of London, one feels one is drinking in the pure air our Lord intended."

Marie de Courcy pointed at the spots on the hillside below the painted cliffs. "What are those?"

Emma was frightened. "Not — Indians, I hope? They are red!"

Emile laughed. "No, my dear. Those are cattle — red-and-white cattle — Charles's cattle! He has now almost a thousand, and is bringing others here. They are a new strain, bred for more meat and less skin and bones."

"But whatever do the poor things find to eat when the land is covered with snow?"

"I am a lawyer, dear child, and not a farmer. But it says in Charles's book called *The Beef Bonanza* that they root with their cow noses under the snow to find grass. It is hoped the cattle have also read the book."

There was laughter at the dry remark. With all the champagne, everything seemed amusing. The merriment waned when Murdoch stalked near, hat in hand.

"Sir?"

"Yes, Murdoch."

The Scot waved his bowler at the scud of cloud. "We are several miles from the chateau, and it looks as if it might snow. Perhaps we ought to be heading back."

"Snow?" Emma asked, excited. "A snowstorm? Oh, I want to stay, Emile! In London all we have is a few dirty flakes, stained with soot. Can we stay? We have a fire, and there is plenty of champagne left!"

Emile shook his head. "In this country the snow comes with a roar, and can kill. Snow in the Dakotas is not a pretty watercolor hanging on the wall. No, I am afraid Murdoch is right. We must return, quickly. Charles left you in my care, and I do not want to present him with a wagonload of frozen corpses."

After Murdoch had packed the picnic things, leaving a pile of champagne bottles in the snow along with the smoldering remains of the fire, they piled again into the wagon. On the homeward track the snow started to fall, at first only a few lacy flakes, but rapidly growing thicker. Under the steady downpour the ruts of the road began to blur. To be sure of the way, Murdoch turned toward the river. Emile looked over his shoulder at his charges; the company were dozing, wrapped in blankets and burrowed into the straw.

"How far?" he asked Murdoch.

The baron's man pointed with his whip at a jagged sandstone peak barely seen through the increasing snow. "The local people call that the Mitten, because of the side peak that looks somewhat like a thumb. Once we round that, it is only a mile or so."

They passed near a scraggly burr oak that stood like a withered sentinel, limbs black and witchlike. Beneath the tree, almost directly in their path, lay a bulky object dusted with snow. A log? What? Emile, peering through the downpour, said, "Hold up, please, Murdoch. What is that, lying there?" When the wagon stopped the company came awake from their dozing, peering over the sideboards. "What is happening? Are we lost, then?"

The Scot set the handbrake and tied the reins about the handle. "I don't know, sir," he said, "but I shall find out." Jumping down into the snow, he floundered as the thin crust broke under his weight. Emile, following him toward the thing, stared as Murdoch's hand brushed away a veil of flakes from a face. The eyes were closed, the visage pale as if carved from marble.

"A girl!" Murdoch exclaimed.

"*Mon Dieu!* Is she — is she —" Emile helped the Scot clear snow from the clothing, picked up a frosted handkerchief made into a bundle. "Is she — dead?"

"I do not think so, sir." Murdoch spoke to M. Dessines. "Sir, will you bring what brandy is left, quickly?" He laid his ear to the breast. "I hear a faint fluttering, it seems to me. And her body is still somewhat warm."

Emile took the slender wrist in his fingers. "There is a pulse. Weak, but —" He turned to the females. "Please bring some blankets, ladies."

Marc Dessines, the hunting piece still in the crook of his arm, stared down at the girl. "Whatever is she doing here, in the snow?"

"She is the one who will have to tell us," Emile said, lifting the body in his arms. "If she lives, that is."

They bedded the warmly wrapped body in the wagon. Mme. Dessines tried to force some brandy between the pale lips, but the teeth were tightly clenched. Emma, unfastening the knot in the kerchief, discovered only a comb, some underdrawers and stockings, a handful of small coins in a leather bag, and a worn volume of poems by an unknown American poet. Touched, the English girl warmed the icy hands in her own. "So young, so fair!" Valerie fingered the sleeve of the cloth coat which had been the girl's scanty protection against the weather. "A very poor cut, and the material is inferior. In this country they do not know fabrics, let alone style!"

Murdoch whipped up the mules. In a few minutes they were mounting the hill toward the chateau. When the big iron tires of the baron's hunting wagon ground in the gravel beneath the porte cochere, Mme. Boucher, the housekeeper, shawl about gray head, ran into the yard followed by the servants and Ike Cooney, the baron's new foreman.

"Been right worried about you all, Mr. Emile," Cooney said. "With the storm coming on, we was about to send out someone to see if you all was all right!"

Mme. Boucher frowned at the blanket-wrapped bundle in Emile Durand's arms. "What is that, monsieur?" Suddenly she stepped back. "Dead?"

"I don't think so, madame," Emile said over his shoulder. "Please prepare a bed for her, quickly, and heat some water!"

Marc Dessines, in response to a nod from Emile, herded the curious guests into the great hall where a blazing fire had been laid and warm drinks were ready. Emile, followed by Mme. Boucher, carried the girl up the broad staircase and to a bedroom, discreetly leaving while the housekeeper and one of the upstairs maids undressed the unfortunate female and put her to bed with bottles of hot water at her sides and feet. Dr. Cromie was sent for. Emile, returning to the hall, was faced with a barrage of questions.

"And what was she doing out there in the snow, that poor girl? Is she dead? Who is she? Does anyone know?"

Emile poured himself a brandy. "I don't know. But she is alive, and in good hands. We are doing all for her that can be done. And the doctor will be here soon."

"She is pretty, that girl," Marie de Courcy mused, twirling Charles's fine brandy in a glass and staring through it at the fire. "A good nose, nice firm chin, beautiful hair of a certain coppery tinge. I wonder if it is dyed."

"Pregnant, too, I think," Mme. Dessines murmured.

Emile put down his glass, startled. "Pregnant?"

"*Oui*. At least, I think so. Not many months along yet, but —"

"How do you know? It — it seems indelicate to make such a judgment!"

Mme. Dessines shrugged. "When one has had six children, one has a certain sense about these things."

Dr. Cromie, a rider reported, had gone to Wibaux to treat a sickly baby. Mme. Boucher sighed, folding hands before her ample bosom. "It cannot be helped, then. But the child is breathing better, and her body is warmer. Also, she moves a little, and mutters things."

Emile, meeting her descending from the upper story, asked, "What things, madame?"

"I do not know. The words do not make sense."

Very concerned, Emile fondled his long mustaches. "There is no identification?"

"No, monsieur."

"The book of poems?"

"It was wet, the pages wet. Inside, what was written is blurred."

"No — distinguishing marks?"

The housekeeper looked puzzled.

"I do not know exactly what I mean. Something — anything — that might help identify the poor child. Even now her parents might be searching for her! She cannot be over eighteen or so."

Mme. Boucher coughed, delicately. "You are a family man, monsieur, and I can speak of this to you. She is going to have a baby, and —"

"I know that, madame."

"*Bien*. And on the inside of her thigh there is a large scar, a triangular scar, well healed. Aside from that, nothing."

Emile sighed. "Well, I will go and sit with her awhile. I pity the poor creature. Perhaps I can find out something when she wakes. In the meantime, madame, I am sure you have many duties, with all Charles's guests here."

"But —"

"That will be all."

Mme. Boucher inclined her head and shuffled away, the black sateen of her dress rustling dryly. Emile watched her go, then mounted the stairs. Turning the heavy brass knob, he entered the bedroom on tiptoe. The girl lay quietly, eyes closed, the only sign of life the slow rise and fall of her bosom under the lacy bodice of a borrowed nightgown. Emile sat quietly on a chair beside the bed, chin in hand, looking down with compassion at the face — pale yet, but with a growing flush to the cheeks. She coughed once, a quick spasm, but did not wake.

136

So young, so fair! She reminded him of Yvonne, his eldest, now almost thirteen — the same straight aquiline nose, the full sensitive lips, the long eyelashes over high cheekbones. An interesting face; a child's face, really. What did children know about carnal knowledge, giving birth, such things? Still, there it was! What a wicked world!

Lutie heard him sigh. She had heard much that went before but judged it better to keep her own counsel, for a while, at least; she was in strange territory. Still, the sigh intrigued her. She knew it was a man's sigh. In spite of her weakness and the uncomfortable feeling in her chest, she determined to orient herself. Slowly she opened her eyes, and saw — Emile Durand.

For a moment they stared at each other, Emile not quite believing she was conscious, Lutie not quite believing that she had been miraculously transported to heaven. Emile! The chief angel, with his soft blue eyes and taffy mustaches, was watching over her! Was she really dead? Had she perished in the snow in her flight?

"You are awake, eh?"

Lutie blinked, uncertain still, modestly catching a fold of the blanket about her bosom. "I — I — where am I?" Trying to sit up, she fell to coughing, and dropped back. Her chest seemed filled with molten iron; it hurt.

Gently Emile tucked the coverlet about her. "Do not worry, mademoiselle." Mademoiselle was a guess on his part. Probably she had been raped by one of the uncouth hands Charles had hired. He would deal with that later.

Lutie's eyes scanned the room, marveling. She had thought the Griffins' big ranch house a marvelous place but what she saw now caused her eyes to widen, her breath to draw in sharply. The room was larger even than the Griffins' parlor. Emile drew back the heavy velour curtains and the hard winter light brought into rich relief the ornate carved chairs, the deep-piled Wilton carpeting, a diamond-bright pier glass, carved-mahogany chests, graceful ferns in shiny brass buckets with bas-relief figures of dancing youths and maidens.

"We found you in the snow," Emile said in his charmingly accented English. "We were out in the baron's hunting wagon, friends and I, when we found you lying half buried under a withered oak tree."

With a painful effort Lutie turned her head. The headboard of the bed was of rich dark wood, and more nymphs cavorted across it, most of them undraped. "My goodness!" she said faintly. After her straw pallet behind a flour-sack curtain in a corner of the dark and gloomy soddy, this transport was magical. Quickly she glanced at Emile. Did he recognize her? In a way, she hoped this handsome man *did* remember her from the day he and the baron helped bury poor mad Uncle Milo. Still, she did not want to be discovered. She had run away from home, and stumbled into incredible good luck. The last thing she wanted was for Mama to find out where she was.

"What is your name, *s'il vous plaît?*" Emile asked. Then he laughed. "You must forgive me! I speak so much the French that I forgot!"

"I know those words," she said quickly. "It means 'please.'"

"That's right."

"Ah — my name is Lutie. That's for Lutecia. Lutecia is the old Latin name for the city of Paris."

"I know *that*," he smiled. "So we are even, eh? But — Lutie what?"

"Smith," she lied. "Lutie Smith." To forestall embarrassing questioning, she closed her eyes. Her head *did* ache, and something in her chest seemed to grate when she breathed.

"Lutie Smith, then." Emile rose. "Well, Lutie, you must rest now."

Eyes still closed, she said, cautiously, "I know where I am, though. This is the chateau. The baron's chateau."

"Yes."

"Then where is he? The baron, I mean."

"Charles? Oh, he has gone to St. Louis to see about some business. Refrigerator cars. He will not return for several days. Until then you must rest, eh, and eat nourishing foods? Charles and I will talk things over when he returns."

Charles and I will talk things over. Lutie swallowed hard, thinking of the baron's dark visage, his mocking eyes. In a way, the baron had killed Buck, and her lip trembled. But now she must sleep, rest, gather her mind, her strength, for the time when the baron returned. She would make her case, find a way to stay on in this great house. She would leave behind forever the poverty and shabbiness of life in the hated soddy and somehow take her place where she firmly believed she belonged: among rich and elegant people who spoke French and rode out to hunt in gaily painted wagons.

Returned from Wibaux, Dr. Cromie looked at his thermometer and said, "You've got quite a fever, Lutie, and shouldn't be moved from here until that inflammation in your chest clears up. But I don't see why I shouldn't tell your pa and ma. They're crazy with grief for you. Your pa isn't well anyway, you know. Jake Sigafoos and a passel of others have been out looking for you till they're plumb tuckered out."

Lutie coughed, putting a borrowed handkerchief to her lips. Was this how it was to be delirious? Dr. Cromie's face looked queer and distorted. There was a high-pitched ringing in her ears, like a lot of tiny bells.

"I don't care!" she cried. "I — I don't want them to find me!" Miserably she added, "Doctor, I'm going to have a baby! Mama practically drove me out of the house. I can't go back! I *won't* go back! Don't you understand?"

Dr. Cromie put the thermometer back into the case and sat heavily beside her. "I suspected, I must admit. Buck, of course."

Eyes swimming with tears, she nodded.

"Ah, Lutie, I'm sorry." He shook his head, and ran a hand through his tight gray curls. "Well, I'll talk to your folks anyway, tell them you're all right. I've got to do that. But —"

"But what?" She was suspicious.

"You're pretty sick, Lutie. The best I can do is tell them that, and when you're better, perhaps you can see them, talk to them. Your pa is sick, you know, and your ma is a good woman, though a trifle outspoken."

Mutely she nodded. For now, it was probably the best she could manage. Lying back on the pillow, she let her taut muscles relax, starting at her toes, through her limbs and hips, through the place where Buck's damned baby lay, finally through her breast and arms and shoulders and neck. She must rest, to be strong when the inevitable happened, when the baron returned, when Papa and Mama came to take her back to the soddy. The heavy brass latch clicked, and she knew Dr. Cromie had gone.

I'll beat them, she said savagely, clenching her fists. *I'll conquer them all. I have power, my own kind of power, and I'll use it!* Moments later, when the woman in black sateen came in, Lutie played possum again. For a long moment the woman stood silently by Lutie's bed, hands folded before her. Lutie did not let on. She lay quietly, thinking only that the woman — Madame something-or-other that sounded like "butcher" — looked like an old alligator. Still, she would need all the friends she could muster. She stirred slightly, sighed, and tried to look as fetching and innocent as she could.

After that, there were a lot of things Lutie was not sure of. Probably it was because of the inflammation Dr. Cromie said she had in her lungs. Dimly she was aware of activity about her — low voices, drafts of bitter medicines, someone attempting to bathe her while she twisted restlessly in the big carved bed and cried out.

Mama! she remembered crying. *Papa! Sid! What am I going to do? Why am I here?* In fevered dreams she saw her parents, Emile's gentle smile, the baron's wry twist of brow and sardonic face. As in another dream she felt someone near, bending over her, and heard the rustle of black sateen. Madame was bending over her again, staring, calculating. Another time she woke, or thought she woke, and was sure the servant Murdoch, the dark beetle-browed Scot, was peering at her through the open door. Screaming, she sat up, clutching the coverlet about her. But no one was there.

She did not, however, dream of Buck Griffin. Resolutely she had set that face out of her life. And one day she woke, clear in her mind but still light-headed, the hot bitter pain in her breast gone, and feeling a strange peacefulness. Very weak, she managed to sit up in bed. Rolling to the edge, she put bare feet on the thick carpet and swayed to her feet.

"Oh, my!" Dizzy, she sat down again, bracing herself with arms thrust back. For a long time she remained thus, feeling, listening, filled with a heady sense of returning strength. Bathed in sunlight, she was content for a while just to *be*. The brass latch of the door must have clicked, but she did not hear it. Still sitting, quiet and content, she felt rather than heard the presence. It was Charles de Fleury, the baron.

"Mademoiselle," he said, bowing. "You are better, I hope?"

Embarrassed, Lutie flung herself beneath the coverlet and stared at him with wide frightened eyes.

142

"*Pardon*," he said, closing the door after him. "I did not think — How is it said? I did not mean to *scare* you, young lady." He wore rough and shabby clothing, like one of Pa Griffin's Slash G hands: stained and torn jeans, a flannel shirt open at the neck to show a bush of wiry black hair, a loose-hanging vest with several buttons missing. Big-roweled spurs clinked and clanked as he strode across the carpet, tossing his wide-brimmed hat on a chair. Seeing her stare at him wide-eyed, he chuckled.

"My apology for how I look so — so *déshabillé!* But Ike Cooney and I have had troubles — shooting troubles — with M. Griffin. I have been on a horse two, three days."

For the first time she noticed the blood-stained cloth wrapped about his hand. He did not sit, but continued to prowl about the room, intense and alert, shaggy brows twitching.

She watched him pass into the sunlight, then out again, shadows etching his face in hard lines. She had not expected him. Still — she had lost track of time during her illness.

"I — I heard you were in St. Louis."

He stopped pacing. "*Oui.* I was. But hearing of troubles, I returned."

His English was still heavily accented, awkward, but it had improved greatly since the last time she had seen him, at the birthday party. But he did not seem to remember her. Well, she *was* thinner, peaked, and her hair must look awful! Choosing her words carefully, one hand trying to smooth down her hair, she said, "I — am grateful to you for letting me stay here."

He sat down wearily, booted legs crossed, fingers scratching at his untrimmed beard. "It is nothing. When a man comes to a new place like this, it is only *comme il faut* — damn, this English is so hard for me! — It is proper I be a good neighbor." He stopped scratching, peered at her. "Now I know! Mme. Boucher told me your name, but I did not — what you say? — connect. That is it. I did not connect. You are that girl — when we buried the man that day —"

She nodded. By now it must be no secret who she was.

"And at the *fête* — the birthday party. That day, too!"

"Yes."

When he grinned, she flushed.

"Aha!" He pointed a finger. "You have been naughty, eh? A baby!"

Angry, she bit her tongue. This was a delicate piece of business; the baron was no simple Buck Griffin. Letting herself sink languidly back on the pillow and closing her eyes, she stalled for time. For a moment he did not speak. Finally he came to her bedside with a clink of the big spurs.

"Again, *pardon*. I am sometimes a rough and unthinking man. But everything will soon be all right. Dr. Cromie has arranged for your people to come and see you. Perhaps soon you will be able to go home again and be with them. I will send you in my new hunting wagon. Did you see it? Ah, no! Emile said you were senseless when he found you. Well, it is very big, with immense wheels painted yellow and brown. There is leather upholstery and built-in chests and lockers for guns and bottles and provisions. I designed it myself, you see, and —"

Her careful tactics were shattered. "No!" she cried. In despair she rolled her head frantically on the pillow, clenched her fists. "I don't *want* to go back! I *won't* go back! Please, don't send me back!"

He stared at her. "What? *Mon Dieu*, I did not mean to make you cry, mademoiselle!"

"I can't go back! Let me stay, please! Let me stay here, in your chateau!"

Upset, he scowled at her. "For God's sake, stop your shrieking! Do you want to alarm the whole household?"

Not caring that the coverlet fell away, she sat up. Reaching out, she snatched his unwilling hand. "Please! I'll do — anything! I can work! I'm a good worker! Just let me stay, and I'll —"

"Nonsense!" He drew his hand away. "You talk foolishness, you know! There is no place here for a young girl, already in difficulties. My house is not an academy for young and wayward females!" Groping for words, he avoided her eyes, making awkward gestures with the bandaged hand. "This is a place of pleasure, you see, for me and my friends. We — we drink, we entertain each other in a certain way, we — we —"

"I don't care! I am very adaptable, you'll see. All I ask is —"

"A — dap —" His brows drew together. "I do not know that word! Anyway, we smoke hashish also, when we please. We —"

"Smoke it then! But please —"

"No!" he protested, temper rising. "Damn it, no, mademoiselle! I have been very accommodating of you, or for you, or however it is said in this barbarous language of English. But enough is enough! You will have to go home as soon as you can travel."

Throwing aside the coverlet, she ran to him in the lacy nightgown, throwing herself at his booted feet, clutching his knees. "I *won't* go! You can't *make* me go! I'm going to stay and wash and scrub floors and empty the chamberpots and do everything! You don't need to pay me. Just let me stay!"

Astonished at her passion, he stared down. Groaning, he slapped his thigh with the wide-brimmed hat. "Damn!" he cried. Then the door opened. Mme. Boucher peered around Emile Durand's shoulder. Emile spoke quickly to the baron, in French. Lutie, arms still clasped about the baron's muddy jeans, saw Emile stride forward, push the baron roughly aside. Kneeling, he lifted her, carried her to the canopied bed. Mme. Boucher adjusted her pillow, pulled up the coverlet, while Emile and the baron seemed to quarrel about something. Lutie knew little French, but was pleased to think they were arguing about her.

Angry, the baron finally stamped out, slamming the door after him. Emile gestured to Mme. Boucher. The housekeeper bowed her head in acquiescence and rustled out. For a long moment Emile stood in the sunlit window, fingers caressing the soft fair mustache. Finally he turned to Lutie. Her heart ached. She did not like to see him troubled, but right now there were larger issues to be considered.

"We will talk this over later," he said. "For now, child, there is nothing to fear."

Exultant, she slept that night a deep and dreamless sleep. In the morning, when her folks came, Lutie was very calm; she knew she had won — at least for the time being. Of course, she was sorry for Papa. He looked so old and worn. But that did not move her, even Mama's tight-lipped statement that she had misspoke herself, that she should not have called Lutie that — that name.

"In Virginia," she explained, "we ladies did not use words like that, I want you to know, daughter. It was just that — just that —" Face working, she turned her head away, and wept. In spite of grief and trouble and backbreaking labor, Mama practically never wept. She was made of some kind of iron, Lutie guessed. Finally Mama said, "Well, I'm sorry, Lutie. That's all I can say. You were always a difficult child. I think it was some of your Uncle Milo's bad blood."

Hair neatly done, a fresh *peignoir*, Mme. Boucher called it, about her shoulders, Lutie lay in the big bed, feeling very well indeed. *She* was made of some kind of iron, too.

"I'm sorry too, Mama," she agreed. "And Papa." They had not brought Sid, whom she *did* want to see. "But I've got a job here now, living at the chateau." She did not, really, but she was sure of herself. "I'll be all right. In a few days I'll be up and around and earning my own way, so I won't be a burden on you."

Papa cleared his throat. "You were never a burden, child." But Mama stood up, and said, "Lorenzo, we'd best be going."

After they left, she did cry for a little bit. But the tears did not last long. A new life had opened for her. She was going to make her mark in it, somehow.

CHAPTER
EIGHT

The baron's chateau was a rambling structure of wood two stories high, containing almost thirty rooms. Painted gray, with roof and shutters vermilion red, it faced south, giving a sweeping view of the river and the grasslands. It was surrounded by a wide veranda for taking the sun, from which in clear weather could be seen Little Misery, miles distant, and the buildings of the Griffin ranch far upriver. Several hundred yards from the main building the abattoir was taking shape, the slaughterhouse where the baron intended his beef to be processed for shipment to the hungry East — though lately it was rumored that the Northern Pacific Railroad, in concert with the jealous "meat barons" of Chicago, were causing difficulties.

Still weak, Lutie extracted from Dr. Cromie permission to let her walk slowly about, "so long," Mme. Boucher warned, "as you do not get in the way, or come into a place where there are guests."

The living room was almost as spacious as outdoors. The great fireplace opened on all four sides so that the blaze could be seen from any quarter. Over the fireplace hung weapons: battle-axes, guns, a pair of crossed sabers, medieval pikes, daggerlike knives, others with crooked and sinuous blades. On the floor oriental rugs mingled with buffalo robes, and the walls could scarcely be seen for the profusion of oil paintings and hunting trophies. The baron, one of the maids told her, played the piano. On a slightly raised dais was an ebony piano almost as big as the interior of the old soddy where Lutie once lived.

There was a library, too, where she often stole to read the books that seemed otherwise to be untouched: works on travel, the social sciences, economics, political processes. The dining hall, a long high-ceilinged room papered in a kind of red velvet cloth, occupied most of a separate L. Glass-fronted cabinets held several services of Sèvres and Limoges; Lutie dared to open a cabinet and read the legend on the bottom of the plates. Silver, too, massy knives and forks and spoons with what she judged was the baron's crest worked cunningly into the metal.

Upstairs sprawled several bedrooms — she was never sure how many. Each had that marvel, a bathtub, in an alcove. In what she thought must be the baron's own room there was a huge one of enameled tin, painted by Italian artists with scenes of a leaping stag pursued by huntsmen. The baron was a big man, much taller and heavier than Emile Durand.

Lutie was allowed to take her meals with the servants in the spacious kitchen. The help ate well, though certainly not as well as the waves of guests that came and went at the Château de Fleury. In the kitchen she saw exotic items being prepared; lamb with *sauce aux câpres* — the "capers" being little black buglike things

150

in cans from Park and Tilford, all the way from New York — fish, rack of lamb, wild ducks *saignant*, slightly bloody inside. There were venison and elk, and the guests particularly enjoyed the local prairie chickens. M. Guillaume, the chef, discovered a way to braise them in an iron kettle with wild onions, along with a dash of brandy to make a succulent broth. M. Guillaume also kept the keys to the wine cellar, a dark and mysterious cavern filled with bottles bearing faded and watermarked labels; Château Lagrange, Haut Brion, Latour, and Margaux. Dishes were often returned to the kitchen hardly touched. Lutie became familiar with what M. Guillaume called his *chefs-d'oeuvre*, his masterpieces — fillets of flounder amandine, salmon in court bouillon, a Syrian dish of lamb called ristaya of which the baron was very fond, and a host of opulent desserts: *crème brûlée*, raspberry *bombe*, steamed date pudding rich with figs and walnuts.

"You like good food!" the chef said to Lutie. "You have taste, girl, and appreciate fine things!" He even complimented her on her French when she slavishly imitated his Parisian trill of the tongue speaking of *vin rouge* or *coquilles St. Jacques*.

But with all the fine living and luxurious surroundings, with all the gay and lively guests and the hunting parties and late-night *soirées*, all was not well in the baron's Dakota preserve. As in any great house, the servants knew a great deal about what was going on. It was an item of kitchen gossip that the baron had greatly overextended himself in borrowing from

Eastern banks. The chambermaids spoke to each other in hushed tones of troubles in getting needed materials and machinery to finish the slaughterhouse. The ranch hands, usually tight-mouthed, sometimes let slip word about confrontations with the Griffin riders; even pitched battles at the edge of the baron's twenty-five thousand acres along the meandering Little Missouri. Old Griffin, it was said, had sworn to drive the foreign intruder from Dakota. Since he had Sheriff Holland in his pocket, along with the local justice court, Griffin was a formidable opponent. Still, it was hard to imagine the baron, with his immense land holdings and luxurious establishment on the bluff, being driven from what he had started. Charles, Baron de Fleury, was not that kind of man.

Emile Durand worried a great deal about the situation. A man of the law, he counseled Charles to patience, to gradualness, to moderate his client's breakneck approach to establishing his barony. He and Charles had been childhood friends. They had both gone to St. Cyr and served in a smart regiment, Charles going on to a military career while Emile turned to the law. Now, in spite of their long friendship, they often quarreled.

In late winter the baron held a birthday party for Marc Dessines, with guests from Chicago, St. Louis, New York, even from Paris and London. For days the kitchen help toiled to prepare the menu Mme. Boucher brought down from the baron. Lutie could not sleep for all the noise and excitement. It was near dawn when the last guest made an erratic way up the grand

152

staircase and tottered into bed. With the first streak of dawn fiery red on the inlaid parquet floor of the dining room, Emile and Charles lingered at the long table, littered with empty champagne bottles, soiled plates, a broken wineglass lying on its side in a red puddle.

"I am glad," Emile sighed, "for the opportunity to speak to you in private, *mon cher*. You are so busy; it is either a trip East, or you are surrounded by people. Have you time for a little talk about business affairs?"

Charles had been matching his guests drink for drink, and adding a few for good measure. Draining his glass, he spun it between thumb and finger, watching it gyrate on the stained Madeira lace.

"Come to my parties more often then! You are too much of a sobersides now. You were not that way when we were at school together!"

Emile shrugged. "I am a quiet man, with a family. How would it look if I were to dance on the table with that Jeanne whatever-her-name-is, and she half undressed?"

"You are too phlegmatic, my friend! Life is passing you by." Pulling the cork from a bottle, he tried to fill Emile's glass, but the lawyer put his hand over it. "As you wish," Charles shrugged.

Emile reached into an inner pocket and withdrew a folded sheet of paper. "This is the latest accounting of your financial situation. It is accurate: I prepared it myself."

Sighing, Charles picked up the document. Pulling a guttering candle closer, he scanned it, heavy brows drawing together.

"You know I am not good at figures!"

"Then look at the last line. You are fast running out of cash, and the interest you are paying to the banks is mounting at an incredible rate! Until your beef undertaking begins to bring in some money, you must conserve, my friend — conserve!"

"Conserve? What do you mean?"

Emile waved his hand. "Minimizing such entertaining is perhaps a way to conserve — a small way, but a start." Retrieving the account, he pointed to a column of figures. "Last month, over ten thousand francs for wine alone! And do you really need all the servants? Housemaids, parlormaids, a butler, cooks and subcooks! Too many laundresses, and more riders in the bunkhouse than the U.S. Cavalry, I think! The wages" — he ran a finger down the column — "for last month they come to —"

"I need them!" Charles objected. "I like people about me; men of quality and beautiful women! It takes a considerable staff to care for them, doesn't it? As for the riders, it is my personal army, my answer to that ugly old Griffin. It will come to a war, a real war, and I must defend my lands, Emile! I tell you, that miserable old man has threatened me, and I have given orders that on no account are my men to retreat!"

Emile put a hand on the baron's sleeve. "No need to shout, my friend. I have only your best interests at heart; it is as your lawyer I speak. While I defer to you on other things, at business you must listen to *me*." Though trained to handle difficult matters, he had never liked quarrels, loud voices, animosity. "As in the

154

management of the chateau, I counsel moderation in your beef operation. After all, you are a stranger in this new land. The local people are hard men, who have wrested a living out of a difficult land. It is only natural they should be at first suspicious, especially after that unfortunate incident with young Griffin."

"But *how* can I moderate my progress? Am I to abandon the slaughterhouse, stop fencing my land, buy no more cattle for spring delivery? You yourself have told me I must soon bring in money to pay for the undertaking!" Shoving back his chair, Charles strode about the room, hands clasped tightly behind his back. "My friend, you do not understand! Brave undertakings require brave men, men who move and act and make decisions! When I undertook this project, I knew that I myself was a principal asset! I risk, I dare! That is my way! You have seen me risk a hundred thousand on the turn of the wheel at the casino! I did not win the *Médaille Militaire* at El Ouatia by conserving either my men or me!"

Emile was becoming annoyed. "I am not talking about war, *mon ami*. This is business, simply business. If you did not know I was such a sobersides, as you put it, I did not know you were such a mule, such a stubborn brute. They say, you know, that no man is so blind as he that *will* not see."

"Oho!" The baron's face flushed, he chewed at a corner of the bristling beard. "So I am a brute, eh? A blind mule, to use your unfortunate phrase. Let me tell you, Emile Durand, that I am beginning to believe you were against me from the start!"

"That is not true!"

"All you have done of late is put obstacles in my way! Damn it all, do I not have enough obstacles? Pah!" The baron kicked a smoldering log in the fireplace and it burst quickly into flame.

"You are being unjust, you know that! And it is no use to try to talk sense to you when you are in such a mood!"

"It is you who are in a mood, with mealymouthed talk about conserving and moderating and drinking weak tea instead of good French wine!" He pounded a fist on the table. "It is my way of living you don't like! You are a penny-pinching timid man, and I don't know why I ever took you for a friend!"

Determined to control himself, Emile folded his hands in his lap. "You will regret those words, I know. You are too good and generous a man, Charles, to mean them! But let us abandon that prickly subject. I must ask your opinion about another matter."

Glowering, the baron sprawled in the high-backed chair. When he did not speak, Emile went on.

"A small matter, but one which is important to the girl."

"Girl? What girl?"

"Lutie. The Hamlin girl. The one we found on the prairie after the storm."

"Pregnant."

"Yes. As you know, she refuses to go home. She is a stubborn young lady, and insists on staying here. I have talked with her many times lately, and she is willing to take on any task — parlormaid, vegetable scrubber in the kitchen, laundress — just so long as she can remain. Guillaume says she is a good worker."

Charles was still upset. Pouring another drink, he said, "Pretty, isn't she? That high bosom, those clear blue eyes?"

"I suppose so."

"You advise me to discharge half my servants, and then are in favor of putting on a new one, is that it?"

"I think it would be a charitable act."

Charles's grin was saturnine. "Oh, come, my friend! You suppose I know none of what goes on belowstairs! In spite of the fact that you believe me incompetent to manage my holdings, I tell you I have a sharp ear. I hear many things *sub rosa*, to speak in the lawyers' Latin gibberish! The reason you want Mlle. Lutie to stay on is that you have plans of your own for her!"

Emile was astonished. "Plans? What plans?"

Roguishly the baron stroked the glossy beard. The words were thickened with liquor, but clear enough. "You hypocrite! With a wife and children in Chicago, you intend to dally with my help! Emile, I would not think it of you!"

Red-faced, Emile sprang to his feet. "That is an insult, Charles — a grave insult, not only to me but to my family!"

Charles sprawled deeper in the chair. "Don't take on so! It was only a joke, a little joke."

"It was no joke!"

Weary, the baron shrugged. "Emile, you know how I am. When I have had too much wine, I become quarrelsome. I apologize." He waved his hand, chin sunk on chest, eyes closing. "Let the girl stay. I don't care!"

Lutie worked hard, first as kitchen help and then being advanced to parlormaid when the chef spoke to Mme. Boucher. M. Guillaume was very sentimental. "She tries hard, but for a girl soon to be a mother the work in the kitchen is bad. Perhaps you can find a place for her upstairs." M. Guillaume liked Lutie. Most of the servants did, though the housekeeper remained distant and aloof. Murdoch, too, the baron's man; Lutie did not like the way he watched her with his deep-set eyes under heavy brows. Tall, gaunt, slipping silently about the great house, she felt always under Murdoch's scrutiny. Yet he was very correct, always calling her "Miss Lutie" in spite of her lowly position.

Actually she had not minded the kitchen work. There was a cheeriness about the kitchen: the warmth of the big range, the steamy smells, cheerful bakers white to the elbows with flour, assistant cooks stirring pots of soup, all a pleasant clatter and *bonhomie* — that was a word she looked up in the dictionary, finding it meant "simplicity, good nature, cheerfulness." Already she had a smattering of French; she was a quick learner. Physically, too, though well along in her pregnancy, she felt fine, happy with the realization that at last she was close to the seat of power, that at long last she was getting someplace. And about time, too, she thought — she was twenty years old.

The upstairs duties were not too demanding. Mme. Boucher had evidently been instructed to go easy on

158

her. For most of the day Lutie dusted furniture, watered houseplants, and polished silver. During the morning hours, at least, everyone — the baron and guests — slept off a late revelry, and abovestairs the chateau was silent and peaceful. Drawing open the curtains, she stared out at the snowy world. All was deep in white, the only evidence of activity a few cowhands near the barn, squatting in a sheltered alcove to repair harnesses, and some carpenters sawing and pounding on the rising structure of the abattoir. The word sounded ever so much more stylish than "slaughterhouse."

The cowhands were rough untutored men, brawling and troublesome on payday when they returned from Little Misery liquored up, but devoted to the baron. Some were "hardcases," it was said, fleeing from charges in Montana or Colorado. Their idea of humor was crude: a much-appreciated joke was to fill a bunkmate's boots with water which hardened to ice during the night. The carpenters at the abattoir were mostly Scandinavian, local people who jabbered in an unintelligible nasal language and went about with lower lip bulging with "snoose," they called it — snuff.

Some of the workers were Indians, too, Sioux Indians. In Dakota Indians were anathema, useful only as butts of cruel practical jokes. But the baron, long familiar with the native peoples of Algeria and respectful of their character and culture, hired old Yellow Hat's Sioux at good wages. They responded by working hard and becoming trustworthy. Not mingling with the cowhands or the carpenters, they preferred to camp in their own *tipi* village on a rise a half mile or so from the chateau. Lutie wondered how they ever kept warm in the flimsy buffalo-hide tents, but somehow the Sioux seemed to manage. In spite of the heritage as hunters and warriors, they took readily to farming, sowing and cultivating and harvesting the new Russian wheat from the Crimea with which the baron was experimenting.

In her work Lutie was exposed to the amused stares and gibes of the baron's guests. They all knew her story; in fact, her bulging waist could hardly conceal her condition. The beautiful women looked on her with a gay contempt, the men stared knowingly and talked behind their hands. Disregarding them all, she assessed them as parasites and hangers-on, with no real standing of their own. They were — what was the word? Going again to the unused library, she found it: "sybarites." But she did make one concession. Listening avidly to their talk, she improved her French, more carefully enunciated her English, stored in memory details of the London theater, the Paris Opéra, the current price of beef — nine dollars per hundred pounds on the hoof — along with the badinage, the chitchat, that seemed their chief occupation. Finding once a half-smoked hashish cigarette in the parlor, she went to a dark hall closet and lit it, having observed that smoking the stuff seemed part of the social ritual. She got sick, and when she reeled into the kitchen, sitting down with pale face and trembling hands, M. Guillaume was sure she was near her time. A cup of tea finally calmed her, and she smoked no more hashish for a while, although later she

160

came to enjoy it. Reflecting on the incident, she almost giggled in spite of the horrible nausea. What would Papa and Mama — and Sid — think of her now? Smoking hashish! Then she felt a sudden wave of remorse. Weeping, she put her head on the scrubbed-white table. Resolutely she had stricken them from her thoughts, but she did miss them. M. Guillaume, mistaking her emotion, patted her gently on the shoulder. "There, there, *ma petite*, collect yourself. It is difficult, I understand, to carry a child, but you will come through all right." To comfort her he fixed her a piece of *weinschnitte* — bread dipped in grape wine, fried, and sprinkled with cinnamon and butter. It was too much. Nauseated again, she fled the kitchen with a hasty "*Merci, monsieur!*"

Emile — the gentle Emile — had gone back to Chicago for a visit with wife and family, but was expected to return in a few weeks. The baron was again in St. Louis, wrangling with the ironworks which was building his refrigerator cars. There was trouble, it was said, not only with the St. Louis company, but the railroad interests were rumored to be somehow in league with the "beef trust" in Chicago against him. In March the Little Misery *Gazette* ran an item reprinted from the Bismarck *Tribune*:

The Territory is in some measure grateful to the Baron de Fleury for his considerable investments in the future of this area. He has given employment to many, including our benighted Indian brothers, and spent large sums in the local economy. While many consider his plans grandiose, and others resent the presence of a foreign *entrepreneur* on native American soil, it is the opinion of the editor that, on the whole, his undertaking is bound to be beneficial, and should be supported. It is understood he is presently having difficulties in the East, both with bank financing and with the delivery of needed supplies and machinery, but it is to be hoped that his efforts will eventually be crowned with success.

The Mandan *Pioneer* thought differently:

Rumors of violence along the Little Missouri River have proved correct. Our correspondent at Little Misery reports that on Wednesday last what amounts to a pitched battle took place near Pretty Butte between the Baron de Fleury's men and riders from the Slash G spread, owned by Mr. Henry Griffin, a prominent and well-regarded citizen of Morton County. The affair, which resulted in the wounding of three of the Slash G hands and unknown injuries to the combatants on the other side, was precipitated by a dispute regarding the boundaries of the land along the river which the baron is fencing. The baron's lawyer has filed suit in the Morton County Court, claiming that Slash G cattle are trespassing his lands. The suit will not come to trial for several weeks. Mr. Henry Griffin has a long reputation hereabouts as a fair and agreeable man. In fact, he was one of the first to settle in this area, coming from Texas in 1859 with his wife and family. We would advise the baron to restrain his men from acts of violence until the case can be legally disposed of.

In late March it snowed, a blinding wind-swept downpour that added inches, then feet, to the blanket that already lay on the land. The baron's cattle — all cattle, in fact — drifted before the snow, holing up in coulees and canyons, rumps to the wind. Many of them died, Lutie heard, and were found frozen stiff, legs grotesquely splayed out, muzzles blood-raw from trying to root through the snow to underlying grass. The baron was still absent, Emile Durand was in Chicago, the trains west blocked by the heavy snows. Ike Cooney, the foreman, had all the hands out, even the Indians and the Swedish carpenters, scattering hay on the snow for the surviving cattle.

Only two guests remained at the chateau — the Dessineses. Mme. Dessines lay in bed with a catarrh, drinking tea laced with brandy and complaining of the inclemency of "the Far West," while Marc Dessines gloomily scanned weeks-old newspapers and cursed the snow. The kitchen was quiet; the hands ate in a corner of the bunkhouse, provided for by the Chinese cook. Wandering through the almost deserted house, Lutie curled up in a corner and read back copies of *Peterson's Magazine*, *New York Saturday Night*, and *Godey's Ladies' Book*. Tiring of that, she ate a sweet Italian orange smuggled from the kitchen. A little splay-footed with her increasing burden, she went to the library. On the wall hung a mandolin. Idly she plucked the strings. It seemed not all that different from her banjo. Taking it down, she lounged on a flowered Chesterfield, being careful of her stomach, and strummed the instrument, murmuring softly. Emile, she thought, dreaming in a golden haze. *Gentle Emile!* Idly she hummed words, trying this combination and that, making up a little song. *Emile's my love. The gentle dove — calls to me and —* What next? What rhymed? Engrossed in the effort, she was not at first aware of footfalls in the deep carpet. Suddenly she looked up, trembled in surprise. It was the baron, standing near.

"Pray continue," he said in his dry tone. "It is very pleasant to hear a woman singing."

Embarrassed, she struggled to her feet. "I — I'm sorry. I didn't know. I mean — I thought you were in St. Louis or somewhere — sir." Nervously she hung the mandolin back on the pegs and tucked vagrant strands of hair into her lace cap. "You see, I — I —"

He raised a hand. "Please. It don't — do not — I mean to say, it doesn't matter." He continued to stand before her, hands on hips, looking at her in a quietly calculating way.

"I'll go. I —"

"No!"

Uneasy, she smoothed the folds of the black sateen skirt, uniform of the parlormaids. Eyes downcast, she could almost feel the weight of his dark eyes. Moments

164

passed. The tall clock in the corner ticked heavily; clearing its throat, it struck the hour.

"Please, sir —" It was not right of him to treat her so, surveying her like a prize heifer bought for breeding. "I am wanted below-stairs, I think. Mme. Boucher said —"

"Hang Mme. Boucher!" He said it good-naturedly. With the same calculating look he took her chin in his hand, drew her close, stared into her eyes. "You have fear of me, eh?"

She did not know what to say.

"I can see it." He released her, looking pensive. "Well, that must be remedied." Going to the door, he added, "You may play the mandolin whenever you like. Perhaps sometime you will play for me, eh?" He paused, stroking the glossy beard. "Tomorrow I shall drive to town in the buckboard to send telegraphs. Is that how you say it?"

"Telegrams," Lutie said faintly.

"Telegrams, then!" He nodded. "*Merci*. At any rate, I will be leaving soon after breakfast. Have Madame get you some warm things. I think it is time you stopped in to have the good Dr. Cromie examine your — ah, your — condition."

"But I feel very well!"

He waved a hand abruptly. "At nine, then — Lutie!"

For a long time she was rooted to the carpet, watching the open doorway where he last stood. Why had he stared at her so? Had he heard her singing about Emile? Why should he bother to take her into town himself? She felt a kind of dread excitement.

The next morning, bundled in a borrowed fur coat, she waited on the veranda for the groom to bring around the team and buckboard. Soon the baron joined her, dressed in his rough frontier clothes: coarse flannel shirt with a scarf about the neck, a buckskin jacket, heavy jeans stuffed into high boots. On his head was a fur cap with a long tail dangling behind.

"Ready?"

"Yes, sir."

Although the temperature was well below freezing, it was a sunny day. The baron drove expertly, hands on the reins seeming to sense the spirit of the matched bays. Overhead, a hawk wheeled in a cloudless sky. There was no least breath of the chill air that had killed so many cattle.

"Lutecia, eh?"

"Yes, sir."

"Emile told me. After my *belle Paris*, eh? Well, it is a pretty name."

She huddled in the thick fur.

"He is fond of you, you know. Emile."

"I — I think M. Emile is a very fine gentleman, sir."

"My friend. My best friend. But sometimes we fight." He laughed. "You see, Emile is very dignified and I am — well, I am different!"

Wheels singing in the crusted snow, they threaded the long defile toward the river and Little Misery, seven miles distant. Midway down the slope grew alder and cottonwood, nourished by a stream in the canyon below. As they were passing the thick stand of winter-dark trees, a shot rang out. Lutie screamed.

166

"*Mon Dieu!*" The baron rose in the seat, sawed the reins at the startled bays, spread his body wide before her. One of the horses sidled too near the edge of the road and the buckboard lurched sickeningly. Still trying to protect Lutie, Charles roared something unintelligible in French while the buckboard slid farther down the slope, going sidewise like a crab, with the frightened horses scrabbling for purchase on the rocky slope. "Damn! Come back here, you horses!"

Lutie was going to faint; she knew she was going to faint. Her eyes stared at the fresh hole in the dashboard, a splintery flower where the bullet had pierced. Hanging desperately to the dashboard, she closed her eyes, feeling sick.

Still cursing, the baron wrestled the team back onto the road. The now lop-wheeled buckboard followed. "There!" he panted. Wrapping the reins about the whip socket, he jumped out to run back down the road, looking into the mingled spidery branches of the trees. Lutie, breathing deep, sat trembling on the seat, hearing the faint tattoo of hoofbeats die away in the draw below.

The baron looked at the lopsided wheel. "Coward! To shoot from ambush! Is that the way they fight in this so-great American country?"

Lutie felt funny. Her insides were acting strangely. "Please," she said, "I — I —" She half rose, but the baron pushed her down again.

"Is it your — your —"

Lips set tight, she nodded.

"Ah, *mon Dieu* — no!" He was pale also, an unaccustomed pallor against the dark bush of beard. "Well, it cannot be helped." Putting a shoulder against the damaged wheel, he strained until it yielded, came back into line. "I don't know if it will hold, but we have no choice!"

On the wounded wheel they finally lurched into Little Misery, the baron muttering to himself. "Cowards! Rascals! Scoundrels! How are you, Lutie? Don't give up! We are there soon. Damn that wheel! Have you a name for the baby, eh? Have courage. It is only a little way now."

Dr. Cromie, fortunately, was in his office. He did the best he could but Lutie's baby — Buck Griffin's baby — died. In a way, she felt relieved. She was shut of Buck Griffin for good.

CHAPTER
NINE

The baron was furious. Gathered on the graveled carriageway before the chateau, his guests listened uncomfortably to an account of the ambush. Charles pointed to the splintered hole in the dashboard of the wagon. "Look there! Think of it — to shoot from ambush, at a wagon in which is riding a young girl! Me, it is not so important; I have been shot at before, by Algerians and other people. But a woman!"

With morbid interest they inspected the hole. Valerie shuddered. "Ah, so close to you!" Mme. Dessines said. "The Far West is a violent country, people told me. Now I believe it!" Emma, the English girl, announced, "In Warwickshire the constables would not allow this!" Marc Dessines paled. "I must admit I am glad Madame and I are going back to New York next week! While I have enjoyed shooting things out here, Charles, I do not like for them to shoot back!" No one laughed.

"They cannot drive me away with such tactics!" The baron shook his fist. "I will fight them!"

Murmuring among themselves, the ladies drifted toward the veranda. All week long the ice in the river had cracked with continued reports like small-arms fire. Geese flew northward in straggly skeins, and the air was nimble with the smell of spring. Marc Dessines, standing beside Charles, was about to light his cigar when he paused, burning match in his fingers. "And who is our visitor, eh?"

Up the grassy slope cantered a rider on a powerful black. He rode easily, reins slack, guiding the horse with the pressure of his knees. As the mounted figure loomed larger, Charles swore softly.

"You know him?"

The baron did not answer. Instead, he drew himself up, folding arms across his chest, staring at old Henry Griffin. Marc Dessines, sensing trouble, hastened to join the ladies.

Reaching the buckboard, the old man drew rein. He sat stiffly in the saddle, the spring wind blowing long white locks about under the stained brim of the high-crowned hat.

"I come to speak to you."

The baron stared at him, arms still folded. "Talk, eh, instead of bullets?"

The patriarch flushed, a deepening copper in the leathery skin.

"That's what I aim to talk about! I want you to know that ambush in the canyon wasn't no part of my doings, nor of my crew, so far as I can make out. I don't like you, de Fleury, but I ain't the kind to dry-gulch a man."

The baron had some difficulty with "dry-gulch."

"If I beat you," Henry Griffin went on, "I'll beat you fair and square! But I got to warn you there's others around here don't like your guts ay-tall. I'm not responsible for *their* actions."

170

The baron's gaze was unblinking. "You have encouraged them against me."

Griffin spat tobacco juice in the gravel. "Didn't take much encouragement. Folks out here ain't used to fences!"

"The railroads, too. It is heard you have traveled East to use influence against me."

The old man shrugged. Taking off the big hat, he wiped his forehead; the sun was hot. "I'm a big shipper. I got to admit they listen to me."

"The beef packers, too."

Henry Griffin put the hat on again, settling it against the wind. "They got their own way of working and they ain't about to change it for no foreigner comes in here and sets up his own slaughterhouse." He looked at the big building, the tall brick chimney, the cattle being prodded through a chute for the first batch. "Well" — the black skittered nervously, and the old man gathered the reins in a gnarled fist — "guess that's all I got on my mind. Come on, Nig." He kneed the black; together they ambled down the sunlit slope toward the river.

The baron remained, chewing at his mustaches. Ike Cooney, approaching him, stopped at a respectful distance. "Baron, I wanted to —"

"Another time!" Charles turned on his heel and strode away. "Insolence!" he muttered. Brushing past the awed spectators on the veranda, he mounted the grand stairway to his upstairs office. *Where is Emile, now that I need him? Off to Chicago again! He should be here! There must be a proper legal action to bring such ruffians to account!*

171

In the hallway Murdoch was softly closing the door of the room where Lutie was convalescing after the loss of her child. Charles shrugged. Too bad! *Eh, bien* — he frowned at Murdoch.

"Just looking in on Miss Lutie to see if she needed anything," Murdoch said, and slipped silently past the baron.

"She is not to be called Miss Lutie!" Charles called after him. "She is only a servant!" Murdoch was already gone, disappeared into a palm-lined alcove. Feeling put upon, the baron knocked on the door and walked in.

"*Bonjour, mademoiselle.*"

The girl lay back on a fat pillow, gingery ringlets bound with a blue ribbon, her face pale as the bed linen.

"You are feeling better, I hope?"

Looking at him through half-closed eyes, Lutie nodded. "*Plus bien, merci, monsieur.*"

He was pleased she had learned some of his own language. "A good accent. I congratulate you." For a moment he stood above her, one hand stroking the wiry beard, the other jammed in a pocket.

"Do you know — Emile is right! You are a very handsome child."

Something sparked in the blue eyes, and she drew the covers more tightly about her shoulders. "I am not a child!"

He laughed. "Young lady, then — woman — what you like! You are a female, in any case." Playfully he took her chin between thumb and forefinger, shook her. "I am glad you are improving. Do not hurry!"

172

She turned her head away from his hand, petulant. "I don't intend to stay in this bed much longer, like a dead weight! There are things I should be doing about the house."

"There is no need for you to —"

"But I must!" She sat up, still clutching the coverlet about her. "I am not a charity case, *monsieur!* I work for my keep, I can tell you!" She looked suddenly beyond him. Charles turned. Emile Durand stood in the doorway in a travel-stained broadcloth suit of Paris cut, portmanteau in hand.

"So there you are!" Charles complained. "Emile, I expected you back a week ago. There have been so many things —"

"I'm sorry, Charles. There were delays." Emile looked from one to the other. "I was just passing when I heard voices —"

"This young lady," Charles complained, "is very obstinate! I have just been saying her — telling her — she must rest."

Emile nodded, sat down wearily near the bed, portmanteau at his feet. "That is right, Lutie; you must gather your strength. When I arrived Mme. Boucher told me of your misfortune."

Charles frowned at the sudden pleased look on Lutie Hamlin's face. The countenance cleared; it was as if the sun had suddenly entered the room to warm and cheer her.

"I suppose I must," she sighed. "But I *will* be up and about soon!"

The baron bit his lip. "Emile, you must come to my office as soon as possible. There are many things to discuss." Turning on his heel, he left.

When he had gone, Lutie made a face at the door. Emile smiled wryly and fondled his mustaches.

"You do not like him a great deal, I take it."

She tossed her head. "I am grateful to him for taking me in, but I intend to give him back good measure." Stretching out her hand in a graceful gesture copied from Mme. Dessines, Lutie smiled in the languorous manner of the tall brunette, Valerie. "I am glad you are back, *Monsieur* Durand."

Emile opened the valise and searched within. "Chicago, I must tell you, is a barbarous place. And those men of money, the bankers there —" He grimaced. "They can be very hard to deal with." Poising the package in his hands, he sighed, shrugged. "*Bien* — I must not bother you with dreary business details!"

"But I *enjoy* talk about business and cattle and the railroads and things like that!" Watching the package, she added, "Women can be good at business, too, you know. For example, right now I can tell you that cattle are selling at the Chicago yards for nine dollars a hundredweight!"

He smiled; her breast seemed to fill with warmth as the sun backlit his head, fired the blond hair and mustaches with golden vapor.

"You are a very remarkable young woman, Lutie. You never cease to astonish me." Handing her the package, he added, "I am sorry about the loss of your child. Perhaps this will help a little, to know that someone

174

remembered you all the way from Chicago. I ordered it from Tiffany and Co., on Fifth Avenue in New York."

With eager fingers she unwrapped the package. "I know all about Tiffany and Co. too! Mr. Tiffany was the man who got hold of some extra pieces of the Atlantic Cable right after they laid it and sold them to the public for ever so much money!" Delightedly she held the thin gold chain up to the light. "Oh, thank you so much!" Carefully dropping it over her hair, she felt its light touch on her neck. "It — it makes me feel like a great lady!"

He sank back in the chair, clasping hands behind his head. "Really you are amazing!"

Something in his gaze puzzled her — a sudden reserve, a restraint she felt rather than observed.

"Amazing?"

Rising, he paced the floor, paused at the window, looking down at the activity around the abattoir. "Do you not grieve for your child? I mean — you seem so gay, so happy."

She fingered the delicate links of the chain. "From now on, I *mean* to be happy!"

He sat down, took her hand in his. "I am afraid this is a kind of façade, a mask you wear for a little while. Do not hide your grief, Lutie. Believe me, it is better to let it out and thus dispose of it, rather than sealing it in to cause bitterness as time goes on."

She trembled at his touch, but spoke resolutely. "It is not a mask. I don't care about it. It happened, and now it's over. I just don't care, that's all!"

175

A good family man, Emile was taken aback. "But the child —"

"I don't care about the child! It means nothing to me, except that I'm free of it! I tell you I don't *care!*"

Emile rose, looking at her in puzzlement. "If that is what you think —"

"It is what I think."

He shrugged, picked up the valise, carefully closed the brass catches. "Well, I must go see Charles." He shook his head, looking tired. "He is not in the best of moods, and I have bad news for him."

She could not bear to see him distraught. Also, she had behaved badly, and he had not understood the simple truth she had blurted out. Snatching at his hand, she held it to her cheek in a sudden impulse, closing her eyes in anguish. "I didn't mean to talk that way — about the baby, I mean! Please —" She began to weep.

He was uneasy, his hand limp and unresponding in her own. "If you wish — certainly!"

"Don't feel badly on account of me, Emile. You're the only real friend I've got anymore. Please! If — if you aren't my friend I haven't got *anyone!*"

He dropped the valise, knelt beside the bed. "Don't cry, Lutie! Of course I'm your friend! A very proper friend, you must understand — sometimes such friendships can be misinterpreted. But I am your friend, always, and you may count on me."

Kissing his hand, her tears fell wetly on his wrist. Opening her eyes, she saw Mme. Boucher's stern face in the doorway. Madame coughed, discreetly.

"Monsieur Emile?"

176

He turned quickly, rose, dusted the knees of his trousers. "Yes?"

"The baron must see you in his office at once, sir."

Emile nodded. "I am coming."

At the door he paused. For a young man he looked old. "Goodbye, Lutie."

She felt weary and spent. Still fingering the golden links of the Tiffany chain, she saw him through tear-wet eyes.

"Goodbye," she called. Her heart ached for him — and for herself.

Full spring arrived, buffalo peas blooming in pink and purple masses along the roads. The brown river shimmered gold in the warm sun, and dogwood and wild grapevines bordered it in rich green. Windmills hummed in the wind. Already the sod was being turned by grasshopper plows to show the black earth, steaming and fragrant in the golden light. Old Yellow Hat's Indians abandoned their soogan blankets and worked in the fields and outbuildings bare to the waist, grateful for the return of Sun, one of their primary gods, along with Rock, Thunder, and the rest of the pantheon.

Lutie, fully restored, resumed her duties as parlormaid. Though her duties were never onerous, she now had even less to do. The many guests were reduced to a few. After the ambush of the baron's buckboard, many began to feel the West was too dangerous a place, and departed for other pleasure palaces. Valerie, prior to her own departure, announced that on a shopping visit to the general store at Little Misery she had heard rumors of a coming armed assault on the chateau itself, but this was discounted. Still, there was enough trouble to make Charles's friends uneasy, especially since Charles himself had taken to drinking heavily and almost nightly quarreling with Emile Durand. The baron did not sleep well. At night he often stalked the silent house, staring out at the moonlit meadows; M. Guillaume had seen him. The cook sighed, fat cheeks wobbling.

"This is an unhappy house! I do not know how long I stay here!"

Lutie was sad also. The beautiful people she admired were leaving, one by one. It was only Emile's continued presence about the echoing halls that made life tolerable. Too, she missed Papa and Mama more than she cared to admit, but she would not go back to that sod hut for anything. She longed to see Sid, also. None of the servants knew how to play Old Sledge, or even cooncan. But one warm day, while she was shaking out a dustmop on the kitchen stoop, her brother trudged around the corner, carrying her banjo.

"Sid!" Dropping the mop, she flew to embrace him. "Oh, Sid — is it really you?"

His shirt was wet and black with sweat, boots dusty. Suffering her embrace, he croaked, "Can a man get a glass of water hereabouts? It's a long ways up the hill from Little Misery!"

Taking ice from the zinc-lined chest in the kitchen, she put it in a glass and pumped water into it. "Here — sit beside me on the stoop!" Eagerly she snatched up the banjo. "Oh, I'm glad you brought this! There are

178

mandolins and balalaikas and such around here but there isn't anything like a banjo to raise the spirits!"

Savoring the water, Sid drank while she fondly watched, then squeezed his arm. "My, you have gotten strong!" He had gotten bigger and heavier, too; at fifteen he was a young man, at least an inch — maybe two — taller.

He flexed his arm proudly. "When the weather's real dry, it takes a lot of force to pull sheets of paper off the stack. Electricity in the paper, Mr. Oates says."

"Tell me all the news! What have you been doing? How are Papa and Mama? Got any sweethearts in town?"

Sid's face changed. "Papa's pretty sick, I guess."

The chord on the banjo died away. "Oh, no!"

"Yep."

"He never was real well, you know."

"Well, he's worse now. Dr. Cromie thinks it's the consumption."

"Oh, no! Poor Papa!"

"Mama's uncle died in Virginia and left her some money, the telegram said. She wants us to go back home — what she calls home — but Papa's bound and determined to make a go of Uncle Milo's place. But hell, that sandpile ain't never going to grow nothing."

Lutie was shocked. "That's awfully bad grammar! And don't swear!"

"That's the way people talk out here. I been working for Mr. Oates at the newspaper office and people come in all day and say worse things than 'hell.'"

"Working for Mr. Oates?"

"He pays me a dollar a week." Sid was silent for a moment, drawing patterns in the dust with a twig. Then he said, "Wish you'd come home, Lutie. There isn't anybody for me to talk to anymore. Mama's always getting mad, and Papa's too sick to say much, especially after he works all day at the sawmill."

Her hand sought his. "I miss you, too."

"Is it true, what they say — you had a baby, and it died?"

"Yes. That's true. But I don't care."

Sid reflected on this. After a while, still drawing designs, he said, "If I had a baby — I mean if my *wife* had a baby — I guess I'd care."

She looked at the heart pierced by an arrow that was being traced in the dust. "Are there many pretty girls in Little Misery?"

Abashed, Sid threw the twig away, settled back on the stoop, elbows propped on the step, long legs thrust out. "I guess."

"Any particular one?"

He grinned, ears reddening. "God damn it, Lutie —"

"Don't swear, I told you!"

"I been kind of sparking Marie Oates. She's Mr. Oates's daughter. We went to church with the Oateses last Sunday, and they had me to supper."

Aware of a looming black-clad presence above her, Latie saw Mme. Boucher, hands folded over the dark bosom, lips set.

"The parlor," Madame said, "is very dusty, Lutie."

Lutie rose, shaking out the folds of her skirt. "Yes, ma'am. I'll come right in." Dustmop in one hand,

180

banjo in the other, she embraced Sid. "I've got to go now. But — but remember me to Papa and Mama. Tell them — tell them I love them both, dearly, but I" — she groped for words — "I guess you'd have to say I've got a different road to travel. You understand that, don't you, Sid?"

Awkwardly he kissed her cheek. "I suppose so, Lutie. You was always — different."

From the stoop she waved until he had turned the corner by the springhouse. "Thanks for the banjo!" she called. Then Sid was gone, and a part of her had gone with him. But that was the way it had to be; she had set her course, and would not deviate.

The baron, too, had his course. As the Territory cattlemen grew more hostile, as the "grangers" protested his beef herds trampling the land they had always thought theirs, as the Chicago packers fought to keep de Fleury dressed beef out of the East, he gave them back shot for shot. In an indignant notice paid for in the *Gazette* he trumpeted defiance:

All men should know I have legally purchased, and records in the Morton County Courthouse will show that I own, twenty-five miles along the west bank of the Little Missouri River to a depth of five miles inland. I will not brook trespassers of any kind, whether they be cattle or men. I am a man of my word, and mean action.

CHARLES DE FLEURY

Already he had ordered Emile Durand to leave for Chicago again for the purpose of instituting a civil suit against the "beef trust," which, in conjunction with the Northern Pacific Railroad, was opposing him. The Northern Pacific, it turned out, was a principal stockholder in the St. Louis Refrigerator Car Company, which had contracted to supply the baron with fifty cars using the new Hamilton patent. Consequently, a large shipment of dressed beef was now spoiling in the icehouse, dug deep into the slope behind the abattoir, for lack of refrigerator cars promised for Little Misery by the first day of June. Not only that; much of the Crimean wheat was rotting in the ground, and the new cattle driven in from the Black Hills developed troubling symptoms at the change of pasture.

By this time the only guests in the great house were the Dessineses, and they were thinking of leaving soon for California. Marc Dessines wanted saltwater bathing for his rheumatism. Mme. Dessines was more truthful. "There is not fun here anymore, Charles," she protested. "The gloom is centimeters thick, *mon cher!*"

"Nevertheless," the baron insisted, "I shall prevail!"

Mme. Dessines shrugged, lit a Havana cigarette. "Of course, Charles. But there are limits."

On the night preceding Emile's departure for Chicago, a full moon shone. Lutie, desolate at her friend's departure, could not sleep. Near midnight, sweltering in her attic room, she sat on the edge of the bed and lit a candle against the dark. Her nightgown was damp and hair plastered wetly against her brow. The room was sweet with the scent of early June: bee bush and rose mallow, gaillardia that later would be matted red on the ground like a Persian carpet. Rising, Lutie watched the white-clad body in the mirror above the washstand. Gathering her hair with both hands, she held it above her head, imagining she was with Emile. He would *like* her hair that way, high and soft, Grecian — faintly Grecian, a conceit borne out by the long white nightgown. Catching the hem, she belted a fold about her waist, trying to look proud and aristocratic, as befitted Emile's lady. Of course he had a wife already, and children, but they were in Paris. *Emile*, she breathed. *Ah, Emile* . . . Loving the image, she watched the great lady in the glass. That was how it would be, someday. After all, she *was* different, Sid had been right.

In the soft night air she heard distant voices. Slipping on bare feet to the window she knelt, listening. She was too far away to make out the words, but the tones were clearly quarrelsome. Closing her eyes, she finally heard one word. "Damn!" Charles shouted, and banged a dissonant chord on the piano below.

Half curious, half fearful, she continued to listen, but could not catch anything more than the rumble of male voices. Opening the door, she peered down the stairway to the second floor. Like a wraith she hurried down the stairway, past the portraits of de Fleury ancestors staring woodenly into the gloom, and lifted the heavy brass latch of the door opening on the high balcony that surrounded the immense parlor. Many times she had gone there at night to watch the scene below — beautifully gowned women, handsome men in starched shirts with lace bosoms and long-tailed coats. They laughed, they smoked hashish, they drank champagne, they played naughty games. Like the cat that could look at a king, Lutie frequently crouched among the fronds of potted palms, peering with mingled apprehension and delight — watching, listening, learning.

The heavy door closed behind her. She made her way cautiously, like the cat, through the almost tropical profusion the baron's gardener had laid out on the narrow balcony. Below, Emile and the baron faced each other in the rays of an oil lamp. Emile sat on the oriental divan, nervously smoking a cigarette. Charles stood spraddle-legged before the smoke-stained fireplace, now vacant and bleak in a Dakota summer. One hand clenched behind his back, he raised the other to point at Emile Durand.

"You lawyer fellows! You become tiresome, you know — always ranting on and on about commas and periods and paragraphs!"

Emile drew hard on the cigarette and the tip glowed in the dimness. "You should sign no contracts unless I approve them first!"

"What am I then, a child? A mewling infant that has to have its nose wiped every few minutes? I know what I am doing!"

Emile stubbed out his cigarette in a bronze ashtray made to resemble a tortoise. "You do *not* know what you are doing! That is why this immense enterprise is close to ruin! I have warned you before!"

"Warn me?" Charles's face flushed in anger. In the half-light from the oil lamp Lutie could see the dark

184

tide. "Warn me? I do not take kindly to warnings, my friend! The Griffins and their lackeys have found that out!" He picked up a book from the table. Lutie recognized it, had read it. It was called *The Beef Bonanza*, written by a man named Brisbin. "This book says that cattle are gold! It says that —"

Emile rose, his voice shaking with anger. "That book is a great lie, Charles, and I am surprised you should be taken in by it!"

"This book —"

Emile knocked the book from Charles's hand; it sailed through the air. "I am tired of your damned book! You are an idiot!"

For a moment the baron stared at his book, lying on the Turkey carpet in a sprawl of white pages. Then he slapped Emile hard across the face. "Ingrate!"

Fists clenched at his sides, the lawyer stood his ground. "Fool! You great fool, with your playthings!"

"Fool, am I? Well, no man calls me a fool!" Seizing a chair, the baron climbed up and pulled the crossed sabers from the wall above the fireplace. The heavy crest at their juncture came loose and tumbled down, ringing metallically on the hearthstones. Kicking it aside, the baron offered one of the heavy swords to Emile. "Defend yourself!"

White-faced, Emile pushed aside the heavy pommel. "I am not afraid of you, Charles, but this is really too much!"

"Too much?" The baron laughed, scornfully. "After the way you have maligned me? No, sir — in Paris I would send my seconds to you! Here we must dispense with such formalities. Will you fight?"

Lutie, horrified, became aware of footsteps in the hall outside the door to the balcony. Someone — perhaps Mme. Boucher — was awake, hurrying down the stairs to the parlor.

When the baron raised his hand as if to slap Emile again, the lawyer seized the saber. Furious, he stepped back, flexed the steel, held out his left arm in a pose Lutie had seen in an illustrated French romance.

"*Alors — en garde!*"

There was a clang of steel as the baron attacked, slashing, thrusting, head lowered like a charging bull. Emile gave ground while Lutie, white-faced, gnawed at her knuckles. She wanted to cry out, to stop them, but her voice would not come.

"*Messieurs!*" Mme. Boucher stood in the doorway below in a night robe, hair done up in curlers, wringing her hands. "*Messieurs!* Stop it! *Mon Dieu,* what are they doing?"

The combatants paid no attention. Emile backed steadily away, eluding the baron's headlong rushes, parrying and blocking with great skill. Lutie admired his grace.

"Is this not enough?" he panted.

The baron's only response was to lunge again, knocking over the table in a desperate maneuver. Annoyed by Emile's expert defense, he slashed wildly, muttering under his breath.

Marc Dessines, sleepy in gown and nightcap, joined Mme. Boucher in the doorway. "What the hell is going

186

on here?" he demanded. Quickly he rushed to part the duelists, then retreated as a slashing blade tore a rent in his nightgown. Finally Lutie found her voice. She screamed.

For a moment — a tragic moment — Emile Durand looked up at the balcony. At that instant the baron swung his saber in a clumsy arc. The blade bit into Emile's wrist and he dropped his own weapon. Slowly he sank to his knees, looking with awe at the fountain of blood gushing from the wound.

"My God!" Marc Dessines rushed forward to kneel beside Emile, trying to stanch the blood with the hem of his nightgown. Mme. Boucher fainted. Lutie, hurrying from the balcony, ran into Mme. Dessines, who was also descending the stairs. "What is going on?" she demanded, but Lutie brushed past her.

"So much blood!" Marc Dessines babbled. "Someone send for Dr. Cromie, quickly!"

Charles did not move. Saber hanging from his fist, he stared down at his late antagonist with lips set and eyes hard. Holding his slashed wrist, Emile raised his eyes to the baron's.

"So much blood," he agreed. His hand was red, his sleeve was red, the Turkey carpet was stained with red; it lay in a growing puddle on the thick nap. Lutie pushed through the crowd at the doorway — M. Guillaume, parlormaids, assistant cooks, one of Ike Cooney's hands. Her bare feet were sticky with blood as she knelt beside Emile. Brushing aside Marc Dessines, she took Emile Durand's blond head in her arms, pressed her cheek to his.

"What has he done to you?"

Emile's forehead was cold. He rolled his head toward her; she felt his body grow slack in her arms. Glazed, his blue eyes stared into hers. "Why, there is Lutie," he said in a bemused voice. "Come closer, child. I cannot see you too well!"

Ike Cooney, rushing in from the bunkhouse, had dealt with both animal and human wounds; the foreman did the best he could with a tourniquet Lutie tore from her own gown. When Dr. Cromie arrived Emile was unconscious. He lingered in an upstairs bedroom for another few hours, and then passed away from loss of blood. The embalmed body was shipped to Paris for burial. Charles, Baron de Fleury, was charged with murder. The trial was set for district court in Mandan for the eighteenth of July, 1883.

CHAPTER
TEN

Because of the baron's difficulties in obtaining a suitable defense attorney the trial was delayed. In the meantime, he was free on ten thousand dollars' bail to carry on his business enterprises. The breathless summer heat had burned the Crimean wheat that had not rotted; the heads were scanty and poorly formed. Hailstorms stripped the corn. Meat spoiled in the few refrigerator cars. For some mysterious reason, the railroad crews responsible for icing the cars did not report for work. Wells on the ranch failed, and it was necessary to haul water from the river for the stock. But the river ran slack and muddy, bound in shallow pools and eddies. One of Ike Cooney's few remaining hands — the rest had left for higher pay offered by the Slash G — remarked that the river "had got so low a man couldn't drown hisself." With no guests, the chateau was a gloomy place. Many of the staff were dismissed. M. Guillaume, the chef, also quit, though desired by the baron to stay on. "I cannot cook for a handful of people," he complained. "It is not a challenge!"

The baron himself, mover and shaker of the place, had lost his spirit. Grieving over the death of his friend, he stalked the empty sunlit rooms, immersed in his thoughts, paying little heed to affairs that cried out for attention. Without Emile Durand to superintend affairs, to demand decisions, to bring him papers to sign, Charles was ineffectual. A large part of the management of the ranch fell on the shoulders of Ike Cooney. The foreman was a good worker, but wanted first to be told what to do.

"I don't know, Ike!" the baron murmured, shaking his head. "Use your good judgment, eh?"

"But, sir —"

The baron waved him away. Muttering, Ike went back to where the hands were loafing about the derrick and sand bucket brought out to dig a badly needed deep well.

"So where do we start drilling?" someone asked.

"God damn if I know!" Ike grumbled. "The old man don't seem to give a hoot! Right here, I guess, is as good a place as any. I ain't no dowser!" Moodily he watched the growing pile of mottled brown and yellow mud. "Damned if I don't go over to Slash G myself before long! This outfit sure as hell ain't goin' nowhere!" Of the once-huge chateau staff, now only Mme. Boucher, Murdoch, and Lutie Hamlin were left; of twenty-six ranch hands, only five remained, including a discouraged Ike Cooney. The Sioux, however, remained loyal, though unpaid.

In the latter part of August Mr. Edward Chilton arrived to conduct the baron's defense in District Court at Mandan. He was a plump little man with a fringe of gray chin whiskers and a bright ferretlike glance over half-moon spectacles. One of his first acts was to move for a change of venue from Mandan to Bismarck. The baron fidgeted in discomfort as Mr. Chilton read the editorial in the Mandan *Tribune* as a basis for his motion:

"The Territory has long been scandalized by the iniquitous doings of the Baron de Fleury at his so-called chateau on the banks of the Little Missouri River, as well as by his rapacious landgrabbing and utter disregard for the citizens and customs of this area. The death of the baron's lawyer, M. Emile Durand, under suspicious circumstances, only serves to reinforce the bad impression given by this foreign entrepreneur. It is hoped that quick and certain judgment will be rendered by the court in this matter, so that counts, marquises, and dukes will be discouraged from entering this country to plunder and ravish. The soil of America belongs to Americans only!"

Mr. Chilton peered at Charles over the rims of his spectacles. "It's clearly inflammatory. You can't get a fair trial in Mandan."

The baron shrugged, bit listlessly at the end of a fresh cigar. "I am not likely to get a fair trial anyplace in this crude representation of a nation! They are all against me!"

"That's no way to talk, Baron. If we go into this fight thinking we shall lose, then we shall certainly lose!" The lawyer edged his chair closer. "Now tell me, sir, what happened the night M. Durand was —" He cleared his throat.

"There is no need to mince words. Emile was murdered. I killed him."

"Let's not use the term 'murder'. That's a word for the prosecution. Just tell me, in simple words, what happened."

"Emile was bothering me with details — how we were losing money, how this was going bad and that was going wrong, how I must practice economies, how —" He broke off, pinching the bridge of his nose between his fingers, eyes closed.

"You had been drinking?"

"Yes."

"Heavily?"

"I am afraid so." The baron opened his eyes, stared at the smoldering cigar. "I became angry. There was a quarrel. I lost my head." He gestured at the empty brackets above the fireplace. "I snatched down the sabers and tossed one to Emile, daring him to fight. I — I am a military man, you see, and that was my way to settle an argument."

"Did he accept the weapon?"

"He did not want to, but I bullied him into it." The baron swallowed hard, laid down the cigar as if it tasted bad. "You see, Emile was a very gentle person, although he had been trained for the Army at St. Cyr as I had. Then —" He shrugged. "We were *corps-à-corps* —"

"Explain that to me, please."

Charles made a picture in the air with his hands. "I rushed at him. We were shoulder against shoulder, too

192

close to use our weapons. He withdrew, and for some reason his attention seemed diverted. I saw the opportunity — *mon Dieu*, I regret the moment! — and rushed forward in a running attack. I caught him across the wrist as he stood in second parry, and he — he fell."

"Bled to death?"

"Yes, the artery spouted blood."

"There were no witnesses to the fight?"

"None. That is to say, some of my guests were attracted by the sound of the sabers but they arrived — too late."

"Are they available as character witnesses?"

Charles shook his head. "They do not relish public notice. Foreigners, you see — as you have read me, foreigners are not very welcome here in the land of the free and the home of the brave!" He spat. "Pah!"

Mr. Chilton removed the spectacles and huffed, polishing the lenses with a handkerchief. He looked thoughtful. After a while he hooked them again over his ears. "Well, it is not a very good case, baron, but we will see what we can do. What you have told me is, of course, privileged information. The face we turn to the court will be another matter."

"I will not lie!" Charles protested.

"I will not ask you to lie. But if I am to defend you properly, you must cooperate. Things are not always what they seem, you know! 'What is truth?' Pilate asked."

Charles sank deeper into his chair. "I do not know this M. Pilate."

The change of venue was denied. When they arrived in Mandan, horse droppings were flung at the windows of the rooms in the Empire Hotel occupied by the baron and his lawyer. Crowds outside the courtroom were sullen, and reluctant to give them passageway into the courthouse. The baron saw faces: Sam Oates from the Little Misery *Gazette*, Jake Sigafoos from the livery stable, Sheriff Holland, even a crazy "spiritualist" lady who had traveled all the way from Little Misery, someone said, to pray for him. Henry Griffin was in Mandan also, attending each session of the court, with his hawk's nose, stained white mustaches, and hard-eyed stare. *Will he testify against me?*, the baron wondered. *I am hardly responsible for his son's death.* Still, respected as old Griffin was in Morton County, he could damage the baron's case.

The trial went badly. Charles was a poor witness in his own behalf, continually referring to his bad temper, against lawyer Chilton's admonitions. At the lawyer's insistence he finally admitted the fight with Emile Durand had been a fair fight. But since dueling was proscribed in the United States of America, he was still at a disadvantage. In their hotel rooms Chilton became angry. When a waiter knocked at the door with a bottle of Cuban rum the baron had ordered, the lawyer sent the man away.

"You have drunk enough, Baron!"

Charles stared through red-rimmed eyes. "*Moi?*" He laughed. "I have not drunk nearly enough!"

"Either you sober up, and quickly, or I ask the judge to be relieved of your case! Why didn't you tell me you

194

had settled so much money on M. Durand's widow and children? That was a patent admission of guilt, damn it all!"

"Did I not kill the husband and father? Do I not owe the family reparations? Do I not —"

"You owe them nothing until this trial has settled the matter of your guilt or innocence! After this, Baron, take no action that may prejudice your trial until you have my consent! Is that clear?"

Charles poured a glass of water, stared at its murky depths. "*Bien*; I agree. But I have lost the trial already, we both know that. There is no chance. I have no will to fight these ignorant *paysans* any longer. They and the railroads and the beef trust have assassinated me just as surely as I killed my good friend Emile Durand!"

In early September came the time for the summing-up. The prosecutor was in fine form. His condemnation of foreign invaders bringing unwanted customs to the shores of America was applauded by the courtroom spectators until the judge splintered his gavel by repeated hammering. "I will clear the courtroom if there is any further demonstration! This is a court of law, not a damned barroom!"

Mr. Chilton did his best but he was also a kind of foreigner, an interloper from east of the Mississippi. When he stepped down, discouragement plainly showing on his sweating face, the judge turned to the jury. "Gentlemen of the —"

"Wait!"

There was a rustling as the spectators turned. A young female, modishly dressed in a green paletot buttoned down the front and a well-tailored balmoral skirt, hurried down the aisle.

"Your honor —"

The judge summoned the bailiff to eject the woman, then thought better of it. She was an attractive young woman with blue eyes and gingerish hair showing under the brim of a flower-trimmed straw hat tied in place with a scarf. In her hand she held a travel-stained valise, and her boots were dusty. The judge eyed her. "Young lady, what the hell are you doing in my courtroom?"

Lutie took off the big hat to fan her sweat-pearled brow.

"Well? I want an explanation before I give you a week for contempt of court!"

Eyeing the judge, the bailiff edged forward.

"I'm what I guess you call a material witness," Lutie said.

"You're what?"

"I saw the whole thing." Lutie waved the hat toward Charles, sitting thunderstruck at the defense table. "I came to testify in the baron's defense! He was *provoked* into the fight! He and Mr. Emile —"

"Your honor!" The prosecutor was outraged. "This woman has no place in this courtroom! I have never seen her before! From the looks on the defense counsel's face, neither has he. I demand —"

"Overruled," the judge advised. "I know how to take care of things like this." Rising, he arranged his robe.

"Ma'am, I will ask you to come with me into my chambers to discuss the matter." He banged the gavel. "Court is recessed till this afternoon!"

Shaken, the baron and Mr. Chilton returned to their rooms. The lawyer, a teetotaler, sipped at a sarsaparilla with ice. He did not even object when Charles drank whiskey from a bottle under his pillow.

"Christ Jesus!" he said, mopping his brow, "this trial is going to be the end of me! I've got palpitations." He hiccuped. "That breakfast doesn't set so good, either. Who *is* this female?"

"A maid in the chateau. Really, a nobody."

"A very important nobody, if she can get us out of this mess!"

"She doesn't know anything."

"Was she there?"

"Perhaps she came in later, while Emile was — bleeding. I didn't notice; there was so much confusion."

"She says she can help you."

Charles was silent, staring moodily at his bottle. Then he asked, "Will the judge allow her testimony?"

Chilton finished his sarsaparilla. "All we can do is wait and see."

That afternoon the judge announced that because of the arrival of a new and important witness, the trial of the County of Morton, Dakota Territory, and the People versus Charles, Baron de Fleury, would be opened to further testimony. Mr. Chilton, after a long and private talk with Miss Lutie Hamlin, put her on the stand. Calm and composed in a Paris frock, wearing white gloves and waving a lace handkerchief against the buffalo gnats, she answered counsel's questions firmly and unequivocally.

"Yes, sir. I am a parlormaid in the chateau."

"Then you had a great deal of freedom to move about and observe and overhear matters."

"Yes, sir, I did."

"What were the relations between Baron de Fleury and the deceased?"

"They were the best of friends."

"The baron would not do anything to harm a good friend?"

Lutie shook her head. "Of course not!"

"On the fatal evening, however, they quarreled, did they not?"

"Yes, sir. I could hear them from my room upstairs."

"About what?"

"Business matters. Oh, there was nothing personal in it. It was just a business discussion."

Mr. Chilton took off his pince-nez, rubbed his eyes, walked slowly about the courtroom. Finally he said, "And now to the — shall we call it a duel? You saw it, you say, ma'am. From where?"

"There is a balcony that surrounds the big parlor, with a lot of potted plants on it in brass pots — palms and vines and things. I heard the loud voices, and was afraid. I knew and liked both the baron and Mr. Emile; they had been kind to me. So I crept out on the balcony in my nightgown — I had been asleep, you see — and watched."

"They were fighting, with the swords?"

"Not yet." Lutie paled, and clasped the handkerchief tighter. "Ah —" She broke off, for the first time somewhat distraught.

"Yes?"

"Mr. Emile" — she swallowed hard; her breast rose and fell quickly — "Mr. Emile had been drinking. He became angry. The baron tried to restrain him, but he snatched a sword off the mantel and challenged the baron to fight."

The room was quiet, the only sound the dusty buzzing of the gnats and the far off whine of a sawmill. The baron half rose from his chair, about to speak, but Mr. Chilton waved him back.

"And what was the baron's response?"

"He — he tried to reason with him. But Mr. Emile claimed he had been insulted, and wanted satisfaction. When he rushed at the baron, of course the baron had to defend himself!"

There was a stir in the courtroom. The judge pounded his gavel and looked fiercely about.

"And so the quarrel was provoked by Emile Durand?"

"Yes, sir."

Lutie's voice was faint, and the judge leaned forward.

"How was that again, miss? What was your answer?"

She turned a troubled face. "I said — yes, sir. That Mr. Emile provoked the quarrel."

The prosecutor tried hard to break her story but Lutie Hamlin answered all his questions with the same hard resolve. The trial ended in a hung jury, with many questions unanswered. The weather was hot, the expense to the county onerous, and the prosecutor wearily agreed to dismiss the defendant. There was not even talk of a retrial, though many citizens of the county were indignant. *It's the Frenchman's money got him off! That girl is a born liar! Who knows what goes on in that big place on the hill?* Men leered behind cupped hands, whispered that Lutie Hamlin was the baron's paramour. The women sniffed, drawing their skirts aside when she passed.

"Lies!" the baron stormed in the privacy of the hotel room. "All lies, to besmirch poor dead Emile! I never agreed to lies!"

Mr. Chilton, restored to equanimity by victory, beamed. "You would rather hang, then, would you? That jury would have done it, too. I have seen many juries, and that one was meaner than an alligator with bound-up bowels!"

Charles ran a hand through unkempt hair. "But why did she do it? I thought she was in love with Emile."

Mr. Chilton, seated at a desk, was making out the bill for his services. "Payable in cash," he said, handing it to Charles.

"But why?"

The lawyer shrugged. "I don't concern myself with affairs of the heart. Charles, you are not an unattractive man yourself. Perhaps she fancies you, my friend."

They traveled back to Little Misery together, Charles and Lutie, on the Northern Pacific. His manner toward her was scrupulously correct; he did not know where to begin, what to say. In fact, she rather frightened him. Handing her off the train at Little Misery, he took her arm and led her to the buggy where Murdoch awaited their arrival. People watched silently; one man spat very near the baron's boots, and there was a general atmosphere of hostility. When they reached the chateau Mme. Boucher was waiting on the veranda, arms akimbo.

"There you are, you little bitch!" she said to Lutie, and slapped her face.

Quickly the baron intervened. "Madame!"

"Thief! Strumpet!" Madame added some malevolent French. "Monsieur, this woman must be arrested immediately! I came on her stealing money from your desk. She ran away then, and when I went over the valuables, I found she had taken a valise and toilet articles and many articles of expensive clothing left here by Mme. Dessines and Mlle. Valerie and the other ladies."

Lutie was very cool. "Of course! How was I to pay the fare to Mandan without money? And I could not appear in court to testify for Charles in a parlormaid's uniform."

Madame was thunderstruck. Her thin-lipped mouth dropped open like a fish gasping for air.

"*Oui, madame*," Charles soothed. "I do not wonder at your feelings, but it appears it was all for the best."

"But — but —"

"Please have coffee brought to the library. Miss Hamlin, will you come up as soon as you have had an opportunity to — freshen up, as they say."

Eyes downcast, Lutie curtsied. When she saw that the baron had gone up the great staircase inside the door, she straightened and stuck out her tongue at Mme. Boucher. Running upstairs to her garret room, she rouged her lips and powdered her nose with some of the cosmetics left behind by Emma, the English girl, whose complexion she greatly admired. She did not hurry; Charles could wait awhile. She found time to pick up her banjo and strum a few chords, singing an old song she had picked up somewhere. It began:

"My love has gone, he sleeps away.
I love him yet and forever a day."

When she knocked at the library door Charles was sitting at his desk, shades drawn against the hot afternoon sun, a glass of cognac at his elbow. In the gloom his bearded face was weary, cut by sharp planes of light and shadow. He motioned for her to sit near.

"Mme. Boucher has given notice."

Lutie looked down at her folded hands.

"I cannot blame her," he continued. "This is a dreary country, and the chateau is like a tomb, with everyone gone. Mr. Cooney has given notice, also. It seems old Griffin has offered him more money." He cursed between tight lips, and drained the glass. "The fall roundup is coming on, and there are only a few hands left, mostly the Indians, who at least have some concept of loyalty, if no one else does!" Drumming fingers on the polished wood of the desk, he stared at her. "Speaking of loyalty, why did you do what you did, Lutie? I mean — speak up for me, lie for me?"

"I love you," she said.

He seemed not to hear. Pouring more cognac, he went on. "You understand I am grateful, in a way. Yet — it is shameful to escape a deserved punishment. I killed Emile — I was to blame —" He paused, glass halfway to bearded lips, astonished.

"I love you," she repeated.

He put the glass down.

"I have always loved you, since that first day I saw you shaving in the private car, back in the varnish."

"But — but —" Dazed, he clawed at his beard. "Emile —"

"It was Emile who found me, brought me here. It was Emile who persuaded you to let me stay. Emile was a nice man, indeed, but no more than a means to an end. I love you, Charles. I know it is presumptuous —" She lowered her eyes, looking again at the modestly clasped hands. "But it is true!"

"I — I cannot believe it! You, Lutie — love me?"

"I risked everything to protect you. People don't think much of me anymore. My reputation is ruined. But I did what I did for love. You must believe it!"

Slowly he got to his feet. The delicate glass fell over as his sleeve brushed it, spilling the cognac on the papers littering the desk. Charles did not notice. "Lutie, I seem to have misjudged you." He took her hands and drew her close. "Ah, Lutie! But I am twice your age, child."

"I am no child!" she said defiantly. "I told you that before." Allowing him one quick embrace, she pulled herself away, looking at the ormolu clock on the desk.

"Look what time it is getting to be! You must be hungry, after that long ride on the train."

He was reluctant to release her. "But how can we talk of food, after such a declaration, *ma chère?* I say — this is the first time for months I have been able to smile!"

"There is no one in the kitchen anymore," Lutie went on. "I believe even the Chinese cook for the hands has left. But I am a good cook. I will go down and fix you something."

"Something, anything!" He kissed her hands. "Whatever you prepare, Lutie, is bound to be ambrosia."

Going downstairs, she paused at the front door. The sun, low in the west, painted the ranch outbuildings with a bloody brush. The tall brick chimney of the abattoir pierced the darkening sky. High above, a hawk sailed, a lonely figure against the scattered crimson clouds. The baron's lands stretched as far as she could see.

Lighting a lamp in the silent kitchen, she started a fire in the range, apron about her waist. Soon she found eggs and ham in the larder, and boiled coffee. Bustling about, feeling almost proprietary, she became aware of someone watching. Turning, she saw Murdoch, the Scotsman, standing in the doorway to the cellar, a dusty bottle of cognac in his hand.

"The master wanted another bottle."

She turned her back. "Well, take it up to him, then."

Not aware he had moved so close, she started as he patted her bottom. "You're a cute little trick," he said. "And smart, too!"

204

The palm of her hand caught him squarely on the mouth. Staggering back, he juggled the precious bottle for a moment.

"You don't need to take on so!"

"Get out of here!" she spat.

Rubbing his mouth, Murdoch grinned a rawboned grin. "I've never been slapped before by a — a parlormaid!"

"I'm not a parlormaid anymore!"

Still grinning, he backed away. "No. That's right. I guess you're not. Not anymore."

CHAPTER
ELEVEN

Between the baron's land and the river, high sandstone cliffs ran like a parapet, crowned by the jagged needle of the peak called the Mitten. They were multicolored, freakishly splashed red and brown, gray and ochre, with alternating black bands of lignite. Over millennia of geological time the bluffs had eroded into fantastic shapes: cones, obelisks, spires, Moslem minarets, even a grizzly with hulking shoulders and a snout foaming saliva when the rains came. The baron's Sioux feared the wild buttes, not wanting to pursue cattle into the winding canyons. *Macha sicha*, they called the cliffs: the Badlands, where dwelt an evil god. Now it appeared the evil god had cast a spell on the baron's undertakings.

The chateau, only a little more than a year old, began to look shabby and neglected. Paint peeled, a window broken by a confused magpie was unrepaired, dust gathered on the expensive furnishings. Coyotes raided the long sheds where the baron had kept chickens and turkeys to be dressed for market. The bunkhouse was abandoned, a door swinging idly to and fro in the wind. The pile of mottled earth by the uncompleted well melted away in the autumn rains. The last of the hands had departed, offered more money by Henry Griffin to help in the fall roundup. Now only the Indians remained loyal to the baron. There were not enough of the Sioux to herd and tally the beef animals, but old Yellow Hat and his people tried hard; the baron had been good to them. From the veranda Lutie could see, far up the river, the great cloud of cinnamon-colored dust where Slash G was gathering its cattle for market.

Brandy glass in hand, the baron stared at the small fire Murdoch had kindled. "Is it possible, Lutie, that all my work has come to this? Nothing?"

Sitting beside him on a needle-pointed stool, she clasped hands about her knees. Yes, it was possible. But *she* knew what had to be done. A person could make fate holler uncle, if that person knew what he — or she — was about.

"Madame?" Murdoch leaned over, another brandy snifter on the silver tray. The crystal bowl caught the firelight to illuminate a smoky liquor in its depths. Graciously Lutie accepted, murmuring a casual "Thank you," the way the English girl, Emma, had done. Emma's wasn't really *thank you*; it was more a kind of 'kyu, with the first syllable swallowed as if of little importance.

Murdoch withdrew. It was, she realized with a small thrill, the first time the baron's man had called her "madame." Sipping the liquor, comparing it with Buck Griffin's rotgut, she felt good. Even Murdoch had conceded her place in the baron's household.

"Look at this!" Angry, the baron turned up the wick of the Argand lamp to show a headline in the Chicago

Tribune: DRESSED BEEF PROMOTERS INJURE CATTLE INDUSTRY. Voice thick and choleric, he read:

"The Fink Commission has taken note of the recent efforts of foreign entrepreneurs to ship dressed beef directly from the West instead of the usual and normal practice of sending live animals to the Chicago stockyards to be slaughtered there and prepared for market. Armour and Co. is reported to be filing suit against this competition. The railroads also are protesting the diminution of traffic, dressed beef requiring much less car space compared to live animals."

Furious, he threw the *Tribune* into the fire, watched it char.

"I am a benefactor of the American working man, *n'est-ce pas?* He can buy my dressed beef at half of the price charged by the meat packers. That is why they, and the railroads, pillory me!" He stared at her. "Pillory? Is that a good word, Lutie?"

"Yes," she said. "A very good word, baron." His English had become excellent. He knew German and Italian, and even Algerian dialects.

"Ah, Lutie!" He reached out to put his hand on her knee. Under his touch she trembled slightly, but otherwise did not move. "Do you pity me?"

He wanted sympathy. Finally she granted him the necessary amount, no more. "*Oui, monsieur.* Fate has been unkind."

208

His grasp tightened. He looked at her with sad dark eyes. "Then —"

Quickly she rose, smoothing her dress. "I will see to your supper. There is very little in the pantry. Have you any money? Tomorrow I must send Murdoch into town to buy some chops, a loaf of bread, and a few eggs."

Withdrawing his wallet, the baron took out a bill. "*Mon Dieu!*" He peered into the leather folds. "I thought there was much more." Shrugging, he handed her the note. Then he turned to the side table, pulling out the stopper of the crystal decanter and pouring himself more cognac. Holding up the bottle, he peered through it. "Much more serious, the cognac is almost gone!" He grimaced and sank back on the flowered sofa, chin on chest, watching the fire. The brimming glass spilled drops on his ruffled shirtfront, but he did not appear to notice. "Why?" he asked, absently.

On her way to the kitchen, she paused in the doorway. "Why — what, monsieur?"

He drank the cognac, wiping an unshaven chin with the back of his hand. "Don't call me *monsieur!* You know I have given you leave to address me as Charles."

"I am sorry, Charles."

"Why, you ask? Why did you do it, Lutie? Why did you lie for me in the courtroom at Mandan?"

She stretched up her arm against the richly carved doorframe, tightening the fabric of her waist against her bosom, knowing that the backlighting from the lamp in the dining room outlined her figure.

"I have told you. Because I love you."

Slowly he turned the empty cognac glass in his fingers, watching her with approval. "You are a handsome woman, Lutie. I am indeed flattered. You love me, eh?"

"I have told you so, many times."

He shook his head. "No. It is impossible."

"What do you mean?"

"My luck, the luck of the de Fleurys, has changed. All is going dim. You do not love me. It is a — what we say in French, a *mirage*, a — a —"

"The same word in English, Charles — a mirage."

"A mirage, then, like my plans to become the beef baron of the New World! All a mirage, swept away by the winds of chance. So you — you are a mirage also."

Again she felt excitement in her bosom, the thrill of playing with a man, bending him, moving him to her will. It was a dangerous game, she knew; Charles had an unpredictable temper. But she knew how to handle him.

"I am not a mirage, Charles. I am flesh and blood."

"Damn it, you are, indeed." Rising, he prowled toward her. But she only laughed and fled toward the kitchen, calling over her shoulder, "Now I must see to your supper!"

In the golden days of autumn Papa died. The baron drove Lutie to Little Misery to attend services in the Baptist church. People were unfriendly, watching the pair with narrowed eyes and whispering behind their hands. Lutie stared fiercely at the spiritualist lady, who seemed to be casting some kind of curse on her. Mounting the steps to the church, Sid intercepted her.

"Sid! Why, how — how tall you've got!"

Her brother's face was troubled. "Lutie, don't come up front. Don't sit with Mama."

"Why?"

"She's real upset. She's like — crazy! She says it was all your fault, Papa dying. He died of a broken heart, Mama says."

"But —"

The baron took her arm. "Maybe it is best, Lutie. We sit in the back, no one notices. Then we leave, quick."

Angry and hurt, she assented. They sat in the utmost rear pew. The church was crowded; Papa had been well liked. The Sigafooses were there, and Sheriff Holland and his wife and grown spinster daughter, along with the Oateses and Mr. Larson from the sawmill and a lot of farmers and ranchers who did business in Little Misery. There had to be over a hundred. Lutie never imagined that Papa, so quiet and meek, had made so many friends. Mama and Sid sat alone in front, Mama stiff and severe, Sid grown up now.

The reverend preached a compelling sermon, dwelling on Papa's friendliness as well as the knowledge and learning he brought to Little Misery's citizens. Lutie was surprised to learn Papa had given a talk on the geology of the Dakota Territory before the Ladies' Literary Society, and for a while, before he became so ill, sang in the choir. Her lips tightened when the pastor spoke of the reverses Mr. Hamlin had suffered, including the tragedies inflicted on him by the death of his brother Milo, and the "thoughtlessness of another family member." Heads turned to look. Lutie flushed.

"I — I must get out of here," she said, taking Charles's arm. "Please! I feel faint."

They waited around the corner of the church for Sid. "I've got to talk to him!" Lutie insisted.

Charles shrugged. "If you wish. But I would feel better back at the chateau."

Mourners gathered in the slanting autumn sunlight to comfort Mama. Lutie could hear murmured comments; "He was a good man, sister"; "We'll surely miss him, Miz Hamlin"; "Many's the time he went out of his way to be nice." Lutie grieved for Papa, but she was proud of him also. Finally Sid saw her beckoning and trudged toward them, hands in his pockets.

"What is Mama going to do now?"

Sid's copper-toed boot traced a circle in the dust. "Papa had a little insurance policy. When the money comes, Mama's going home."

"Home?"

"Virginia. You know that's always what Mama meant when she talked about home. There wasn't ever any other home for her but Bedford County."

"But what will you do?"

Sid squared his shoulders. "I'm most grown. Mr. Oates is giving me a place to sleep in his shed out back, and I'll take my meals with them. I'm going to be a newspaperman. Mr. Oates says I've got what it takes."

In spite of a heavy heart she had to rag him a little.

"And you'll be close to your sweetie, too — the Oates girl! What was her name?"

212

"Marie. Marie Oates." He did not blush and stammer and protest, the way he used to; he *was* growing up.

When the baron took her arm, Lutie held back for another moment. "Sid, you won't be a stranger? You'll come up and see me — see us? I mean — you're all I've got now!"

"Sure," he said. "Sure, Lutie." But she was afraid he would not.

" *'Voir*, Sid," the baron said, handing her into the trap.

"Goodbye, sir. Goodbye, Lutie. I'll —" He broke off, at a loss for words. "I'll tell Mama —"

The baron slapped the reins over the matched bays; the trap wheeled swiftly away in the golden dust. Lutie didn't know what Sid was going to tell Mama. What was there, after all, to say? Papa was dead, Mama was going home, Sid had changed. There was nothing left but the baron. Stiffly she sat beside him, ignoring the stares of passersby, fingering the gold chain Emile Durand had given her. It felt fine and warm on her neck, the way his hand had once been on hers. Almost, it seemed, she heard his voice, his gentle voice, speaking to her.

Distraught, beset by creditors, the baron talked gloomily of abandoning everything, leaving the country, going back to Algeria to rejoin his old regiment, now fighting the Touaregs in places with names like El Oued and Zougabat and Garaal Kabda. Moody, he recounted previous exploits of arms, and recalled old comrades.

"Emile, too —" His speech was slurred, and he had become more careless about his dress and toilette, in spite of Murdoch's attentions. "Ah, Emile — he was a prince of a fellow! Lutie, did I ever tell you about the time at Saumur when we — we —" He hesitated, train of thought lost. "I have forgotten. What was I saying?"

Sheriff Holland appeared on the veranda one day with a writ attaching a parcel of several thousand acres of the baron's lands for an unpaid bill. Blinking, Charles peered at the document. Lutie finally read it to him.

"It's for three thousand head of cattle you bought, at forty-five dollars apiece. The broker wants his money."

"Money?" Swaying a little on his feet, Charles glowered. "I haven't got any money anymore. Besides, forty-five dollars a head was too much. I was robbed, I tell you!"

Sheriff Holland's paunch wagged as he shifted position, uncomfortable before the baron's anger. "Can't help that, Baron. You contracted for the animals, and the man ain't been paid."

Charles tore the writ into shreds, threw the bits into the air. "There, *monsieur!* That is what I think of your writs, your legal foolishnesses!"

When the sheriff protested, Charles ran to the library and took a Belgian fowling piece from the cabinet. Jamming shells into the breech, he hurried out on the veranda. The sheriff ran, scrambling awkwardly onto his horse, the animal snorting and bucking as the baron discharged the piece into the air.

"And don't bother me again with bits of paper!" he shouted.

Lutie shook her head, took the weapon from him. "That was not wise."

Charles shrugged. "If I had been wise," he said, "ah, Lutie, if I had been wise! If I were wise, I never would have come here."

"But you *are* here."

"And so, *ma chérie*, are you, and that is my one blessing!" Unsteady on his feet, he groped for her. Pushing him away, she went back to the kitchen. The time was not yet; she would know when the time was, and so would he.

One morning Dr. Cromie came by, sitting his claybank heavily. To Lutie he looked older, much older. Climbing stiffly down, he took her arm in his as they walked up the steps onto the veranda.

"Keeping well, Lutecia?"

"Of course I'm well, Doctor! There's so much to do around here I don't have time to be sick." Curious, she asked, "Why did you come? Not that I'm unhappy to see you — you were such a good friend to Papa and Mama — but —"

Sitting on the porch swing, he took off his hat, fanning himself. "Warm for October."

"There's cider in the springhouse. Would you like a glass?"

"No, thank you. Ah — the baron's man Murdoch stopped by the office when he was last in Little Misery. He was worried about his master's health. Drinking a lot, is he — the baron?"

215

"Yes."

"Where is he now? Perhaps I could see him."

She lied. "He's out on the range, I guess, looking at the few cattle we have left." The baron was asleep. With the better part of a quart of rum the night before, along with a bottle of Château Haut Brion at supper, it would be noon before he woke. She had sent Murdoch down to the river to fill the barrels with water. In the long summer drought their one well had failed, and the other had never been finished.

"I'm sorry about that. According to Murdoch, the baron is a sick man. Perhaps I can help him."

"The baron," Lutie said evenly, "is well. He is, of course, discouraged at the turn of events. But Murdoch should not have troubled you, Doctor."

"Are you sure?" He looked at her keenly.

"Very sure."

He took her hand in his. "Lutecia, I'm worried about you too. I don't know what's going on up here — there are a lot of rumors — but you're not looking well."

Touched by his interest, she was still annoyed. "How do you mean?"

"How old are you?"

She had to think for a moment. "Twenty. Or is it twenty-one next month?" She laughed, embarrassed. "Actually, I haven't thought too much about it."

"You look a good thirty. Your face has lost that innocent bloom and there are lines in it. You're harsh, not at all like the fresh young girl that came out from — where was it? — Columbus?"

216

She said nothing, only pushed the porch swing a little to keep it moving. That was what she must do always, keep moving, be alert, watchful. "Yes, Columbus."

"The Territory ages women fast, my girl, but not *that* fast. What's wrong? Would you like to tell an old man?"

She had hardened her resolve and carefully acted a role, but now felt something weakening in her. Papa dead, Mama gone, Sid —

"Tell me about it, Lutecia."

Her eyes misted. When he put a fatherly arm about her she let her head rest on his shoulder. He smelled of cigars and carbolic acid and old clothes.

"That's better," he murmured.

It had been a long time since she had wept. A few tears came, but not many. Perhaps her tear ducts had dried up with what she had been and seen and done — and would do, before she was *really* old. Gradually she straightened, pushed up a few straggles of the ginger hair.

"Gracious! I — I don't know what came over me!" Taking a handkerchief from her bosom, a scrap of lace left behind by Mlle. Valerie, she dried her eyes. "I really didn't mean to do that."

When he looked at her she avoided his gaze, once more alert and armored.

"You don't want to tell me, eh?"

"Tell you what, Dr. Cromie?"

He shrugged, picked up the worn leather valise. "It's your decision, Lutecia. Well, I must be going. Got to ride downriver and see a colicky baby at Rainy Butte."

Climbing onto the claybank, he hooked the handle of the valise over the horn of his saddle, peered at her through his gold-rimmed spectacles. "When a doctor can't help folks, I guess it's up to the good Lord." He waved, and the claybank moved stolidly down the sun-scorched hill toward the river, shimmering brown and muddy in unseasonable warmth.

Anxiously she rushed into the parlor to gaze at herself in the gilt-framed mirror backed with diamond dust. Another Lutie stared back, face illumined with a probing light that defined every feature, every blemish. Still and all, she thought, fingers exploring the anxious visage, Lutecia Hamlin was a beautiful girl. No, a woman! A woman, with knowledge of mysteries unknown to males. Of course, there were hollows under her eyes, dark shadings accounted for by what she had been through; Buck's tragedy, her miscarried child, Papa's death, Mama going home. Still, perhaps the dark circles gave her a kind of allure, made her look like the Egyptian ladies Papa had read about, females with stuff called *kohl* painted around languid eyes. However, there *were* new lines around her mouth she had not noticed. Trying to rub them away with her finger, she tensed when she felt hands grasp her waist, and smelled the sweetish odor of bourbon.

"*Ma chérie*, what are you doing now? Admiring yourself?" Charles pressed rough whiskers against her cheek and tightened his grasp, moving his arms higher, to her bosom. "Ah, leave the admiring to me, Lutie! When all is cold, you warm me, like a fire."

218

This time she allowed him more freedom; it was necessary to play the bait carefully. When he became too rough she begged off and left him standing by the pier glass, biting a corner of his mustaches in frustration. From the stairway she looked back. She could not see him directly, but in the mirror he picked up a carafe and poured out the dregs of wine left in the bottom.

On Sunday morning Murdoch went to church in Little Misery, dressed in his somber black. Lutie was alone in the big house; practically alone, anyway, since Charles was in a mood and had sequestered himself in the parlor, playing gloomy chords on the ebony piano. He was very curt with her, relenting only when she gave him a bottle of brandy; the cellar had long been empty. In fact, the brandy had not come from the once well-stocked cellars. With her own money, saved from her meager salary as housemaid, Lutie had sent one of the Indians to bring it from the saloon at Little Misery. The saloons did not ordinarily sell liquor to the Indians, but she forged a note with a fair representation of Charles's signature. She had practiced the signature often. Someday that skill could be useful.

Roaming about the silent house, footfalls soft in the dusty pile of Wilton carpeting, she plucked a bouquet of withered flowers from a vase and walked outside to cut fresh blooms. The baron's gardener had long since departed; carefully manicured beds were now a rampant confusion of color as nasturtiums fought with gloxinia, roses struggled against peonies. With scissors poised, she frowned as her ear caught a distant rumbling. Thunder? No, the day was blue and cloudless. A delayed Indian summer bathed the land in unnatural warmth.

Cutting a handful of blossoms, she paused again, listening. The rumbling grew louder. The south, along the river — it seemed to come from the south. Shading her eyes, she stared in that direction. Because of the intervening bulk of the abattoir she could see nothing. Soon the sounds became louder, more distinct, and she could make out individual contributions: drumming hooves, stock bellowing, shouts of men. Like a tidal wave, running cattle suddenly burst around the abattoir, dim forms in a mantle of dust, rolling white-rimmed eyes, bawling in terror. Riders on swift ponies galloped among them, slapping right and left with their hats, hallooing and cheering.

Terrified, Lutie shrank back into the flowerbed. Part of the flood veered off to clatter up on the veranda, milling about. A red steer with a lopped horn pranced uncertainly, and a bulky shoulder shattered the colored glass of the door. Another became entangled in the porch swing. The chains snapped and the steer crashed down, splintering the oaken swing, colored cushions flying.

"Hi, there! Hiyi, you brutes!" a rider shouted, grinning as he worked his mount around the churning mass of beef. Instead of trying to turn the stampede, the rider flapped his sweat-stained hat and screeched joyously, adding to the animals' confusion.

"Stop!" Lutie screamed. "Oh, stop them!"

220

Another tributary of the fleeing herd had flowed into the abattoir. She heard a metallic crashing as the panicky beasts plunged into the complex machinery; the scalding baths, traveling carcass hooks, pumps and valves and steam pipes. "No!" she cried, a dismayed hand at her mouth. "Oh, no — please!" In panic herself, she fled through the prickly rosebushes, tearing her dress and lacerating her arms, to huddle on the porch amid the wreckage left by the departing herd. A few animals still wandered aimlessly about. Some, judging from the bawls, were entangled in the works of the slaughterhouse. Dust lay heavy in the air; the noonday sun shone redly through the veil. The stampede had passed on.

"Charles!" she screamed. "Charles!"

One or two riders remained. They rounded up the few stragglers. Several lay threshing on the ground, probably, she thought, with broken legs.

"Charles! Oh, come!" She wept with anger and frustration. "Look at what they've done!"

The last rider, a tall man with a bandanna over his face against the dust, or possibly for concealment of his identity, tossed something at her as he rode off.

"Morning, ma'am!" he jeered, and was gone.

The object bruised her breast. Shaken, she picked it up, a paper wrapped around a rock. Charles shambled out on the veranda. His speech was thick. "*Alors*, what is happening?" He rubbed bleary eyes with a knuckle. "*Mon Dieu* — such noise, such commotion!"

He was too late to do any good, even if he had not been drinking. Spreading the note flat, she read:

FORRINERS GET OUT OF MORTON CO. BEFORE ITS
TOO LATE

"Let me see it."

Silently Lutie handed it over. While he was staring at
the note, lips working, she overcame her reluctance and
walked to where a dead cow lay, legs stiffly outthrust.
Beside her a red calf nuzzled the mother's teats,
skittering away as she approached. Kneeling, she
examined the brand on the flank: Slash G.

"Bastards!" Charles shouted. Crumpling the paper,
he flung it down. "Ghouls! Assassins!" English could
not contain his anger, and he broke into French.
Though she had become somewhat fluent in the
language, she did not comprehend what he was talking
about. Staring at the maimed cow, some of the words at
last registered in her dazed mind; *quitter, laisser,
revenir* — Finally she understood.

"You will not!" she said coldly, returning to the
littered porch. Some of the dust had settled. The sun
shone with returning warmth. "I'll be *damned* if you
will give up!"

Slack-jawed, he stared at her. "What?"

"We've just begun to fight!"

He shook his head. "I have had enough! I cannot
fight this whole county, and the railroads and the beef
barons of Chicago into the bargain!" He scowled. "And
who are you, mademoiselle, to tell the Baron de Fleury
how to conduct his business?" Angry and saddened by
the destruction, he was turning his fury against her.

222

"You are a big man, a great man," she said quickly, putting her hand in his. "What difference if you lose a battle, when you win the war? And we *can* win, I know!"

"We?" He grinned a sardonic grin. "Have you declared yourself a full partner? Perhaps, Hamlin woman, you forget your place!"

She drew him into the parlor, where a new layer of dust coated everything. As she closed the shattered door, some of the broken glass tinkled to the floor and lay in jewellike disarray, illumined by a shaft of sunlight. "There!" she cried. "That's a good omen. Don't you see?"

Charles slumped on a sofa. "A good omen! Pah!" Reaching for a decanter, he returned it when he saw it was empty. "Can't you see it is hopeless? These people, these crazy people" — he plucked at his beard — "they are animals, not at all like we French. They hate anyone with a clean shirt."

She picked up her banjo and sat close beside him, legs curled under her. "If you leave, what will happen to me?"

He seemed perturbed, and pondered a long time. "You," he murmured. "Yes, you. What about you, Lutie?"

"I love you, you know."

"I have never been sure, nor am I any more sure about why you lied for me at the trial. Sometimes it seems to me — it seems —" He broke off, fingering his unkempt beard, looking at her in a calculating way.

"Listen," she said quickly. "We can do it! We can beat them!" Twanging a defiant chord, she sang the little ditty Papa had once taught her:

"Are we downhearted? No, you bet!
We've hardly yet begun to sweat!"

In spite of himself, he began to laugh. "Ah, Lutie, you are a champion."

"Then you'll stay?"

Twining fingers about the delicate gold chain Emile had given her, he jerked at it. The slender chain broke. Tossing it to the floor, he said, "I do not like even dead rivals, Lutie. You are mine, and I am jealous of you!" Gathering her in his arms, he carried her to the bedroom. *On Sunday morning*, she thought, a little appalled. Nevertheless, she gave herself to him quickly and wholly, becoming in fact as well as appearance his mistress. It was much better than that stolen moment with Buck Griffin.

Afterward, he lay sleeping in the huge gilded bed. Putting on a robe, she stole down the stairs and retrieved the broken necklace. Then she sat for a while on the porch, very pleased with herself, smoking a hashish cigarette. The sun was quartering down into a gray-flecked sky but the air was still warm. A few late flies buzzed about and heavy-bodied bees lurched through the ruined flowerbeds. The little red calf had abandoned its dead mother and was munching grass down the slope toward the river. Content, she descended the steps and pulled a drooping blossom, holding it to her nose as she strolled about the yard. It was then she saw the snake, the diamondback, gliding from the ruined abattoir. Uncertain, it raised its head, the red forked tongue darted questioningly about. It struck a course directly for her. Oddly, Lutie was not frightened. Smelling the blossom, she watched the rattler almost idly. When it was within two or three yards she held up the flower like a scepter.

"This is our property!"

The snake paused, body lying again in the straggling loose-W pattern she remembered from that long-ago encounter, when Buck had come on her in the meadow.

"Go, sir! Go away!"

The snake raised a dusty head, seemed to consider. Then the thick body contracted and it rolled looping toward the thick grass at the edge of the yard. Satisfied, Lutie watched it disappear in hoof-trampled grass.

CHAPTER
TWELVE

Another Dakota winter came on, swiftly and merci-
lessly, like the horde of riders Papa had once told her
about, the wild riders of Attila, pillaging and
destroying. This time the marauders were snow and ice
and howling winds that prowled about the lonely
chateau, looking for a breach to swarm in and
overwhelm. Water left in basins froze. Sometimes, in the
middle of the night, a window would inexplicably
shatter. Lutie would struggle up, put on the baron's
wolfskin coat, and nail a sheet or blanket or bit of
tapestry, whatever she could find, over the hole. The
baron, sunk in despondency, did not care, only
burrowing deeper into the blankets with a muttered
curse. In Ohio it was the winter custom to pile hay
against the foundations of a dwelling to protect against
the cold. They still had a few bales, doled out handful
by handful to the cow-brutes that clustered about the
house looking for food. But Lutie was not up to it, the
baron only shrugged, and Murdoch said angrily it was
not his job. The sole island of warmth in the house
was the fireplace where Lutie and the baron spent most
of the waking hours. Charles had lost all his spirit, what
the French called *élan*. Only occasionally could he be

226

cajoled into searching for bits of firewood, or the cow chips the Dakotans called "prairie anthracite." They smelled bad when the frost melted out of them but they did burn, smokily, giving out a feeble warmth.

Still the Indians remained. Most of the time they huddled in their snow-banked *tipis*, wrapped in soogans, venturing out only to snare rabbits or shoot an antelope, a quarter of which they invariably brought to Lutie. The few chickens roosted in the barn, snuggled down in the moldering seats of the once-elegant hunting wagon. Each day Lutie found an egg or two, and somehow they survived. But when one of Yellow Hat's people slaughtered a bony steer, Charles was furious.

"They had no right!" he shouted, slamming his fist down so hard on an ebony table that a spidery leg snapped. "*Mon Dieu* — the whole world is against me!"

To placate him she lay a long time with him in the great carved bed. Winds tore at the roof. A shingle dislodged and whirled away like a gray bird into a gray afternoon. She knew his moods, and felt again the exultation of that power she had over him. She could make him do what she wanted.

"Everything will come out right, you'll see."

"Pah!" He shook his head. "I come to the end of my string, as these Dakota louts say. No, soon I must make a decision! Every day a new lawsuit is filed against me. All this" — he swept out a brawny arm — "soon all this will be gone. *Pouf!* It will be the end of Charles, Baron de Fleury, once a great and respected gentleman, soldier, patriot, friend of royalty." Head sunk on chest, he sighed, untrimmed mustaches flying out with the force of the exhalation.

"Decision?" Lutie was wary. "What kind of decision?"

He did not answer; instead, his finger traced the V-shaped scar on her thigh. "You have never explained this, *ma chérie*."

Drawing away, she sat up, arranging the bedclothes around her. "A — a wound."

"From what, pray?"

The wound in her heart was greater. Already she had repaired the broken necklace, the one Emile had given her, with a bit of silk thread, but was careful not to wear it in Charles's presence.

"You spoke of a decision." He tried to reach for her again. She pulled the quilts tighter about her, refusing his passion. "Not until you tell me about this decision!"

Balked, he lay back and clasped hands behind his head. "There is no use in fighting any longer. Yesterday when I rode into town there was no mail, only further lawsuits — notices of actions filed by the railroads, the refrigerator-car company, the packers Schwarzchild and Sulzberger, Nelson Morris, and Hammond. They have attached all my lands, tools, machinery, what cattle remain — everything."

"But you have friends! The Dessineses, your old comrades at Saumur — Pétain, Mazel, Dortas — surely they will lend you money." Hoping to incite him, she threw aside the quilts, sat up with her legs under her, determinedly gay. "Winter won't last long! Soon it will

228

be spring. Some of the Crimean wheat is bound to survive. You can buy more cattle and we'll start all over again!"

When he shook his head, she pouted. "But you *must!* You can't just walk away from all this and admit defeat. *I'm* not afraid."

"I'm not afraid, either. It is only that there is no use throwing good money after bad."

"But —"

"You forget your place!" he protested.

"What is my place, then?"

He only glowered.

"Listen," she said, choosing her words carefully. "Listen to me, Charles. I have loved you. I have lied for you, in court, risked going to jail for perjury if I were found out. I demeaned myself to cook for you, wash your dirty linens, kept this place habitable in spite of bad fortune." She held out her hands. "Look how rough and red, and the nails split and ugly! Don't my wishes mean anything to you?"

"Of course I am very grateful, but —"

"Grateful? Is that all?"

"Woman, do not shout at me. I do not allow it!"

"Allow! Allow!" She mimicked him. "Who are you to allow me anything?"

For a moment he seemed uncertain before her anger. "I intend to take you with me," he muttered. "In the mail was a draft from Marc Dessines. He has loaned me enough to buy passage for us and Murdoch to Paris. Once there, I have relatives who —"

"I have no intention of going to Paris with you. No, monsieur. If you have no stomach for a battle, then I will take your place. I will stay here and make a success of this undertaking. I will fight them — old Griffin and his Slash G brigands, the railroads, the packers — Schwarzchild and Hammond and all the rest!" Taking him by the shoulders, she shook him as a parent shakes a fractious child. "Can you stomach that? Can you run away from the battlefield and leave a woman to fight for you? Can you?"

Goaded, the baron threw her violently from him. "Woman, shut your mouth! How dare you speak to me like this?"

Throwing aside the covers, she stood in bare feet on the cold floor, defiant. "Coward! You are a coward! The Dakota people were right about you after all. You are a dabbler, a wealthy troublemaker, a vain and shallow man. When matters take a bad turn, when a real man is needed, you whimper and turn away with your tail between your legs!"

Towering over her in his nightshirt, torn and mended by her own hands, and torn again, he slapped her, hard. "Stop your gabbling! I will not have it!"

In response she cursed him. From Sid and from Clarence Sigafoos she had learned many filthy expressions, and knew also a few from the French. She lost her head; she was losing the game, and did not like to lose.

"Really," he said coldly, "you are a very common woman, Lutie. I suppose I knew that from the first, but you were — pretty." His lip curled. "Now you are not so pretty. You have become" — he paused — "slatternly, I think that is the word." He took her by the wrist, forcing her to kneel before him. "I know your game, mademoiselle!"

When she tried to bite him, he twisted her wrist harder. She bent in pain. "I — I have no game, except to shame you."

"I know your game," he repeated. "Look at me, Lutie!"

Unwilling, she raised her eyes.

"You are still in love with Emile, *n'est-ce pas?*"

"Emile is dead."

"Of course he is dead. I know that; it was I who killed him! There is not a day the sun rises that I do not rue the act. But you loved him, and you hated me for killing him. So you played your little game!"

She was silent, only listening, and hurting from the tight clamp on her wrist.

"You want to ruin me! You want to entice me to stay on here, sinking deeper and deeper into debt, until I am penniless and dishonored. You want revenge against me; you want to see me brought low, see the de Fleury name dragged in the mud."

"I hate you," she gasped between set teeth. "Let go my wrist, you beast!"

Smiling, he let her go. "I have always wondered why you lied for me in court. You wanted a more delicious fate for me. You wanted your own personal revenge, to drag me in the mire, to stretch out the torture, to humble me and put your pretty little foot on my neck. That is why all this talk of further loans, begging of my friends and old companions, staying on to fight a losing battle with old Griffin and the railroads and the rascally meat-packers and the rest of the jackals, along with the accursed weather! Well, you have failed, Lutie, and I pity you."

She had one last card and played it recklessly, sure of triumph. "Leave me here and I'll go to Mandan and tell the judge my testimony was false. I'll tell him I lied, and that you provoked the quarrel, which as you know is God's truth. I'll see you hanged before you run away from me, Charles de Fleury!"

For the first time in a long time he laughed, a loud and boisterous laugh. "Lutecia Hamlin, you have lost your mind! You are demented! Your hatred has warped your mind, that I once thought innocent and childlike." Thrusting his bearded face close to hers, there was no laughter in his voice. "Who would believe you? Having lied once, would the judge not consider you likely to lie again?" Casually he sauntered past her, looking out the window. To the north flared the northern lights, a wall of reddish light, flame-colored tongues wavering toward the zenith, rising and falling as if fanned by an Indian soogan. He turned to face her, countenance saturnine, lit redly by the northern glow. "There you are — your claws drawn, my little cat!"

She watched him dully, trying to comprehend.

"Tomorrow," he said, "I start packing. Next Monday I leave on the Pacific Express for Chicago and the East. Then the Cunard *Etruria* to Le Havre, and so home again. My home, my always home, France — a civilized country, not like this stupid America with its dolts and savages and" — he stroked his beard, amused — "and with its scheming whores like Lutecia Hamlin. Although named for France's fairest city, she is an American type, pure and simple. Lutie, it has been an education."

Head bowed, she stood as though struck into stone. Charles leaned forward, kissed her on the crown of the head.

"Goodnight, Lutie. I am going down to the parlor and enjoy the last bottle of wine."

Not turning when the door of the bedroom clicked, she remained immobile, staring at the window where he had lately stood. His image, like a dark shadow, seemed to persist. As she watched, it faded, the sharp edges softening, blackness giving way to the glow of the arctic illumination. Rose, pale rose, deepening gradually to a deeper hue — red, scarlet, finally a saturated crimson. Lutie thought of blood, human blood, the vital fluid flowing out and away as the vessel that once contained it shriveled into a husk, fragile and lifeless. Blood, Emile's blood! Almost in a trance she spoke. *Don't worry, Emile. Everything will be all right. I'll make it right for you.* She raised a hand, feeling the smoothness of his cheek, the silkiness of his blond mustache, the touch of his lips on the tips of her fingers. *It will be all right*, she whispered. *Trust me.* As if in response, the northern lights burst forth in a shower of color, great leaping banners of light, flagging the night with approval of her decision.

"I'll make it right for you," she promised, and crept back into bed, comforted.

★ ★ ★

Murdoch and the baron quarreled bitterly. The Scot had not been paid for several months. When he presented the baron with a detailed accounting of the debt, Charles was furious. "How dare you bother me with these petty demands, when I am beset on every side by debtors!"

Murdoch was respectful, but dogged. "Sir, I have relatives in Scotland who need the money I send them. Can you not —"

"No, I cannot! That is an end to it. I must say, Murdoch, I am disappointed in you. I had hoped for loyalty, at least!"

"Sir, I consider myself loyal to you and the de Fleurys, but there are over seven hundred American dollars due me."

"When we return to Paris, I will —"

"I am not going to Paris," Murdoch blurted.

"What?"

Murdoch's jowls set in a stubborn cast. "I have met a widow lady at the Presbyterian church in Little Misery, Baron. Mrs. Tully and I have a — an understanding. I had hoped that with what I have saved and what you still owe me, along with the moneys left from her late husband's estate, we could start a millinery store. I know fabrics, you see, and she is an expert seamstress. This country is growing, and fashions are bound to become important."

"Damn fashions!" Charles exploded. "Damn your millinery store! You belong with me, Murdoch! How can you think of such a thing? Look here, man — who

234

will take care of my clothes, lay out things, see that my linens are washed and folded? Who will —"

"I beg your pardon, sir, but do not yell at me."

"I will yell all I damned please! What kind of a world is this, when everyone seems to forget his place?" Charles raised clenched fists over his head. "The world turned upside down! The old values lost! *Mon Dieu*, it is enough to turn a man into a lunatic!"

"But the money —"

"Get out!" Charles shouted. "Damn it all, get out! Marry your damned widow and turn into a shopkeeper!"

Lutie heard the quarrel from where she crouched, unseen, behind a withered palm. Murdoch's defection surprised her, also; she had thought of them as inseparable. But the Dakota Territory changed people. It had driven Uncle Milo mad, killed Papa, broken her mother, made a man out of Sid, and turned stiff-necked Murdoch into a millinery clerk. She giggled, almost giving herself away, and Charles looked suddenly up, freezing her into immobility. But soon he sighed, lit a pipe with the few crumbs of tobacco remaining in the jar, and stared moodily into the ashes of the fireplace. After a while he laid down the pipe and went to sleep. Lutie crept back into the hall.

The gun cabinets were always kept locked. She had found a key on the painted Limoges tray where the baron kept his watch and shirt studs and miscellaneous articles on the bureau. Opening a glass door, looking cautiously around to ensure that she was not seen, she inspected the array of arms. He had taught her how to load and fire the Swiss Vetterli rifle, the expensive custom-made one, but a rifle would not do. Perhaps one of the revolvers; gingerly she picked up a well-oiled one that said "Williams and Powell, Liverpool" on the butt. It was, Charles had told her, what they called a pepperbox, a curiosity that could be concealed in the palm of the hand but which fired large bullets. Thinking she heard Murdoch in the hall, she closed the door and hid behind a dusty velvet curtain. After a moment, hearing nothing else, she returned to the cabinet and rummaged among the boxes until she found a dog-eared carton that said ".40 calibre." Carefully closing and locking the cabinet, she fled to a dark corner of the cellar. By the light of a candle she tried the shells in the rotating barrel of the pepperbox. The greasy brass bullets slid smoothly into chambered recesses. Shivering in the dank cellar, she pulled the shawl tightly about her shoulders and aimed the weapon at a rat that watched with button-bright eyes from a recess in the stones.

"Ma'am?"

She started. It was Murdoch, peering from the stairs, holding a basket of empty wine bottles.

"Miss? Is that you? Whatever are you doing down here?"

Fortunately she had been facing the wall. Quickly she dropped the weapon into her bosom, shoved the box of cartridges into a niche among the ice-rimed stones, and snuffed out the candle.

"Yes? What do you want?"

He descended the rest of the steps, peering into the darkness. His tone was surly, edged with suspicion.

236

"What are you up to?"

She rose, elegantly, chin high. "It is none of your business! I am not obliged to explain my actions to a servant!" When she tried to sweep past him, he caught her wrist, stayed her.

"Now what mischief are you planning?"

Angrily she twisted away. "Take your hands off me!"

"I was only wondering what you were doing. The cellar is my business, miss. You shouldn't even be down here." His tone was apologetic, but still suspicious.

Lutie didn't answer. Heart pounding, she shook off his grip, climbed the stairs, and slid the loaded pepperbox among the silken things in her bureau. When he had the money, the baron had been generous with her, delighting in decking her out in expensive underclothing.

The week fled and Monday approached. The baron was busy packing, whistling as he worked, and casual with her, almost as if they were on good terms again.

"Ah, to be in France, in the spring! Saumur is in the Loire Valley, you know. Dortas and I used to ride over to Vouvray. The wines of the valley are like — distilled sunshine. And there was a little restaurant in Vouvray, with exquisite cuisine. We were young officers, then." Frowning, he held up a lace-bosomed shirt. "How in blazes does one —"

"Here!" She took it from him. "Men do not know how to fold clothes."

"Ah — merci, chérie!" Holding the carefully folded shirt, he stared out the window at the snowy landscape. "There was a girl, there — daughter of the mayor —"

He shrugged, laid the shirt in his valise. "What will you do?"

"What do you mean?"

He looked at her. "When I am gone, I mean. What will you do then?"

She spoke softly, not wanting to rouse him from the careless reverie. "I don't know. Maybe I can get a job of some sort in Little Misery."

"With Murdoch, perhaps, in his millinery shop?" He roared with laughter while working the shirt into place among the drawers and handkerchiefs and his embroidered Chinese dressing gown.

"Perhaps," she murmured. He did not hear her because he was still chuckling.

"You know," he went on, "in a way I am still quite fond of you, Lutie Hamlin. I think you hate me, and would destroy me if you could, but there is something in you I admire." He paused, finger to bearded lips, pondering. "You think like a man. Yes, that is it! The women I have known were simpleminded creatures, more interested in the latest fashions and gossip about who is cuckolding who. Whom?"

"Whom," she confirmed.

"But you think like a man, and that is part of your charm. If you were a man, and had a man's makeup, you would be a very dangerous person!"

She swallowed, her throat constricting. "But I am not a man. I am a woman."

"Yes," he said, "you are a woman. I used to have a mare at Saumur, a wild and unpredictable mount named Belle Julie. I enjoyed riding her, though she bit me many times. She appeared sweet and gentle, all rosewater and thistledown. Then when I wasn't looking, she would bite me." He showed her a scar on the back of his hand. "But I even enjoyed the biting. It showed Belle Julie cared for me." He pulled her unwillingly to him. "And you care for me, too, in spite of yourself, Belle Lutie, *n'est-ce pas?*"

"So you compare me to your horse!"

He grinned, maliciously. "Not really. Belle Julie was a thoroughbred."

Passive, she permitted him to kiss her, not moving as the rough beard raked her neck, her shoulders. At last he released her, holding her by both arms and looking into her eyes.

"What might have been, eh, Lutie? Well, it is too late for all that." He turned from her. "Of course, you are welcome to stay on here in the chateau after I leave. In time the lawyers will take it over, too, as they have robbed me of everything else. But until then, it is your home."

"*Merci,*" she murmured.

Suspecting sarcasm, he looked at her sharply, but her face was bland.

"Now where is that damned Murdoch? I mean, after all, he could still help me pack these few things! I am not used to work of this kind."

"He has gone to Little Misery to see his Widow Tully," she reminded him calmly, "and is staying the night with her father so they can all attend the Sunday-evening services. I believe the Baptists are christening some Indians or something."

★ ★ ★

Monday dawned with eye-blinking whiteness, unexpected sun gleaming on the endless snow. Lutie woke before dawn. Face burrowed into the pillow, Charles still slept. Quickly she drew out the little pepperbox from among the silken drawers and camisoles in her bureau.

Outside, in the sunlit morning, a bird called — a plaintive *kee-wit* kind of sound. Lutie, hiding in the dressing alcove, wondered what kind of bird it was. *Kee — wit, kee — wit* — the innocent sound calmed her. She looked down at the instrument of death in her palm. So small, so really — insignificant! It could not have weighed, even with the leaden bullets, more than a few ounces. It did not even look deadly; it looked more like a child's toy of some sort. Once, a long time ago, in Columbus, Papa had given Sid a little gun like that. It was meant to be loaded with soapy water, and only puffed gossamer bubbles. She remembered that Christmas. It had been cold then, too. The windows of the little house on Third Street were etched with frost. One errant bubble drifted onto the window and, miraculously, did not break. It hung there, shimmering and swaying in the light from the candles on the tree, until it froze into a perfect icy sphere.

Hearing a small sound, she tensed herself. Had Charles risen? Chancing a quick glance around the corner, she saw him still wrapped in quilts, rolled up like an Egyptian mummy, her own side of the bed bare. He did that, often, and she hated him for it, too. Oh, he had so many things to account for! But now the books would be closed. Papa was good at keeping books, and had carefully explained to Lutie and Sid some of the mysteries of trial balances and double-entry and other arcane procedures. Well, in a way this was like keeping books for a bad business. There were credits — some — and a lot of debits. Now she was going to account for everything, and close the books for once and for all. Emile was — had been — a lawyer. He would appreciate how neatly she had totted up everything and come out even.

Holding the gun before her, surprised her hand did not even tremble, she moved from the alcove, bare feet making no sound on the parqueted floor. Charles lay still in the cocoon of quilts, his back to her. Should she call out first, let him have one final moment of horrified recognition? Shaking her head, she moved soundlessly on, closer and closer. She would send him unaware and unshriven into perdition, without opportunity to repent.

The muzzle of the little gun was only inches from the gaily patched quilt. She remembered that quilt. It was one that Emma, the English girl, had worked on and given to the baron as a Christmas present. It was composed of small delicate squares: some solid colors — red, green, blue, yellow, some plain white, ornamented with figures of soldiers and horses and cannon. One square, in the middle of Charles's slumbering back, was delicately embroidered with the image of a man on horseback, galloping. Perhaps that was Charles himself, at Saumur, riding Belle Julie.

"Charles," she said. She did not say it, really; instead, she spoke the words in her mind; she could not take a chance on waking him. "Charles. Die, Charles!"

Putting the muzzle of the pepperbox against the tiny embroidered figure, she pulled the trigger. She pulled it again and again, until the spinning cylinder was empty.

CHAPTER
THIRTEEN

In the sunlit silence of the empty chateau, the reports of the little pepperbox were deafening. Echoes caromed off the bedroom walls, roamed the deserted halls, seemed to round through the house and then roll back, still loud and deadly but diminishing. Lutie, holding the weapon, stared at the unmoving bundle, wrapped in its final coverings. As the echoes died like a summer storm dying away in the distance, she became aware the little bird was cheeping on the cottonwood tree outside the window. *Kee — wit, kee — wit.* Aware of another sound, she whirled.

Charles, in nightgown and slippers, emerged from the closet that held the gaily painted Italian bathtub.

"Charles!"

"*C'est moi, chérie.*" Chuckling, he leaned against the bureau. "*Ma foi*, but I know you well!"

Unbelieving, furious, she pulled the trigger again and again. Nothing happened. Charles reached out and took the tiny weapon.

"No more bullets, my dear. I was careful to count them." Picking up the quilt, he held it to the light. "Here — here — and here. There, also. Quite a neat ring of hits, Mademoiselle Lutie." With thumb and forefinger he pressed out a spark where powder burns had ignited the material.

"But —"

Casually Charles tossed the pepperbox on the bureau. "I knew, of course, that you planned to kill me. It was in your eyes, your voice, your manner. Ah, to me you are like a pane of glass, Lutie Hamlin. Today, you see, was the last day to exact your vengeance, so I was especially watchful. When you rose and sneaked out, I smelled Monsieur Rat. So" — he grinned, pleased with himself — "I got out of bed, rolled up the covers into a fair approximation of a body, and waited. I did not have long to wait."

Her bare feet were cold. The chill seemed to have permeated her vitals, seeping to her belly, her heart, her brain. Charles unbuttoned his nightshirt, rubbed an unshaven chin.

"So, Lutie, we are even, eh? One accidental killing versus attempted murder."

"You cannot prosecute me," she whispered. Her throat was tight and constricted. "There were no witnesses!"

"Prosecute you?" Pulling her to him, he kissed her gently on the forehead. "A mad child like you, Lutecia Hamlin? I am a soldier, you know, and used to greater dangers. No, I have not time or inclination to make anything of this. Besides" — he took his gold watch from the bureau — "we have nine in the morning already and the Pacific Express leaves Little Misery at ten minutes past noon. There is yet to shave and bathe,

244

finish my packing, saddle up the mare and ride to town."

Seeing her incredulous stare, he answered an unspoken question.

"I do not think I need fear you anymore, Lutie. I will take my bath in comfort and leisure, with no bullet holes in that expensive hand-painted tub. You have done your worst and, as you see, I am intact."

Exhausted, she slumped on the bed, burying her face in her hands. Later she could hear him pouring warm water from the kitchen stove into the Italian tub, singing a cheery French marching song. She was still dazed and speechless when he emerged, rubbing himself with a towel.

"Everything in this house is spoken for by creditors. The furniture, carpeting, paintings, guns — everything! If there is anything you want, Lutie, as a — well, perhaps a souvenir of our time together, I would advise you to take it before the tradesmen come like a swarm of locusts. As for me, I take only what I carry in my valise. I am honest, and owe a lot of money. I suppose my creditors are entitled to what they can get out of this debacle."

When she did not speak, continuing to stare at him with glazed intensity, he bent, peered into her face. "Do you hear me, then?"

Suddenly, overwhelmed by passion, she screamed, beating with her fists at the carved headboard.

"That is more like it," Charles observed, selecting a shirt from the bureau drawer. "Let it all out, *chérie*, and you will feel better."

The world seemed to reel. Panting, Lutie swayed to her feet, fists helplessly clenched. Running from the room, she stumbled to fall headlong in the thick Wilton carpeting. Picking herself up, she fled down the hallway, knocking over a potted palm on a stand. Charles came out on the balcony as she ran through the dusty parlor.

"It is an expected reaction, my dear. You will be all right in the morning."

The pulse in her ears was so loud she hardly heard his words. *Lutie is going out of her mind*, a small voice inside her explained. *Uncle Milo had the same taint!* Standing on the broad veranda, she looked wildly around.

"No, that isn't it," she murmured. "That isn't it at all. I — I am just upset, that's all. And who would not be?"

Crazy, the voice said. It was somehow soothing. *Crazy Lutie!*

"I am not crazy!"

I don't suppose Milo thought he was, either, the voice went on.

She couldn't identify the voice. In a way, it sounded like Emile. Panic-stricken, she ran outside and plunged into the snow. Odd; it didn't seem cold at all. Gasping for breath, heart pounding, she floundered down the hill, past the snow-frosted dead calf, toward the river.

The river is frozen, the voice reminded. *You would have to chop a hole in the ice.*

"I'm not going to kill myself," she gasped. "I — I just want to run, and run!"

246

Down there!

"Where?" Blinking in the sunlight, she stared down the hill.

Not far, perhaps a half mile. The twisted burr oak where I found you that day.

It was Emile!

Elated, she staggered through the snow, when the crust broke. Icy shards lacerated her bare legs but she pressed on.

"Emile!" she called.

It was too far away; she would never make it. Calling, holding out her hands, she floundered on. She was very tired.

Not far now, the voice said comfortingly.

"I hope not!" she gasped.

Just over that rise. You couldn't see the burr oak from the house, remember?

Clothed in purest white, the gnarled leafless tree looked like a beacon jutting up from trackless ocean.

"Emile!" she called again.

He was there, of course, strolling casually about the dark-limbed oak, one hand in his pocket. In the morning sun the rich brush of his mustache showed glints of gold. His eyes were gentle.

"Emile!" she pleaded. "Wait for me!"

Smiling, he nodded.

With a final effort she reached him to fling herself at his feet. All her being dissolved in snowy warmth.

"Emile," she murmured. "Ah, Emile! At last, *mon cher!*"

★ ★ ★

In July of 1906, Mr. Albert Stokes, reporter for the Omaha *Ledger*, came to the thriving town of Little Misery for information about the life and times of the "Prairie Baroness," as the old woman had called herself. Stokes's editor was anxious for a "popular interest" story to lighten the otherwise heavy editorial tone of his paper. "Young Dr. Cromie," he was told. "Young David Cromie knows more about her than anyone living."

Old Dr. Cromie's nephew was a physician in Minneapolis who used to spend summers with his bachelor uncle in Little Misery. Always he admired his uncle's patient ministering to the frontier people. When the old man died in the spring of 1887, David left his practice on Nicollet Street and with his youthful wife Cora returned to the scenes of his boyhood to take up the honored place in the community Uncle Philip had long held.

Dr. Cromie rolled back his office chair and pushed the gold-rimmed spectacles high on his forehead, realizing with a not unpleasant wince that the gesture had been a common one with his uncle. "Old? No, she wasn't so old. Perhaps in her middle forties when she died."

"From the pictures I saw of her, I would have taken her to be much older," Mr. Stokes remarked.

"Well, you have to realize that life on the frontier was hard. It aged people fast — women, perhaps, more than men."

The reporter chewed a fresh point on his pencil. "I'm hoping maybe a piece on her can be a kind of springboard to launch a whole series on the characters that made the West, or however you want to put it."

It was hot in the office; no breath of air stirred. Through the open window came the snorting of a pair of draft horses as they pulled a wagonload of beer kegs from the railroad station to the Empire Saloon. It was Saturday — no school — and urchins played noisy one o' cat in the dusty plain. A fly buzzed in the window and sat insolently on a tin of asafetida. Dr. Cromie lifted the tattered flyswatter from its nail and deftly, surgically, killed the fly.

"So what can you tell me about her?" Mr. Stokes asked, a trifle impatient.

"Well . . ." Dr. Cromie had much of the gentleness and serenity of his uncle. Brushing the fly off the desk with the edge of the swatter, he placed the medicine upright again in the serried ranks. "I was just thinking. It doesn't do to make quick judgments."

"I know the story up until the time the baron left," Mr. Stokes prompted. "Wasn't there a rumor that she tried to kill him?"

"A rumor, yes. Nothing definite. I guess Lutie had a reason. My uncle said the baron treated her like a chattel of some sort. Anyway, after he left —"

"He was killed in Algeria, I believe, after he went back into the French army."

Dr. Cromie did not appear to hear. Instead, he stared out the window in a kind of reverie.

"That spring, the Griffins — I guess it was the Slash G hands, though it was never proved — set fire to the barns and the outbuildings and the slaughterhouse. The house caught fire, too, and one wing was destroyed. When we saw the smoke, Uncle got out his trap and drove up there. Old Jake Sigafoos — he's dead now — came too, and some other people, but it was too late to save anything. Lutie had got a rifle from someplace, claimed she winged one of the Griffin riders. But no one ever came in to my uncle with a bullet hole in him." He shook his head. "I guess it was just the Griffins' way of wiping out the last trace of a man they despised — and a woman, too. Old Griffin hated Lutie worse than he hated the baron, maybe."

"Why?"

Dr. Cromie shrugged. "There were rumors. My uncle had his own theory. I think it was true."

"But why?"

"Some things are better left unsaid. After all, Lutie is dead now, and I don't intend to gossip. Anyway, she lived on in that ruined house — bare, it was, almost completely bare, with creditors taking everything. There was nothing left but her pallet in a corner and some pots and pans."

"How did she live, then? After all, Dakota is a pretty hard place for a lone woman, especially in the winter."

A ball sailed in the open window and bounced against the wall. Dr. Cromie picked it up and tossed it back. "Hey!" he called. "You kids be careful, hear?" Sitting down again, he clasped hands behind his head.

"Old Yellow Hat and his people brought her food. My uncle stopped in every week — he brought me with him when he visited — and helped her. Jake Sigafoos came with wood for the stove. Oh, a lot of people helped. At first Lutie didn't want any help, said she'd do it herself. I remember her banjo; she always played the banjo. When we drove up the hill we could hear her of a summer's day. Old songs — reels and jigs, tunes from the War Between the States, ballads. She had a quite good voice. I remember one song, particularly:

"Are we downhearted? No, you bet!
We've hardly yet begun to sweat!"

You see, she always had an idea she could start up the beef business again and make a go of it."

"But that was crazy! I mean — she *was* crazy, wasn't she?"

Dr. Cromie shook his head. "Not at first. But I guess the whole thing — her uncle's death, her father dying, her mother's going back to Virginia, Emile Durand killed by the baron and all the goings-on at the trial, and then the baron leaving her — it was too much for a young mind. It was said there was insanity in the family, anyway. Her Uncle Milo hanged himself. So gradually she came to live in an unreal world. She insisted visitors — even my uncle — call her 'Baroness.' She stood on dignity, and accepted charity like it was royal tribute. Even her younger brother Sid — he worked for Editor Oates on the Little Missouri *Gazette* before he died of an ear abscess in eighteen eighty-six — had to bow and scrape when he came. She wanted to play Old Sledge, Sid told me, and she insisted on winning. My uncle said she'd sit there in an old kitchen chair, regal as a queen even with newspapers stuffed in her dress to keep her warm and her fingernails broken and grimy and her hair full of knots and snags, and act like she was doing Sid a favor by letting a commoner play cards with her. And by God, she carried it off! In a way, she could have been a great woman."

Mr. Stokes started to ask a question but stopped when he saw the bemused look in the young doctor's eyes. Dr. Cromie went on:

"The thing that gave her the greatest pleasure, she used to beg my uncle or Jake Sigafoos or Mr. Larson to take her down to the station to see the Pacific Express arrive. That delighted her. She'd sit in Uncle's trap or on the seat of Jake's wagon and her eyes would shine when she heard the whistle and the bell. The engine would come chuffing in, hissing steam and clanking and the drive rods sliding back and forth in oil and she'd cry out in joy and clap her hands. All that power and force and might excited her. Oh, she loved the trains!"

"Sounds to me like she *was* crazy," Mr. Stokes commented. "Wouldn't it have been better to have her committed?"

"They tried. Yes, they tried. Angus Murdoch — he was the baron's man when the baron came out here, you know — Mr. and Mrs. Murdoch tried time after time to get her committed. 'She's plainly insane,' Angus used to say. 'I lived in the chateau, and I know.' Mrs. Murdoch always chimed in, 'Crazy as a shitepoke, that woman — dangerous to herself and to the community.' But my uncle would never agree. 'She's all right,' he'd say. 'Lutie's all right. She's just living out her dreams.'"

252

The next morning young Dr. Cromie drove Mr. Stokes out to the ruined chateau. High on the hill above the growing town stood the tall brick chimney of the burned-out slaughterhouse. The wind blew ripples across the ripe grasses, and the shell of partly-burned house stood black and stark in the harsh light. Wires of a new telephone line — part of a transcontinental circuit — glittered in the sun, a thread of light borne on stark new wooden poles, vanishing in the western distance.

"Progress," Dr. Cromie said. "From Little Misery we can talk to San Francisco now on that machine."

"I used to do the farm news," Mr. Stokes remarked. "Isn't that Crimean wheat over there, those few stalks among the grass?"

"The baron planted a lot of it to feed his stock, but it didn't grow well. Too cold, perhaps, or too hot. Dakota is a harsh place." Dr. Cromie stepped on the sagging veranda, careful where he put his foot, and cautioned Mr. Stokes. "I was too young to remember much, but I do recall the veranda being full of well-dressed men, ladies in bright dresses, servants serving punch. They had picnics out there in the grass. Wine flowed like water, Uncle said. Every week the Pacific Express would bring a new batch of handsome young men and beautiful women."

Inside all was dust and decay. A field mouse skittered from sight, a marauding crow flapped out a broken window. In one corner stood empty wine bottles, in another an overturned armchair. A shabby oil portrait on a wall was black with age; when the reporter touched it gilt fell from the frame like golden snow.

"So this is where she died — the Baroness!"

"No."

Mr. Stokes turned, surprised.

"No one knows what happened. One year all of Dakota was snowed in for a week. Uncle wrote that the snow was six feet deep in Little Misery. When he and Jake and some others finally broke a trail up here, Lutie — the Baroness — was gone. There was no trace of her in the house. They searched and searched. In the spring, when the snows melted, they thought they'd surely find some trace of her. They never found anything."

"But — but what —"

"God only knows. Maybe she wandered out into the snow — looking for Emile Durand, perhaps — and froze to death. The animals, coyotes and things, could have finished off the body." Dr. Cromie paused. Carefully he lifted the faded armchair, set it upright. "So, this is all that's left."

For a long time Mr. Stokes foraged about the house, murmuring to himself, writing entries in his notebook, occasionally asking a question of David Cromie. The young doctor sat on the edge of the porch, chewing a blade of grass. Finally, sun low in the west, the reporter closed his notebook, put his pencil in a breast pocket.

"That's it, I guess."

"Listen," Dr. Cromie said, lifting a finger.

Mr. Stokes listened. Then he asked, "What?"

"Music. Listen to it!"

In the rays of the setting sun the wires of the telephone line blazed with glory. Wind played gently through them, sounding like the strumming of a distant banjo.

Are we downhearted? Dr. Cromie thought. *No, you bet —*

Mr. Stokes nodded. "I hear it. I'm not a musical man, but I hear it. Good Lord, what a reprise for my article!"

We've hardly yet begun to sweat —

Both men silent, they walked slowly down the hill to where Dr. Cromie's mare was tethered, past the big dead burr oak, leaving the wires to sing behind them.

Bibliography

Bourke, John G. *On the Border with Crook*. New York: Charles Scribner's Sons, 1891.

Brown, Mark H., and Felton, W. R. *The Frontier Years*. New York: Henry Holt and Co., 1955.

Dresden, Donald. *The Marquis de Morès, Emperor of the Bad Lands*. Norman, Oklahoma: University of Oklahoma Press, 1970.

Foster-Harris, William. *The Look of the Old West*. New York: Viking Press, 1955.

Garland, Hamlin. *A Son of the Middle Border*. New York: Macmillan and Co., 1923.

Pioneer Atlas of the American West. San Francisco: Rand McNally and Co., 1956.

The Pioneers (The Old West). New York: Time-Life Books, 1974.

The Ranchers (The Old West). New York: Time-Life Books, 1977.

Sandoz, Mari. *Love Song to the Plains*. New York: Harper Brothers, 1961.

Old Jules Country. New York: Hastings House, 1965.